T0108777

THE DEVIL'S
WEDDING RING

Also by Vidar Sundstøl
Published by the University of Minnesota Press

MINNESOTA TRILOGY
The Land of Dreams
Only the Dead
The Ravens

THE DEVIL'S WEDDING RING

VIDAR SUNDSTØL

Translated by Tiina Nunnally

UNIVERSITY OF MINNESOTA PRESS | MINNEAPOLIS | LONDON

This translation has been published with the financial support of
NORLA.

First published in Norwegian as *Djevelens giftering* by Juritzen Forlag,
Norway, 2015. Published in the English language by arrangement with
Bonnier Rights, Stockholm, Sweden.

Published by the University of Minnesota Press
111 Third Avenue South, Suite 290
Minneapolis, MN 55401-2520
http://www.upress.umn.edu

ISBN 978-1-5179-0280-3 (hc)
ISBN 978-1-5179-0281-0 (pb)
A Cataloging-in-Publication record for this book is available from the
Library of Congress.

Printed in the United States of America on acid-free paper

The University of Minnesota is an equal-opportunity educator and
employer.

22 21 20 19 18 17   10 9 8 7 6 5 4 3 2 1

Prologue

A SLOWLY MOVING PROCESSION of cloaked figures appears among the pines. A muted murmur of many voices. In the midst of the group, four people are carrying a platform with a small roof above. The platform is fastened to two long poles, which they have hoisted onto their shoulders. A type of palanquin. Beneath the roof stands the wooden figure of a man wearing a tall, pointed hood.

The small marsh is framed by heather-covered rocks, with pines scattered on three sides. A steep crag rises up on the fourth side. The first rays of sun cast a warm light over the crowns of the trees up there, but shadows still reign in the marsh below.

There is a shout—a man's voice—and the cloaked figures begin to take their places in single file. At the front is the man whose shout made all the others fall silent. Otherwise the shapeless cloaks give no clue as to who is male or female. The hoods hide their faces from view.

As they set off, they begin to sing. The song sounds as if it rose up from this very spot. As if it had been formed in the marshy ground, or in the granite beneath the looming crag, or in the trickling water of the stream. As if it's a song that could not be sung anywhere else.

All the participants have placed their hands on the shoulders of the person in front, except for those four carrying the wooden figure. No longer are there any individuals but instead a single organism, large and multi-limbed.

For that reason nothing happens when a clasp fastened to the collar of a cloak comes loose and falls to the ground. No one calls out. No one stops to search. The song merely continues. The movement goes on. Many feet trample the lovely clasp with the two dragon heads, pressing it more and more firmly into the earth.

One

THE RAW SMELL OF FRESHLY DUG SOIL filled the air as he stood a slight distance away from the people who had gathered around the coffin to say a last good-bye. A few had cast searching glances at him inside the church. He was no one they recalled seeing before. But the deceased would have recognized him, even after all these years. Of that he was certain.

Abide with me . . . The solitary voice of the pastor sounded as if it might blow away on the first gust of wind. Between the dark-clad figures at the grave site, the coffin began sinking downward. Somewhere a bird sang, as quick and bubbling as a mountain stream. It was the first Norwegian birdsong he'd heard in many years.

Only when he noticed the sound of slamming car doors from the parking lot did he walk over to the two mourners who were clearly the widow and her son. He waited, his eyes downcast, as a few stragglers paused to offer their condolences.

Finally it was his turn.

The woman seemed utterly exhausted. "I don't remember seeing you before," she said.

"Max Fjellanger."

It took a few seconds before she was able to place his name. "Oh, but you're . . . Knut would have been pleased. If he could have seen us now, I mean. I'm Karoline Abrahamsen." Then she turned to her son. "This is one of Pappa's old colleagues."

Max said hello and offered his condolences. "We were good friends, but we lost contact after I left the police force."

"Didn't you move to the States?" she asked.

"That's right."

"And now you just happened to be in Norway?" said the son.

"Yes."

In reality, the sole reason for his trip was to attend the funeral, but he thought it would sound strange if he told them that. After all, thirty years had passed since he'd had any contact with Knut Abrahamsen. Another former colleague, someone he hardly even remembered, had sent out an e-mail. As soon as Max read of Knut's death, he knew he had to go to Norway. Anything less would have seemed like a betrayal. If not a betrayal of Knut, then of himself, and maybe of what little remained of his youth.

Now that the funeral was over, he felt drained. He didn't regret coming, but it was time for him to return home. The plane to Tampa left early the next morning, and he knew no one here in Skien.

"Did he drown?" Max asked, even though he knew the answer.

That was actually the only thing he knew about Knut's life over the past thirty years: the fact that he had drowned.

She nodded, her eyes suddenly filled with despair. The son cautiously took her arm as he stared at Fjellanger.

Karoline removed her son's hand. "You go on ahead," she told him. "I'll be there in a minute."

The young man hesitated, but a sharp look from his mother made him reluctantly turn and leave.

"Nice boy," said Max.

She smiled sadly. "Very protective now that his father is gone. Let's walk. I can't bear to stand here anymore."

Slowly they moved away from the grave. Gravel crunched under their feet. Some distance away loomed the dark, roughly hewn memorial stone that marked the grave of the Norwegian traitor Vidkun Quisling. Strangely enough, it dominated the whole of Gjerpen Cemetery.

"Was Knut on a fishing trip?"

Karoline kept on walking without saying a word, until Max thought she had decided not to answer. When she finally spoke, her voice had the sound of someone looking over her shoulder. "That's what I think is so odd," she said. "We have no idea what he was doing there."

"At Lake Norsjø? Is that what you mean?"

"Norsjø?" She looked at him in confusion. "He was found in Dalen. In the river that runs into Lake Bandak."

Somewhere inside Max Fjellanger, something was trying to open. A wound that had never healed, a persistent doubt.

"It must feel strange for you, since that's the area where the two of you used to work."

"How long did he stay there after I left?" he asked.

"In Dalen? Only a year."

"Was he still a police officer when he . . . ?"

"No. He'd already left the force before I met him."

That surprised Max. He would have pegged Knut as the type who would stay on the force until he retired.

"So, what sort of work did he do?"

"He hadn't worked in years. He was living on disability benefits."

Max couldn't bring himself to ask why.

They had almost reached the parking lot, where Karoline's son was waiting along with half a dozen other people, presumably relatives.

"We're all going to have a bite to eat now," she said. "You're more than welcome—"

He raised his hands in polite refusal. "Thank you, but there's something I need to do."

And that was true. He needed to go back home.

She didn't even pretend to look disappointed. Who would want a stranger to join the family at a time when they all needed each other most?

"Then let me thank you again for coming. As I said, Knut would have been pleased."

Max doubted that, considering the circumstances.

Karoline Abrahamsen reached out to grasp his hand in both of hers. All the relatives were climbing into their cars. Max was about to move on, in order to get a taxi, but there was one thought holding him back. "Was Knut still in contact with any of his old friends in Dalen?"

"No. I don't think he'd been back since quitting his job. He didn't know anyone up there anymore. And he hadn't said a word to me about going there. When it got close to midnight and I wasn't able to get hold of him by phone, I called the police to report him missing. The next morning they found him in the Tokke River."

There was something defiant about her expression. Or was there a trace of skepticism?

"Do you think something criminal might have happened?" he asked in a low voice so that no one else would hear.

"I have to trust the police," she said. "Who else can I trust?"

Then she went over to the car, where her son was already sitting in the driver's seat. She got in, and the car slowly headed across the parking lot. As it passed Max Fjellanger, she turned her head to look at him.

That was all. Just a look. Trusting. And expectant.

Two

ON THE BUS THROUGH SILJAN and the interior of Vestfold, he had stared out at the fields where the grain stood green and new. The farm buildings sat a safe distance from the road, away from any prying eyes—big structures enclosing a courtyard, the same way farms had been laid out for centuries, surrounded by forest-clad slopes of aspen, birch, and spruce.

He saw a burial mound in a field. A solitary giant oak with branches like tentacles.

Everything had tried to keep him away. This is what you come from, a voice would have told him, if only he'd listened. It doesn't matter what you became later on. This is what you are.

But he had refused to be persuaded. It was all too long ago.

Back at the hotel at Gardermoen Airport, he almost felt at home again. Airport hotels were all the same. As were all airports. When you entered an international airport, you basically entered a foreign country. An unspecified, anonymous land where everything was pared down to the lowest common denominator of comfort and consumerism.

Max knew that's what he preferred. It was reassuring.

He turned on the TV and watched CNN for a while. Nothing but the usual misery. And it did not improve by switching to the Norwegian news channel NRK. He didn't recognize the news anchors or anything else on *Dagsrevyen,* the daily news recap. But he reminded himself it was half a lifetime ago that he'd last watched the show. Even so, the issues were the same everywhere: war, terrorism, climate change.

From now on, the funerals will happen at increasingly shorter intervals, he thought. When people reached their fifties, deaths began occurring more frequently. Last year it was Ann; now it was Knut Abrahamsen. In Max's view, it was cancer that took most people. But not Knut. He had drowned.

In Dalen.

The old wound was throbbing faintly. And the doubt that had never dissipated. He pictured the German shepherd tied to the tree in the yard of the Homme farm, barking and trying to tear itself free. And Jørgen Homme, the district sheriff, who'd said with ice in his voice: *If you use the dog, it'll be the last thing you ever do in this job.*

Max had given in without a fight, and he'd never spoken of the incident to anyone. Not even his friend and colleague Knut Abrahamsen, with whom he worked every day. But the doubt had never let him go. On the contrary, it had gotten worse, and he left the police force only two years after finishing his training. It turned out that he wasn't made of the right stuff, after all. He had failed when it counted most.

A short time later he began a new life in the United States. He met Ann, and they got married. They had twenty-eight good years together, until her death a year ago. Years in which they built up their private investigative agency. By now the business had grown so much that he no longer personally did any of the investigative work; instead, he found himself buried in administrative tasks. In other words, he had become a great success. The American way. And yet the wound caused by doubt had never closed entirely. It was true that for long periods he might not notice it at all. But then it would suddenly reappear. In the middle of a conversation. While he was stuck in rush-hour traffic. In bed at night. The doubt and the cowardice. He should have defied the sheriff, or at least reported the man's bizarre behavior.

Max switched the channel back to CNN but didn't feel like watching the news. Other thoughts had sunk their claws into his mind. Knut's inexplicable return to old stomping grounds. The look on Karoline Abrahamsen's face. The German shepherd standing on its hind legs and yanking on the chain because, as an experienced tracker, the animal recognized the signs that a search was under way.

With a grimace, as if acting against his will, Max opened his laptop and logged on to the hotel's Wi-Fi.

Then he typed "Eidsborg" into the browser. That was the small community close to Dalen where Sheriff Jørgen Homme had lived.

Most of the hits had to do with the Eidsborg stave church. Max had once gone inside, right after he started his police job. He now recalled that there was something special about that church. Something having to do with an old portrait of a saint. He might have known about it when he was an officer, but if so, that information had long since vanished from his memory.

The name Henrik Thue showed up in many of the hits. He was a professor at the college in Bø and author of the books *The Eidsborg Stave Church* and *The Spirit of the Place*, which was also about Eidsborg. Max thought that such a man must know virtually everything about the area. Also about former sheriffs, and the disappearance that occurred in 1985.

A moment later he found himself phoning Professor Thue to set up a meeting with him at his office in Bø for the day after tomorrow. His cover story was that he was writing an article about the stave church for a Norwegian American magazine.

In the silence following that brief conversation, Max felt almost paralyzed by the thought of what he'd just done. "The dog is vicious and can't be used." That's what he'd heard the sheriff say, though without making the slightest attempt to hide the lie in his eyes.

Now something was ripping open inside Max. Abruptly he hurled the remote control at the wall, sending the batteries flying through the room.

"Fuck!" he shouted.

He never should have come back to Norway. It was a stupid impulse, bound to dredge up all sorts of shit from the past.

"No, no, no," he muttered. This was definitely not what he wanted to be doing.

He grabbed the phone to call Thue back and cancel the appointment, but then decided it would seem ridiculous to do that only minutes after they'd spoken. Better to let some time pass. Maybe half an hour, and then phone to say that something unexpected had come up.

In the meantime he'd see what he could find out online about Knut Abrahamsen's death. That turned out to be easier said than done. Apparently it wasn't big news when someone fell and drowned, not even in the interior of Telemark, where usually nothing much happened. At least that was the case when Max had worked there.

Finally he found a brief article explaining that the police had completed their investigation into the circumstances surrounding a drowning in Dalen. The sheriff of Tokke municipality stated that there was no reason to suspect foul play. There was no description of the accident itself, other than the fact that the car key belonging to the deceased had now been found in the river as well. Obviously Knut had not had the key on him when his body was recovered.

As Max was about to close his laptop, something in the brief article caught his attention. The name "Sheriff Jon Homme." He had to look twice to make sure he was seeing correctly, but there was no doubt about it.

Suddenly his hands began to shake, and it took several attempts before he managed to type the name into the browser. At last he got some hits on the sheriff. Photographs too. The new sheriff was almost an exact copy of the old one. There was no question that Jon Homme was the son of Jørgen.

Muttering a curse, Max picked up the phone to call a car-rental agency.

Three

TIRILL VESTERLI WAS SITTING ON THE SOFA with her legs tucked under her as she read a Swedish crime novel. She was aware of nothing but the story in her book as she fiddled with the locket she wore on a chain around her neck.

She loved the silence that descended after her four-year-old son finally fell asleep and she could open a book and get swept up once again in a mystery. It was the only time of day she had a chance to read. Few things annoyed her more than hearing people comment that she must get a ton of reading done, being a librarian at the college in Bø. As if she had nothing else to do during work hours!

No, it was only in the evening, after Magnus fell asleep, that she actually had time to read. And then it was mostly detective stories. She was almost halfway through this one, and she had just decided that the doctor at the children's hospital must be the murderer. Not because there was anything especially suspicious about him, but because it was otherwise hard to see what role he would play as the plot unfolded. He seemed to be a character that the author was keeping in the wings, in anticipation of some major revelation. She could be wrong, of course; she often was. But any theory she came up with wouldn't count unless she ventured a guess at the identity of the killer before she reached the halfway point in the book.

Fictional murders were not the only ones that interested Tirill Vesterli. Whenever the media reported a homicide or a suspicious death, she would prick up her ears, like a hungry female fox that has caught the scent of prey. Murder cases fascinated her, because she liked to see if she could reason her way to who the perpetrator might be in real-life situations. Usually the husband was the guilty party. Rather boring, in the long run, but that's how life was.

She got up and went to the kitchen to get a half-full bottle of Sancerre from the fridge. As she reached for a wine glass in the cupboard, she noticed something outside the window.

Suddenly her heart was pounding as if someone had injected her with pure adrenaline. Her fingers tightened around the stem of the glass. In the bright summer evening she could clearly see the figure partially hidden behind the small shed belonging to the building superintendent.

And here she had just begun to feel safe again.

When Cecilie Wiborg, the student from Asker, had disappeared without a trace on Midsummer Eve last year, the police had launched a full-scale investigation. And this time it was happening practically on Tirill's doorstep. For several weeks Bø had been in the news every day. Not long after the disappearance, she had gone to the police to share her theory about what might have happened. She still thought it was a good theory, but the police were not convinced. They had laughed good-naturedly and given Tirill a patronizing pat on the shoulder as she left the station.

Shortly afterward, the stranger had started showing up outside her building. The first couple of times she had paid little attention, merely registering that someone she didn't know was out there, hanging around the superintendent's shed. But the third or fourth time, she began to feel uneasy. Especially because the man—and she assumed it was a man—had looked up at her apartment as she stood in the window. Then she started seeing him standing there several evenings a week. Always dressed in black, with the hood of his sweatshirt pulled low over his forehead. It was impossible to tell who he was.

Because of the way the police had reacted the last time she'd gone to talk to them, Tirill couldn't bring herself to file a report. She would have seemed even crazier than before. But in October, about the same time that the investigation into the Cecilie Wiborg case had been significantly reduced, the whole problem ended of its own accord. After that the dark-clad observer stopped appearing.

Even so, it wasn't until late in the spring that Tirill finally quit thinking about the man on a daily basis.

And now there he was again. The same slightly hunched figure, dressed in black, with his hood pulled well down over his forehead.

Shaking, she poured herself half a glass of wine and drank it down in big, noisy gulps.

When she looked out the window again, he was gone.

The bad feeling in her gut abruptly gave way to a fiery anger that flared like a struck match. In a few strides she was out in the hallway. She didn't stop to find her keys, which were somewhere in the clutter, and consequently she didn't close her door all the way. She took the steps two at a time, running downstairs from her apartment on the third floor as she snarled curses at all potential enemies. She bent down to pick up some advertising brochures from the floor in the foyer and wedged them in the front door so she wouldn't get locked out.

Then, in her stocking feet, she raced across the parking lot, with pebbles and gravel digging into her soles. But there was no one behind the superintendent's shed. Looking around, she saw only the neatly mowed lawn, a few bottle caps, and a couple of cigarette butts. She squatted down to touch them, but neither of them was warm.

The oldest of the local Somali boys came riding past on his bike. He was wearing a dark hoodie and black jeans. Who else would wear that kind of clothing on a warm summer day? He must be the person she saw.

Tirill ran into the parking lot and stopped the boy.

"Were you standing behind the shed over there just now?" she asked, pointing.

He frowned, looking as if he didn't understand. Tirill knew that he spoke very little Norwegian.

"Was that you standing near the corner of the shed?" she asked again, in English this time.

The boy shook his head, but she had a feeling that wasn't meant to be an answer to her question. Maybe she looked a little crazy, standing here in her stocking feet, still gasping for breath.

"Were you over there a minute ago?" she tried one last time, but the boy merely rode off without replying.

She looked around at the now deserted parking lot, then up at the various apartments. Had anyone seen the incident?

Lowering her eyes, she walked back.

When she was once again inside her apartment, she had the feeling that something wasn't right. She sniffed at the air in the living room. Had someone been here? Of course not, she thought with annoyance. Pull yourself together! But all the doors had been open while she was outside behind the superintendent's shed.

She dashed through the living room to the hallway leading to the bedrooms and bathroom.

The door to her son's room was ajar.

Everything inside her froze. Nothing moved. Not a drop of blood seemed to course through her veins. Everything stood still, waiting for what would come into view when she opened the door all the way.

With a hand that felt as if it were part of a bad dream, she grabbed the door handle and slowly pulled the door open.

His bed was empty. The covers lay on the floor.

Everything that had been holding her upright during the last few seconds suddenly switched off as abruptly as a light bulb. She didn't notice that she was falling until her knees struck the floor with a bang.

The next moment she was ice-cold and clearheaded. Her emergency generator had kicked in, an engine driven by instinct. She got up. Her only thought was to find her son. She tore open the door to the separate toilet room, but he wasn't there.

Not in the bathroom either.

And not in her own bedroom.

She yanked open the doors, one after another, and left them open.

But it was not a big apartment, and soon there was nowhere else to search.

"Magnus!" she shouted desperately as she tried to find her cell phone. She thought she'd left it on the side table next to one of the armchairs, but she couldn't find it anywhere.

"Magnus!"

She screamed his name, and in her voice she heard the abyss that had opened.

"Mamma . . . ," whispered a voice from somewhere behind her.
She spun around. "Magnus?"

She heard a happy gasp in reply.

"Where are you?"

A little tousled head poked out from the narrow space between the sofa and the wall.

"Hide-and-seek!" he shouted, bursting with excitement.

Tirill ran over and hauled him out of the space, so angry she could have flung him against the wall.

"How could you just sit there and not say anything? While I . . . While I thought that . . ."

When his lip began to quiver, she sank down onto the sofa and pulled his small body close. As she sobbed, she thought to herself that she wouldn't have hesitated to kill someone if it meant defending her son.

Four

MAX TOOK THE E18 TO DRAMMEN and then headed west on E134 past Hokksund and Kongsberg. Up near Meheia, surrounded by forest, he crossed into the county of Telemark, and a short time later the view opened up. Rugged forest landscape sliced by winding valleys with granite mountains in the background.

His soul rose at the sight. Or did it actually sink? He felt slightly dizzy, at any rate.

In the town of Notodden, he stopped at a gas station to buy a hot dog. He stood outside, breathing in the gas fumes, and washed down the food with a cola. Overhead a plane left behind a white trail as it headed west, but it was too late to regret his decision now.

He called information and got the phone number for Karoline Abrahamsen. The widow answered at once, as if she'd been waiting for someone to call.

"This is Max Fjellanger. We met yesterday."

"Oh, right. . . ."

"I'm in Notodden, on my way to Dalen."

Silence on the other end. It lasted a long time.

"What are you planning to do there?" she said at last.

"I want to take a look at the place where they found Knut. I think I owe him that much. If I find out anything, I'll let you know, of course."

"Find out anything?" She suddenly sounded anxious. "Why

are you doing this? The two of you hadn't been in touch for thirty years."

"I'm doing it for my own sake," said Max. "It's complicated."

AN HOUR LATER HE REACHED EIDSBORG. The village was situated in a bowl-shaped hollow in the landscape. There were half a dozen farms with green fields arranged in a semicircle near a small lake. And a tar-brown stave church, as organic as an old pine tree.

He parked at the side of the road and sat in silence as he surveyed the scene. He had expected some sort of reaction from himself when he saw this place again, because he was now in the municipality of Tokke. From here it was only a few kilometers south to the center of Dalen, where he would find the sheriff's office. On the other side of the water, he could see the Homme farm, where Jørgen Homme had lived.

Eidsborg was picture perfect, with all the elements ideally juxtaposed. At the center of everything was the round, sky-blue mountain lake, called a tarn. With the houses and green fields on one side, the stave church on the other, and the whole setting enclosed by protective, forest-covered slopes, it was an idyllic sight.

Max Fjellanger reminded himself that perfection was not something you ever encountered in reality.

AFTER RENTING A CABIN IN A CAMPGROUND, he drove around the center of town until he located the sheriff's office, which was closed for the day. It turned out the office was open only two days a week. He'd been told this was not unusual for a small department way out in the country. Back when he worked here, it had been open every weekday.

He returned to Eidsborg, taking the same winding mountain road he'd driven to Dalen. The kind of road that German and Dutch tourists seek out when they come to Norway.

Just beyond the stave church, he turned right toward the Homme place and the other farms.

Sheriff Jon Homme was standing in the yard, his legs astraddle, bare-chested, wearing cutoffs and a cap advertising Zetor tractors. He stared at the rental car as it approached. Behind Homme was the same tree Max remembered from the last time he was here. An ash, as far as he could tell. Again there was a dog chained to the trunk. Not a German shepherd this time but a Norwegian elkhound that barked furiously at the intruder.

Max stopped the car near the barn ramp and got out. Homme came walking calmly toward him. The man bore a striking resemblance to his father, and the barking of the dog could not be distinguished from the sound Max had heard behind him when, head bowed, he'd retreated to his car thirty years ago.

It was as if no time at all had passed in this place.

"What can I do for you?" said Homme in a low and measured voice.

"I was just wondering whether—"

The barking drowned out his words.

"Quiet!" shouted the sheriff, his voice so loud that Max flinched.

The dog stopped barking, so he tried again. But the same thing happened. The second he opened his mouth, the elkhound stood on its hind legs and began barking.

Jon Homme went over to the dog and grabbed it by the scruff of the neck. First he pushed the animal to the ground. Then he squatted down until they were eye to eye. A few unhappy whimpers escaped from the dog, but Homme merely tightened his grip and leaned even closer to the animal's jaws with the white teeth and slobbering red tongue. He stared at the dog until it went quiet and lay down.

It was clearly a power struggle, and there was no doubt who was stronger.

"Sorry about all the noise," Homme said when it was over. "Elvis isn't very patient. He doesn't get enough exercise. It's my fault. So, what is it you were wondering?"

Max held out his hand and introduced himself.

"Years ago I was a sheriff's deputy working for your father. I just happened to be back here, revisiting my old stomping grounds."

The face with the icy-gray mustache thawed a little.

"Come on over to the porch," he said and led the way.

His hair was closely cropped, but down the middle of his back there was a wide strip of curly white hair that started at the nape of his neck and disappeared under the waistband of his shorts.

Homme motioned for Max to take a seat on the porch, which offered a view of the stave church and the museum on the opposite shore of the lake. Then the sheriff went inside to get coffee.

The sunlight reflecting off the nearly round lake was like an on-slaught of arrows to the eye. On the other side of the water, the sun glinted off the cars and buses parked in front of the church. Max felt a long way from home, but he'd felt like that ever since Ann died. Even in his own house. She had been his home, his anchor in the States. In Norway he'd never had an anchor. If he'd had one, he couldn't have left everything behind as easily as he did.

He'd spent his last two years in Norway up here, as a sheriff's deputy in Tokke municipality. Along with Knut Abrahamsen.

And Jørgen Homme.

The first time Max shook hands with the previous sheriff, a shudder had passed through him, moving from his hand all the way down to his toes. He'd never experienced anything like that before or since. It was as if some unknown energy emanated from the tall, gray-haired man standing, his legs astraddle, in the sheriff's office on that summer day long ago. An energy you wouldn't want to try to block.

The present-day sheriff now came out of the house, bringing coffee and a light snack. Cookies. Max couldn't picture the elder Homme ever doing that, but maybe he'd simply never seen that side of the sheriff.

"Father retired in '86," said Homme. "His successor was a man named Rasmussen, who held the job until '95. Then I took over. When was it you worked here?"

"Eighty-four and '85."

"I was working in Oslo back then. Can't recall ever meeting you. Max Fjellanger? I think I would have remembered the name."

"There were two deputies at the time. Me and Knut Abraham-sen. Knut wasn't just a good colleague, he was also my friend. Yes-terday I went to his funeral in Skien."

"I see. I'm sorry."

"He drowned in Dalen last week."

The sheriff's eyes narrowed for a moment. That was the only visible reaction.

"That was him? Odd coincidence."

"Everyone has to die somewhere. Do you know what he was doing here? Out fishing or something?"

Homme shook his head. "According to his wife, there was nothing that would have brought him here. We thought it was strange, and a drowning with no witnesses is always a little . . . Well, you know what I mean. Even if the victim has his pockets filled with stones."

"Knut killed himself?" Max was caught by surprise.

"Didn't you know that? I apologize for being so blunt. I thought you . . ."

That must be why the widow had sounded so anxious when Max told her he was going to Dalen. She didn't want him to find out that Knut's death was a suicide.

"But why would he come all the way up here to do it?"

"That's the reason we were a bit skeptical. But no one in his family mentioned that he had worked here in the past. They just said he'd been a police officer long ago. Maybe he wanted to see the old place one last time. Recall his youth. Who knows what people are thinking when they do something like that?"

The two middle-aged men sat in silence for a while, as if they were both pondering what the sheriff had just said.

"Where was he found?" asked Max at last.

"Right below the bridge in Dalen. On the east side."

"With stones in his pockets?"

"Yes. In the pockets of his pants and jacket."

"Any signs of a struggle?"

"He had a few bruises on his knees, and a small cut on his upper lip. The tech guys concluded that he must have fallen when he made his way down to the river."

Then the sheriff closed one eye as he studied Max with the other. "Tell me, are you still on the police force?"

"No, that was years ago. I have my own business in the States. In the twenty-eight years that have passed since I moved away, I've been back to Norway only twice before now. For my parents' funerals. My sole remaining family member is a brother, but we lost contact long ago."

"Did you grow up here in Telemark?"

"No, I have no real ties to the area, except for the two years I worked here. I grew up in Porsanger in Finnmark and in Evje in Setesdalen."

The sheriff paused to think about that. "So you were a military brat?"

"Yup."

"And you're not going around snooping into these matters on your own?"

"What do you mean by that?" asked Max innocently. "Is there really anything worth snooping into?"

"Not at all," he said.

"Just one more thing, and I'll go," said Max in a disarming tone of voice.

"What is it?"

"Is it true that Knut's car key was found somewhere else in the river?"

"That's right."

"How do you think that happened?"

"I think it must have slipped out of his pocket while he was underwater," said the sheriff.

"But I thought all his pockets were filled with stones."

Jon Homme smiled confidently beneath his mustache as he looked across Eidsborg Tarn at the stave church and museum. It was a smile that seemed to encompass and lay claim to everything in sight. "Except for the inside pocket of his jacket. That's where he must have put the car key."

Max wondered if Jon knew about the rumors that his father had been a corrupt cop. That he'd taken stolen goods, especially folk-art antiquities, and sold them. Maybe Jon wouldn't have been quite so smug if he knew that Max had heard these rumors soon after he took the job here.

"Do you remember the man who disappeared in 1985, never to be found again?" he asked now.

"Sure. Peter Schram."

That was it! The name reverberated like a tolling bell inside Max. "Who exactly was he?"

"As I said, I was working in Oslo when you were here, so I don't know a lot about it. But he wasn't from around here. That much

I know. I seem to recall that he was writing a book. Was it about the stave church? No, I can't remember. Did you take part in the search?"

Max nodded. On the other side of the house, the dog began barking again. It was still chained to the tree in the yard.

Five

VOICES BUZZING IN DIFFERENT LANGUAGES filled the museum's café and reception area. Max walked past the souvenir shop and a moment later entered a room with a display of house gods, primitive wooden figures that had been worshipped on farms in pre-Christian times. Some had been found in the marshes, where they had presumably been hidden from the priest and other authorities. The marsh waters were oxygen poor, which meant they were able to preserve wood for thousands of years. Other carvings had been kept on the farms as family heirlooms all the way up until modern times, before being donated to the museum.

Work was going on in the next room. A man wearing a white T-shirt and jeans was installing what looked to be a photography exhibit. He sported an impressive handlebar mustache. Max nodded to the man and was about to move on when he changed his mind.

"Excuse me," he said.

The man looked up from his work with an expression that signaled he was a person who enjoyed talking.

"Do you work here?" asked Max.

"I'm the head of operations."

"You're from Eidsborg?"

"Born and raised. But my father is from Kviteseid, so I'm considered an outsider. You have to have several generations of Eidsborg farmers on both sides of your family before you're considered the real thing."

He grinned beneath his big mustache, but something in his tone of voice made Max think he might not be joking.

"I'm interested in the stave church, and I have an appointment with Henrik Thue in Bø tomorrow. I assume you know him?"

"Can't say I actually 'know' him. But I know who he is. So where are you from?"

"I'm Norwegian, but I've lived in the United States for a long time. By the way, my name is Max Fjellanger."

"Johannes Liom."

"I used to be a sheriff's deputy here. But that was years ago."

"Oh?" The man looked at him with interest.

"Uh-huh. I have a lot of great memories from all over Tokke municipality. Eidsborg too. And some that aren't so great. Do you remember Peter Schram? The man who disappeared and was never found again?"

"Sure. Are you kidding? I used to see him almost every day. Grew up a few hundred meters from where he was staying. And I still live in the same place. Peter. Hmm. Real sad."

"So you knew him?"

"No, can't say I did. I was a lot younger than him, and he was a few notches above me, intellectually speaking."

"Was he an author?"

"No, he was working on a doctoral dissertation, if I remember right. Something about our stave church and the saint worship that used to go on here."

Max decided not to pursue the topic. Johannes Liom could no doubt tell him a lot more, but he didn't want to seem too pushy and arouse suspicion. Better to come back another time and take up the subject again.

HE LEANED AGAINST THE CAR, observing the hustle and bustle. Another bus had just pulled in, and a long line of tourists streamed toward the open church door, which seemed to lead into total darkness. Max would have liked to go inside too, but he didn't want to stand in line.

"Just imagine if there was a crowd like this for a church service," he heard someone say behind him.

Out of curiosity he turned around and saw a woman standing there, a pensive expression on her face as she stared at all the people. It took a few seconds before he realized who she must be.

"You're the pastor?" he said, as he shook her hand.

She gave him a warm smile. "Julia Bergmann."

"German?"

"Is it that obvious?"

"Only in the way you say your 'r's."

"Ah, the traitorous 'r.'" And she smiled again.

It's actually quite charming, he thought. But he couldn't say something like that to a pastor.

Julia Bergmann wore a white blouse and a knee-length skirt with a floral pattern. A bit old-fashioned for someone her age. Probably in her thirties. Her hairstyle, on the other hand, was much more modern. Cut short in back and over her ears, but long in front, with a swoop of blond hair covering her left eye.

She brushed it back with slender fingers.

"So regular church services are still held here?" Max asked.

"Oh sure. But you don't exactly have to fight to find a place to sit. It's a strange thing. Everybody wants to go inside to see the old image of the saint, but few are interested in the living word."

"Are you jealous?"

"Of course."

"Isn't jealousy one of the seven sins?"

"Yes, it is. And like most people, I'm guilty of all seven."

"So, what's the big deal with this saint, anyway?" asked Max.

"Originally the church was dedicated to Saint Nikolas. The building is very old. From the days when Norway was Catholic. The image of the saint, a wooden sculpture, is still inside. Before the Reformation, the figure, which the farmers called Nikuls—and folks around here still call it that—was of enormous importance to the local community. Every Midsummer Eve the people would carry the sculpture out of the church in a procession. First three times around the church building, then to the small lake you can see down there. Eidsborg Tarn. There, the figure was carried around the lake on a palanquin while the priest and congregation sang and prayed. Finally, they would lower the figure into the water to cleanse it. And that was unusual. A saint is pure, after all, and shouldn't need to be cleansed. But the farmers were convinced the ritual would ensure good crops and many births. In the 1800s the saint statue was stowed away, put in a shed that was later torn down. Eventually the sculpture was restored and placed back inside the church. It's true that the figure no longer holds a prominent position, having been banished to a dark nook just inside the door of the church. But it's a magnet for tourists. As is the church, which is utterly charming. We don't have stave churches in Germany."

Max nodded at the idyllic scene on the other side of Eidsborg Tarn. With all the farms arranged in a semicircle.

"What do the permanent residents think about all these visitors?"

"Their focus is on making a living," said the pastor. "So they're more than happy to see the tourists. Nikuls and the church bring in a lot of money for the community."

A red pickup approached from the museum and pulled up next to them. Johannes Liom leaned across the passenger seat to speak to them through the open window.

"Thinking of going inside?" he asked.

Max shrugged in resignation. "Is it ever possible to take a look at the church without being surrounded by a horde of other people?"

"If you wait until winter," said Liom.

"I don't have that much time."

"Hmm . . . If I was free I'd give you a little tour myself, after closing time, but I'm busy tonight." Then he turned to the pastor and added, "This guy is interested in our church. He came all the way from the United States just to see it."

That wasn't exactly what Max had said, but he didn't try to correct Liom.

"How nice," she said. "You know, I need to come up here later tonight anyway to put some things in the sacristy. So why don't I show him around?"

Liom nodded, looking pleased, and then drove off.

Julia watched the truck as it moved away. "Johannes is very dedicated," she said. "He runs the whole museum practically single-handedly. He comes from modest circumstances. His father was a construction worker. There's such a great word for that in Norwegian."

"For 'construction worker'?"

"No, for that kind of dedication. *Ildsjel.* A soul on fire."

Six

TIRILL REMAINED SITTING IN HER CAR outside the sheriff's office in Bø. She could still hear echoes of the good-natured laughter from the last time she was here. As if, above all else, the officers had been grateful to have a little entertainment on an otherwise dreary workday.

Finally she pulled herself together and climbed out of the car. She needed to find out what was going on—if not for her own sake, then for Magnus.

She was greeted by a polite but reserved woman seated behind the counter.

"I'd like to file a report," Tirill began. "Is there someone here I could talk to?"

"Just a moment and I'll check," said the woman, speaking in a neutral, disinterested tone of voice.

She got up and knocked lightly on a door, waited for an answer, and then slipped into the room. Tirill heard a faint murmur of voices, and then the woman was back.

"Go right in," she said, pointing at the door.

As soon as she stepped inside, Tirill felt her stomach sink. The officer sitting at the desk had been present when she offered the police her theory last year.

He stood up to shake her hand. "Tom Ralle. Lieutenant."

"Tirill Vesterli."

"Please, have a seat," he said.

He was short, with broad shoulders and a three-day stubble on both his face and his shaved head. "I hear you want to file a report. Is that right?"

"Yes. This may sound a little paranoid, but someone has been following me."

"Oh really?" he said, clasping his hands behind his head. He didn't seem to recognize her. "Do you know who it is?"

"No. But it's a man."

"A man. OK. And where has he been following you?"

"Well, he doesn't exactly follow me. He stands outside my apartment and watches me. He looks in my windows."

"Where do you live?"

She gave the lieutenant her address.

"That's a building with lots of apartments. Are you sure you're the one he's watching? If that's what he's actually doing, that is?"

"I'm positive. I could see him staring at me."

"What floor do you live on?"

"The third."

"And where exactly does he stand?"

"Next to the superintendent's shed outside."

Tom Ralle leaned forward to prop his elbows on his desk and lean his chin on his hands. For a moment he sat like that, studying Tirill. He seemed to be contemplating how to phrase what he wanted to say. "Sounds like there's quite a distance from where this person is standing to your apartment," he said cautiously.

"Yes, I guess so. It's too far for me to get a good look at his face, anyway."

"And you have no idea who he might be?"

"No. But I have a four-year-old son, and so of course I'm—"

"You're a single mom?"

"Yes."

"I see. And you're worried about your son. That's totally understandable."

"A man has been looking up at our apartment!" Tirill exclaimed.

"OK. . . . But since you can't get a good look at his face, how do you know he's looking at your apartment? I don't mean to dismiss your concern or anything. It's just that if you can't see his eyes . . .

You can't, right? So how can you tell what he's looking at? Do you see what I mean?"

"But I can . . . feel it." She could have bitten her tongue.

A kind smile appeared on Ralle's scruffy face. "And of course we need to take feelings seriously. But when it comes to police work, it's often a good idea to put them aside. So, here's what I can do. I'll make a note of our conversation, and you should call the police the next time you notice someone outside staring at you. Then we'll send a patrol car up to Breisås to take a look around. How's that?"

Tirill was about to say something scornful about the response time of the local police, but Ralle suddenly slapped his hands on the desktop and pointed at her.

"Hey, aren't you the one who . . . ?" He started laughing. "Tirill Vesterli. I remember now. You had a theory about Cecilie Wiborg's disappearance. Am I right?"

She could have sunk into the floor. "Uh-huh," she whispered.

"What was it now? Something about Midsummer Eve and old superstitions?"

She smiled wanly.

"So, do you have a new theory about what happened to Cecilie? Since you're here anyway, I mean."

"No," said Tirill staunchly as she stood up. "I still think the first one is right."

Then she walked out, leaving the door open behind her.

Seven

THE SMELL OF TAR was overpowering in the outdoor gallery, where only scant light managed to seep in through the small arched windows along the wall. The slanted ceiling was covered with some sort of spikes. Max reached up to touch a couple of them.

"The roof is covered with seventeen thousand shingles," said Julia Bergmann. "And each of them is fastened with a nail. Seventeen thousand wooden nails. Every single one made by hand. Just like everything else in this church. Sometimes I think the whole culture up here is a wood culture. Traditional Norwegian rosemaling designs painted on wood, carvings made of wood, and old timbered buildings. As if only what can be expressed in wood has any value."

The nails, which stuck out from the underside of the roof, reminded Max of a medieval torture chamber. Maybe it was the dim lighting and the almost intoxicating smell of the building itself that had diverted his thoughts onto such sinister pathways.

"I need to remember to give the key back to the church sexton," Julia said as she unlocked the door.

A gloomy semidarkness reigned inside the stave church. In the glow from the pastor's flashlight, Max caught a glimpse of old illustrations painted directly on the walls: cloaked men and women, some of them on horseback, surrounded by an ornamental pattern bearing a slight resemblance to rosemaling.

"Other than a small lamp on the pulpit, there's no electric lighting in here. Only candles are used," said Julia.

The building seemed almost like an unlit torch, impregnated with tar for centuries. It wouldn't take more than a single spark for the whole structure to go up in flames.

The pastor aimed the beam from her flashlight at a spot above the entrance to the choir. "The crucifix is original and just as old as the church. From the thirteenth century."

The cross was the same gray as a pine branch that has lain on the ground drying out for years—somewhere between the gray hue of an eraser and the color of bone. With a gaunt Christ wearing a loincloth. No crown, only a terrible agony tugging the primitively carved lips down into a grimace. And nails through the palms of his hands. Wooden nails, of course. A savior carved from the same material as wooden ladles, buckets, and ale bowls.

"A cudgel," he heard Julia say behind him.

She was aiming her flashlight overhead. Lying across two rafters near the ceiling was a long stick, a little thinner than a fence post.

"A man named Gunnar killed his brother-in-law on Christmas Eve in 1663. Ever since, the cudgel has remained up there near the ceiling. No one really knows why, but it's probably meant to be some sort of reminder."

"Memento mori," murmured Max, thinking of Knut.

"Remember that you will die," Julia translated.

The tar smell was hardly noticeable inside the church. Instead, Max was aware of a smell from his childhood. He had to search his memory before he could identify what it was. The Christmas tree celebrations! This was exactly how the prayer houses in Evje and Porsanger had smelled: of green soap, Sunday clothes, and newly scrubbed hands. A smell that had settled in the walls for generations and greeted the children, filled with anticipation, the minute they stepped inside. He remembered what the pastor had told him. The church was still in use.

She handed him the flashlight. "I have to go to the sacristy to take care of something," she said and then left.

Max shone the light on the illustrated walls. Men on horseback, wearing crowns on their heads. Maybe the three wise men on their way to Bethlehem. And women wearing long gowns with big, crusader-like crosses painted on their chests. They too wore crowns. Lines of text were painted under these images, but Max wasn't able to decipher the worn, Gothic letters, so he had no clue who the women were supposed to portray.

He walked all the way up to the transept and the choir. The altarpiece, which seemed to be of quite recent origin, depicted Jesus wearing a white cloak, with a halo around his newly washed hair. Max was struck by how childlike the image seemed, compared to the primitive wooden Jesus on the wall above. If not for the cross, that figure would have been hard to distinguish from the house gods in the museum.

Max sat down on one of the pews up front, which was no doubt reserved for the local gentry, and stared up at the old crucifix. Personally, he believed it was possible to discover the truth about things. That was his only belief. He had been brought up not as a Christian but rather as a conservative. It was a church membership that was based not on faith but on upholding society. Of the two of them, it was Ann who had been the believer. She had never tried to proselytize, but he'd always known her faith was there, like a bridge he had never crossed, even though it could have brought them together in a new way.

What would Ann have thought about this church?

She wouldn't have liked the darkness. Her Christianity was bright and joyous. Here, the light was dim, and it was so quiet that all he heard were the tiny creaks and scrapes that must be coming from the building itself. Maybe the old timbered structure was stretching after a long, hot day.

He didn't know how long he sat there, but after a while he began to wonder what had happened to the pastor. The door to the sacristy was closed. Max got up and went over to open it. No one was in the room, but he noticed another door on the opposite wall. No doubt it led outside. Julia must have gone out to get something.

He went back to the choir and walked down the center aisle of the nave as he shone the flashlight around. When he had almost reached the front entrance, he aimed the beam at the darkest corner and just about dropped the flashlight when a face stared back at him. A man with a beard, wearing a pointed cap. The somber eyes were focused on something far away, in another world.

Max realized that he was looking at Nikuls. The statue was about a meter high, blackened by centuries of smoke from lighted candles.

Suddenly Julia Bergmann's face materialized out of the darkness next to the saint. She must have exited the sacristy and then come back in through the front door.

"You startled me," said Max, unable to hide his annoyance.

"It's a special kind of darkness in here. As you can see, it's not really pitch dark, yet things disappear from view. People too. I just wanted to show you that," she said, giving him a searching glance. "And by the way, the church has its own ghost," she added. "A monk. He's usually seen leaving the church at night, carrying Nikuls. As if he were planning to carry out the ancient ritual. If you want to understand this place, those are the two things you need to know. About the monk and this special kind of darkness."

Without any further explanation, she went out the door. Max followed, still a bit shaken. It was a relief to emerge into the bright evening.

"How long have you been the pastor here?" he asked.

"Almost ten years."

"A young, female pastor in an ancient church. How did that happen?"

She shrugged, as if it were of no importance.

"Did you ever hear about the man who disappeared in 1985? Peter Schram was his name."

"I think everybody knows about him. Why do you ask?"

"I was involved in the investigation back then. In my former life I was a sheriff's deputy. I've forgotten exactly where he was living. Do you know?"

"On the Tveit farm. It's the one to the left of the sheriff's place," she said, pointing.

Max turned to look toward the farms. It seemed like all of this had just been waiting for him. As if nothing that had happened between that time and now were of any consequence, regardless of how good his life had been with Ann. Because the whole time he had been on his way back here. To the tar-scented interior of Telemark.

Eight

H E PULLED OVER just before the bridge crossing the Tokke River and got out of the car. He peered down at the place where Knut's body had been found. Suicide? The man whom Max had known back in the mid-eighties wouldn't have done such a thing. But anything could happen to a person over the course of thirty years.

The car key must have slipped out of his inside jacket pocket. That's what the sheriff had said.

Max tried to picture the scene. Knut decides to kill himself by drowning in the river. He leaves his cell phone and wallet in the car. Understandable enough, since those items have a certain value, and he has a family. The same is true of the car. No sense in risking having it stolen or vandalized. So he locks the car and sticks the key in the pocket where he always carries it. And that's definitely not the inside pocket of his jacket. Nobody would do that. That's where a man might carry his wallet, but not his keys.

So Knut goes down to the water's edge and starts filling his pockets with stones. Wouldn't he have completed that distressing task even if he'd put the car key in one of his pants pockets? Yes, Max concluded. And in that case the key would not have fallen out.

Of course, it was possible that he put the key in his inside pocket. As the sheriff said, who knows what people are thinking when they do something like that? But Max didn't believe it.

"Old friend . . . ," he whispered to the dark water.

A memory appeared out of nowhere. He was with Knut on the low ridge of Falkeriset, the vaulted sky above and Mount Gaustatoppen like an overturned boat in the east. On their way back down they got caught in a violent thunderstorm. It sounded like cannons being fired indoors, and there was nowhere to seek refuge. Finally they got so scared that they threw themselves down in a small hollow in the ground with hardly enough room for the two of them. There they lay, with their hands covering their heads, as if that would help, while the forces of nature ravaged the open expanse of Falkeriset. At some point they had looked at each other and started to laugh. And they couldn't stop. They laughed and laughed. Two young men surrounded by vast space on all sides.

And then thirty years later: stones in Knut's pockets.

But not his car key.

THE CABIN WAS ONLY A FEW METERS FROM THE RIVER, set slightly apart from the others and with forest reaching right up to the walls on two sides. It looked old and in disrepair, but he was glad to have found a place to spend the night. The windows were open, and fresh summer air filled the room.

From his suitcase he got out his traveling shoeshine case with the brushes, oil, and polish and began cleaning his shoes. His father, Colonel Fjellanger, had impressed upon him that a man with dirty shoes was an unreliable man. A claim that Max had learned through experience was not necessarily true. Yet he was grateful to have had the routine drummed into him.

As he worked, his eyes fell on his suitcase, which was plastered with stickers from various American cities that he and Ann had visited. A veritable logbook of a lifetime together.

In his mind he pictured their yard with the fireflies at dusk and the deep buzzing of hummingbird wings in the daytime. The swimming pool where he used to watch his wife as she swam laps in the evening. The lizards darting across the warm flagstones in search of insects. A whole world that had now disappeared because that one person was gone.

IN HIS DREAM, he and Ann and Knut were fishing in an old well. Knut looked pale and miserable. Personally, Max thought it was disgusting to eat fish that had lived their whole lives in a hole in the ground. The water in the old well could have been polluted from any manner of things. He tried to object, but Ann and Knut both dismissed his concerns. Suddenly Ann pulled a big eel out of the well, and without warning she threw it at Max. The eel struck his arm and latched on, biting him with its tiny, sharp teeth. Desperately he tried to shake the eel off, but it refused to let go. In the meantime, over by the well, Ann had turned into Knut's widow, and Knut had disappeared. The widow pointed at Max with a terrified look on her face. Or was she pointing at something behind him? He turned around to see, and woke up.

The skin on his forearm, where the eel had bitten him in the dream, was slick with sweat. There was a strange smell in the room. Still half immersed in his dream, he thought at first he was smelling grilled fish. Then he recognized the acrid smell of burning paper.

He sat up in bed and looked around. Outside the open window, the sun seemed to have come up. But there was something wrong with the light. It was moving.

Fire! His brain suddenly registered what he was seeing. The cabin was on fire!

He jumped out of bed and ran outside in his pajamas. It wasn't a big fire. Not yet. Only a burning pile of trash right next to the cabin wall. Max rushed back inside and filled a bucket with water. When he came back, the fire had almost gone out on its own. The bucketful of water doused the last of the flames.

He went in and refilled the bucket, just to make sure. He also picked up his cell phone. Outside he crouched down to study the site of the fire in the light of his phone. Among the scorched heather and grass he saw what looked like the singed remnants of a crumpled page from a newspaper. He picked it up and saw that he was right. It was from the Vest-Telemark paper. He poked through the ashes but gave up on finding anything else of interest and then poured the bucket of water over the rest.

What do I do now? he thought.

It was 2:10 in the morning, and someone had tried to set fire to the cabin where he was sleeping.

He shone the light from his phone on the scorched spot on the ground. There wasn't even any soot visible on the foundation. Just some singed heather and grass, and the newspaper page that he'd put back down. He picked it up again and sniffed at it. No hint of gasoline or any other flammable fluid.

If someone had wanted him to die in a cabin fire, wouldn't they have made a better job of it? Was this just some boyish prank? Max looked around, but it was pitch dark around the cabin, and he knew that the forest was close by, as dense as a wall, though he had no idea how far it reached. Possibly tens of kilometers.

He made up his mind to leave the cabin at once and get a hotel room in Bø, about an hour's drive away.

Nine

THE DOOR TO HENRIK THUE'S OFFICE was locked. Max tried to call him, but his phone was switched off. Apparently the professor had more important things to do than talk to some eager amateur.

Max took the elevator down to the first floor and was on his way back to his hotel when he changed his mind.

The only person in the library was a woman sitting behind the counter, tapping away on a keyboard. Her hair stuck out in all directions. He looked at the tag pinned to her shirt and saw that her name was Tirill Vesterli.

She looked up and gave him a perfect librarian smile, the kind that makes it impossible to raise your voice.

"Do you have a book by Henrik Thue about the Eidsborg stave church?" he whispered. "I had an appointment to meet with the professor today, but he's not here."

The librarian got up and headed briskly through the deserted library. Max followed, staring at her hair. Did she just get out of bed and come to work without giving a thought to her hair? Or was it actually some sort of carefully thought-out style? It looked like her hair had exploded.

She found the professor's two books for him and then returned to her place behind the counter. Max sat down and began leafing through the first volume. *The Eidsborg Stave Church* dealt with the building itself, from the time it was constructed, in the thirteenth century, up to the present day. The book was filled with facts about the various restorations and renovations. The other book, *The Spirit of the Place*, focused specifically on Saint Nikolas, or Nikuls, as he was known locally.

After Max had been sitting there for half an hour, the librarian came back to tell him the library would be closing soon. Would he like to borrow the books? Max politely declined, since he had no idea whether he'd have a chance to bring them back.

"Have you lived in the United States a long time?" she asked.

"Almost thirty years." He was about to leave but stopped to ask, "How did you know?"

"Your clothes don't look Norwegian. I see your jacket is from Old Navy. And I assume the rest of your clothes are American too. That alone doesn't really mean much. You could have gone to the States on vacation and used the opportunity to buy yourself some clothes. But I also noticed your ring. It's a wedding band, right?"

Max nodded.

"And you're wearing it on the ring finger of your left hand, which is the custom in most countries, since the left hand is closest to the heart. But in Norway the wedding ring is worn on the right hand, as far away from the heart as possible," she said with a smile. "And it looks as if your ring has left a very visible mark on your finger. So: American clothing. Married abroad. Married for a long time. Voilà." She threw out her hands.

"Very impressive. You should be a detective."

"That's what I am every evening. Between the pages of a book, that is. I think detective novels are enough for me."

"Well, if you ever happen to change your mind . . ."

He was joking, of course. He took out his wallet and handed her a business card that said "Max Fjellanger. Private Investigator."

"Jesus!" she exclaimed. "A real detective!"

"My job mainly involved exposing adulterous spouses or employees who were suspected of stealing from their employers. Not exactly high drama."

"Involved? Does that mean you're no longer a detective?"

He had to pause to think about that. It was years since he'd personally done any investigating. But now there was Knut's death. And the fire someone had set outside the wall of the cabin last night.

"To tell you the truth, I'm not really sure," he said at last.

He could see she was wondering what an ambivalent private detective from Florida was doing in Bø.

"I guess at heart I still am," he added.

Her expression changed when he said that. Quickly she glanced around, as if to ensure that no one was listening, but they were the only ones in the library.

"Are you staying here for long?" she asked in a low voice.

"In Bø? Until tomorrow at least."

"I'm at my wits' end. A stranger has been watching my apartment, and the police just laugh at me."

"Why would they laugh?"

"Because they laughed at me last year too."

"What happened last year?"

"Have you heard about Cecilie Wiborg?"

He shook his head.

"Look up the name. Wiborg, spelled with a 'W.' Afterward I'll explain why the police are laughing at me."

"Afterward?"

"Do you like upside-down cake?"

Max, for the life of him, couldn't think what kind of cake she meant, but he still answered in the affirmative.

Ten

THE BØ HOTEL was only a stone's throw away from the college, and as soon as Max was back in his room, he did as the librarian had said. When he typed in "Cecilie Wiborg," the first hits were dated June 25 of last year. Brief articles about a student in Bø who'd gone missing. At that point no one was mentioning that she might have been the victim of a crime. The following day the police reported that the last confirmed sighting of Cecilie was at 2:55 p.m. on Midsummer Eve. A surveillance camera caught her on her way down Bøgata, the main street in town, carrying a small backpack. Only eight minutes later her cell phone stopped sending signals to the closest cell tower, which meant either that it had been switched off or that it was destroyed. And that's where all traces ended. It was as if she'd vanished into thin air, according to the journalists.

On that day Bø had apparently been filled with both permanent residents and tourists; everyone wanted to be outside in the glorious weather of midsummer. The police had invested plenty of resources in trying to come to grips with the situation in the minutes before and after Cecilie's phone stopped producing any sign of life. After a couple of days, the police announced they were looking for a specific car in which a woman seemed to have been shouting for help. But it turned out to be just a bunch of kids goofing around.

Cecilie Wiborg was from Asker, a suburb of Oslo, and Max wondered why she'd been in Bø on Midsummer Eve. The college classes would have been over long before then. Maybe she had a summer job here, although there was no mention of that in any of the newspapers.

A few of her women friends had been interviewed, and he noted that one of them said it wasn't unusual for Cecilie to switch off her phone for a while, sometimes even for a whole evening. That was why the friend wasn't concerned when she tried to phone Cecilie on Midsummer Eve and got no answer. She didn't start to worry until the following day.

Max jumped when his cell rang. He'd set it on the nightstand. The call was from Henrik Thue.

HE SEEMED YOUNGER than his author photo. In his early forties, Max guessed. A young professor. His blond hair was cut short. He wore jeans and a blazer. His handshake conveyed just the right firmness; the same was true of his gaze from behind the steel-rimmed glasses he wore. His whole lean figure radiated balance and control.

"I woke up with an upset stomach, but I feel a lot better now," he said, gesturing for Max to take a seat. "I apologize for not getting in touch with you. It's not easy to remember everything when you're bending over the toilet."

Max waved away the apology. "I'm just grateful that you're willing to meet with me."

A pint of beer stood on the table in front of the professor, and Max ordered the same. From experience, he knew that most experts were more than happy to talk about their field. Usually the problem was how to get them to shut up.

"Are you a Norwegian American?" asked Thue.

"Born in Norway and still a Norwegian citizen, but I've lived in the United States for so long that I'm not quite sure what I am anymore."

The waiter placed his beer on the table. He took a tentative sip.

"So, you're back here for good?"

"No, I just wanted to make sure I didn't lose touch with where I came from." Couldn't be further from the truth, he thought.

"Hence your interest in stave churches?"

"Exactly. So I thought, why not write an article for the *Viking* magazine? The real Norwegian Americans are crazy about stuff like that."

He glanced around. The closest tables were occupied by noisy families with young kids eating pizza and drinking sodas. A fully loaded lumber truck with a trailer passed by outside, making all the glasses and cutlery clatter.

"I've heard about Nikuls and the ritual of carrying the statue around the lake and then cleansing it. Why did they do that?" asked Max.

"Nobody knows for sure. Some people think it's the remnant of an even older ritual that was carried out in the same place before the advent of Christianity. Bodies of water and springs were often regarded as sacred in pre-Christian times. Rituals were performed to guarantee the year's crops and to ensure that marriages would be blessed with many children. It's impossible to say for sure, but Eidsborg Tarn may have been that sort of sacred place. It wasn't unusual for the church to take over rituals from the religion it had replaced. For instance, Christmas is an adaptation of a pagan midwinter festival. The same is true of Midsummer Day, an occasion celebrated when the sun was at its zenith. That type of celebration may well have taken place in Eidsborg, associated with the lake there. So the people let Nikuls take over the main role after Christianity arrived. Same shit, new wrapping, as the Americans say."

Henrik Thue was clearly the type of person who liked to hear his own voice. Which was just the opposite of Max Fjellanger, who preferred to let others do the talking, because when they did, he always learned something. Ann used to say that this tendency of his made him a difficult person to read.

"Another thing that made the Nikuls ritual special was the fact that it continued all the way up until the eighteenth century. Nearly 250 years after the Reformation and the ban on worshipping images of saints in Norway."

"Why did the Lutheran pastors allow it to go on?"

"Stop and think about it. Even today Eidsborg is a remote location. What do you think it was like several hundred years ago? The pastor was at the mercy of the local population, not the other way around. The people of Telemark were notorious for killing pastors in the old days."

Thue took a big swig of his beer and looked around, as if he were searching for someone.

"What about the ghost? Do you know the story?"

"Of course. An old building like that has to have a ghost. The cloaked monk who is seen coming out of the church carrying Nikuls. If nothing else, the story helps attract tourists."

"And it's the original statue of the saint that's still there today?"

"The real thing. Have you seen the video, by the way?"

Max shook his head.

"A few years ago the ritual was revived. It was supposed to be a historical reenactment. We have a lot of reenactments like that here in Norway, you know. It was done with a priest and the whole shebang. And the genuine statue. That's why some people insisted it was wrong. They said it was worshipping ancient idols, even though it wasn't done as part of any church service. It was meant to be cultural entertainment. Because of the controversy, the Nikuls reenactment stopped after a couple of years. But the first time it was captured on film. As far as I know, you can find the video on the Internet. If you want to understand what Nikuls still means to people, you should watch it."

"Are you familiar with the name Homme in Eidsborg?"

"Of course. The Homme farm is the most important one in the area. The oldest too. The sheriff's farm, going back to the old days. As far as I know, the same family has lived there for as far back as anyone can remember."

"Would you say they're a powerful family?"

Thue shrugged. "What is power? There may be some informal power arenas where the old status still holds true, even though Eidsborg is a very small community. More of a hamlet than a village, actually. So we're talking about very limited, local power."

"I talked to the sheriff, Jon Homme, yesterday," said Max. "Do you know him?"

The professor frowned. "Why would I know him?"

"I thought maybe . . ."

"No." Again he glanced around as if looking for someone, or as if he was afraid of being seen. "I don't know anyone in the Homme family."

"Have you ever heard of Peter Schram?"

"Wasn't he the man who disappeared?"

"Yes. In 1985. Was he writing a doctoral dissertation about the church?"

"Something like that, I think."

"I would have thought that you'd know everything there is to know about him," said Max.

"Schram didn't leave any written work. At least not as far as I know. For me, he's just a name I've heard, a story. And there are lots of stories connected with Eidsborg."

He fell silent and seemed to retreat inward, as if the question had ruined his desire to talk. Max glanced at the noisy families sitting at the neighboring tables. Several of the kids were wearing T-shirts from the local water park. Old legends probably had very little importance here today.

"It's a widespread misconception that the past is past," said Henrik Thue, as if he'd read Max's mind. "The truth is that it's never over."

Eleven

THE TAXI DROPPED HIM OFF near an apartment complex. Three boys who looked like they might be Somalis were riding their bikes around the parking lot. They were shouting to each other in a foreign language and didn't seem especially interested in Max.

He found the right door and rang the bell. Soon Tirill appeared, giving him a nervous smile. He was nervous too. Around her neck she wore a chain with a locket that he hadn't noticed before. It looked intricate and old.

"Come on in," she said.

He followed her up the stairs to a hallway with doors to several apartments. A horseshoe hung on the wall next to Tirill's door.

She had an impressive book selection, he noticed with satisfaction when he went inside. And on the walls hung a row of pictures that he figured must be of her family.

An old black-and-white photo caught his eye. It was bigger than the others and showed a group of five adults lined up next to each other. A child of two or three sat on a small table, reaching out his arms toward the woman who was no doubt his mother.

Then Max realized the woman was Tirill, but with her hair pulled up in an old-fashioned topknot. "Is that you?"

"No," she said, standing behind him.

He could tell that she was used to hearing this question, and that she found it amusing.

"A reenactment of an old posed photograph?"

"It *is* an old photograph."

"But that's you standing there, isn't it?"

"No, that's my great-great-grandmother. The picture was taken in 1898."

"She looks exactly like you!"

"Can you imagine what it was like for me the first time I saw it?"

"As if you were looking in a mirror?"

"As if I'd lived before. But there's something else odd about that photo. Can you see what it is?"

Max leaned forward and studied the photograph carefully.

"Look close at my great-great-grandmother's face."

Max did as she said. While the four other people were looking straight at the camera, the gaze of Tirill's doppelgänger seemed to be drawn to something happening outside the frame of the photo. Or maybe it was more as if she'd simply forgotten about the photographer and the child stretching out his arms in an attempt to get her attention.

"She seems a little out of it."

"Not just a little," said Tirill. "She's dead. People didn't exactly have a lot of pictures of each other back then. A photograph was both rare and expensive. A person might have their picture taken only once or twice during their whole lifetime. Maybe never. When somebody died, it was the last chance to immortalize that person. They often tried to create everyday scenes. For example, the deceased, wearing their best clothes, might be seated with the rest of the family at a table set with coffee and cakes. My son calls her Grandma Death. Isn't she wonderful?"

"Uh, sure. . . . But how did they get her to stand?"

"She's probably tied to a board that reaches from her feet up to the back of her head, and the board is leaning against the wall. We can't see it because of the other people in the photo."

"And the little boy?"

"What about him?"

"It almost looks like he's trying to get her attention," said Max.

"Of course he is. That's his mother standing there."

For a moment he pictured Ann, dead, sitting in a chair next to the swimming pool with a drink in her hand.

"Not exactly what I would have chosen to hang on the wall," he said.

Tirill tilted her head to one side, a pensive look on her face. "I think it makes me appreciate life more. And besides, it's fun to see everyone's reaction. Some people completely freak out," she said and laughed.

They sat down, and Max had high praise for the upside-down cake she served.

"So why did the police laugh at you last year?" he asked after eating enough that he could put down his fork without seeming rude.

"Did you read about Cecilie Wiborg?"

"I've read what I could find on the Internet, yes."

"While the investigation was going strong last year, I went to the police to tell them my theory. I thought there was something they should consider as a key element in their search."

"And what was that?"

"Do you know where Eidsborg is?"

"Yes. Do you mean they should have been looking for her there?"

"I mean that her disappearance had something to do with the saint statue and the old ritual. Do you know what I'm talking about?"

Max nodded.

"You see, Cecilie Wiborg was working on a master's thesis about the Counter-Reformation traits in the folk culture of Vest-Telemark," Tirill went on. "By this I mean the opposition to the great changes taking place when the population had to give up Catholicism, which was the form of Christianity they had been practicing. The people had Protestantism forced upon them by the Crown. The Nikuls ritual is considered a classic example of these Counter-Reformation tendencies, by virtue of the fact that the ritual continued a couple of centuries after it was forbidden."

"Are you saying that Cecilie Wiborg was writing about the stave church and Nikuls?" asked Max with astonishment.

"It was central to her whole thesis. I know that from talking to her fellow students last year. And the strange thing is that she disappeared on Midsummer Eve. Don't you think that's odd? That was the night when they used to carry the statue around the lake and all of that. The supernatural forces were supposed to be extra strong on Midsummer Eve. Especially the effect of all sorts of plants and herbs, and the water in the healing springs. And it was the night when the witches were active, flying on their broomsticks to gather on mountaintops like Bloksberg. And if a young girl picked seven different flowers and placed them under her pillow, she'd dream about the boy she was going to marry. In fact, I've tried that myself, but all I dreamed about was getting stuck inside a pipe. That actually ended up being a good description of my future marriage, so maybe there's something to it, after all."

Max had a feeling that Tirill's wild hairdo was well suited to her personality. But then he remembered how quickly she'd reasoned her way to the fact that he'd lived in the United States for many years, simply by observing him. "So, what was your theory?"

"Simply that it was no coincidence that she disappeared on Midsummer Eve."

It wasn't hard to picture the scene. A young woman disappears without a trace in Bø, and in comes a local Miss Marple, claiming that the police should investigate a lead that has something to do with an ancient Midsummer ritual, which no longer takes place.

"You said that someone has been watching your apartment. Is that right?"

"A man wearing a black hoodie. He was out there a couple of days ago. Come on, I'll show you."

Max followed her over to the window.

"Next to the right corner of the shed down there."

"What makes you think he's watching you?"

"Because I've often seen him there before. But this was the first time in a long while. He first appeared right after I went to the police to tell them about my theory last year. That was in early July. And then he stopped showing up sometime in October."

"But now he's back? When was that, exactly?"

"Day before yesterday. Right before 9 p.m."

At that time Max had been in his hotel room at Gardermoen Airport. "Are you sure it's the same person?"

"Of course I can't be a hundred percent sure, but I think so. And he was standing in the exact same spot. In the exact same way. When I met you at the library, I thought that . . . Well, you told me you're a private detective who wanted to talk to Henrik Thue. I thought you might be here to work on the case. That maybe Cecilie's parents had hired you. And maybe it would be possible to convince you that I'm right, even though the police thought my idea was ridiculous."

"I came here because of an old friend," said Max. "Did you happen to hear about a man who drowned in Dalen last week?"

Twelve

"SOMEBODY MUST HAVE THROWN THE CAR KEY in the river," said Tirill. "I knew there was something fishy about that death. I knew it!"

Max looked at her in surprise.

"I'm interested in anything to do with murder and suspicious deaths reported in the news," she explained, as if she were talking about a normal hobby.

Something began to dawn on him. He thought about the photograph of the dead doppelgänger on the wall, and the interest she took in homicides in her spare time. Was this woman nuts?

When Tirill went to the bathroom, he used the opportunity to take a closer look at her books.

The collection was dominated by two kinds of books. First, crime fiction, mostly in Norwegian and Swedish. And second, books about superstitions and folk culture. He pulled out one volume to take a closer look. *Mysterious Legends from Telemark,* by M. B. Landstad. Another was titled *Sorcery in Norway,* and there was also a book about murders in Telemark during the seventeenth and eighteenth centuries.

Max didn't feel particularly reassured after inspecting her books.

"What is it?" Tirill had come back into the room without his noticing. "You've got such a strange look on your face."

"I'm just thinking," he said, putting the book he was holding back on the shelf.

"About what?"

"About something I haven't told you yet."

She sat down without taking her eyes off him for even a second. Max wondered what was the real driving force behind this intense interest of hers.

"Have you ever heard of Peter Schram?" he asked as he sat down. He could see she was giving the question careful consideration.

"No, I haven't."

"Well, let me tell you about him. When I was young, I spent a couple of years working as a deputy sheriff in Tokke municipality. I worked with Knut Abrahamsen, the man who was found drowned in Dalen last week with his pockets full of stones. In the summer of 1985, we received word of a person who had failed to return from a hike in the woods. We made several searches; people helped us comb the entire area, but Peter Schram was never found. What's interesting is that he was an academic who was writing a dissertation about the Eidsborg stave church and the Nikuls ritual."

"You've got to be kidding," whispered Tirill.

"I also have reason to believe that Jørgen Homme, who was the sheriff at the time, didn't want Schram to be found."

Max told her about the German shepherd the sheriff hadn't requested, and yet the search dog had been sent to assist him. The finest tracking dog of the Telemark police force. He told her how he'd gone to the Homme farm to get the dog right after it arrived, and the sheriff had refused to allow him to take the animal. Homme claimed the dog was dangerous. An argument had ensued, but finally the sheriff had said that Max would lose his job if he used the dog in the search.

"Are you positive it wasn't a vicious animal?" asked Tirill.

"A highly trained police dog? Of course not."

"And yet you gave in?"

He noticed that the wound had now opened completely. All the old hurt had bubbled to the surface. Everything he had suppressed during all those years he'd lived in Florida.

"I was scared," he said. "Scared of Jørgen Homme, and scared of losing my job. Scared and cowardly."

Tirill picked up what he saw was some sort of baby monitor and listened.

"He's sleeping so sweetly. Do you want to hear?"

Part of him resisted, because it seemed like such an intimate thing to do, but he didn't want to offend her.

When he pressed the baby monitor to his ear, he first heard only a rushing sound, like the static you hear when listening to a radio station that isn't broadcasting anything. But he quickly became aware of a slow, steady rhythm. He'd thought that the breathing of a sleeping child would be as light as a butterfly, but Tirill's son was breathing deeply and heavily.

"His name is Magnus, and he's four years old," she said. "I'll admit that sometimes I wish I had a magic wand that would make him disappear for a short time. Instead I ask my mother for help. She lives just down the hill from here. She teaches in an elementary school, and she's great with kids. My parents are divorced. Pappa moved back to Larvik, his hometown."

Max handed the baby monitor to Tirill.

"There are so many reasons not to take a risk," she said. "And nobody can judge the validity of anyone else's reasons. You can only judge your own."

He took this to mean she was trying to console him.

"Was it on Midsummer Eve that this man named Schram disappeared?" she asked.

"I don't remember. I Googled his name but couldn't find anything about what happened. It's an old case, after all, and it was never regarded as anything but a disappearance."

"Do you think it was something else?"

"The only thing I know is that Sheriff Jørgen Homme didn't want me to use the tracking dog. By the way, I did meet Henrik Thue a short time after I saw you at the library. We talked for a while about Eidsborg and the stave church. At the time I didn't know that Cecilie Wiborg was writing a thesis about those things. That must mean that Thue knew her, right?"

"He was her academic adviser."

THEY MOVED OUTSIDE to a small balcony. In the west, where the sun was nearing the horizon, the landscape was dominated by a gap between the mountains, an opening that led to Seljord and onward into Vest-Telemark. It was there that the answers to all his questions would be found. And he had to go after those answers.

"Aren't you scared that somebody tried to burn down your cabin?"

"Hmm," said Max. "Well, whoever lit that fire wasn't trying to kill me. Maybe it was just a boyish prank. It's not certain they even realized someone was inside the cabin. In the worst case, it was meant to be a warning."

"Who knew that you were in Dalen?"

He paused to think about that. "Knut's widow, and potentially other members of his family. Henrik Thue, since I mentioned it to him when I called from my hotel at the airport. And everyone I talked to up there, although that's not a lot of people. The operations manager of the museum. The sheriff and the pastor. A couple of employees at the campground."

"Henrik Thue hasn't been himself since Cecilie disappeared," said Tirill. "Sometimes he doesn't show up for his classes. And apparently he's been drinking too. I'm not much interested in gossip— believe me when I say that—but I seem to hear more than my share. My mother says I'm a 50 percent busybody."

"What does that mean?"

"That I have a busybody's nose for everything that goes on, but I don't pass along what I hear. The only reason I'm telling you about Thue is that you and I are now working together."

Max gave a start. "We're working together?"

"Sure. Aren't we? You're going to help me find out who has been watching my apartment. And I'm going to help you investigate the murder of your former colleague."

"Murder?"

"I can't imagine you would have gone all the way to Dalen if you didn't suspect there was something fishy about his death."

And she was right about that. By now he'd dismissed the notion that she might be crazy. Possibly a little eccentric, but definitely compos mentis. And clearly sharp witted.

"Do you have any idea what you might be getting involved in?" he asked.

She nodded eagerly.

"Then why are you doing this?"

"Because the truth is out there, even though we can't see it."

Max Fjellanger leaned back and took a sip of his white wine. That was the right answer. The truth had always been his lodestar—the thought that it was out there somewhere, no matter how difficult it might be to see. Precisely as Tirill had just said.

The disk of the sun was about to sink below the horizon. For a moment it looked as if the gateway to Vest-Telemark were undulating into the tinted mist, as if it were made of something very different from bedrock. Something more fleeting. Dreams, perhaps.

Thirteen

O N HIS WAY BACK TO DALEN, Max slowed his speed to a mini-mum as he drove past the Eidsborg stave church. Again he saw several big tour buses parked nearby, and outside the church was a crowd of summer-clad people who were apparently just standing there and staring at the building. Max wondered whether going inside to see the old saint statue really meant anything to the majority of these tourists. Most of them had probably been told it was simply what you did on the tour, but maybe it had a deeper meaning for a few of them.

First, he wanted to head for the Dalen Community Center, which was a couple of kilometers away, down a precipitous slope and located near Lake Bandak. As he drove, creeping along the sharp turns down the mountainside, he thought back to 1985, when he'd driven this same route after his upsetting confrontation with Jørgen Homme. On that afternoon, the course for the rest of his life had been set. Without that argument about the dog, he wouldn't have left the police force. He might have left later on, but for other reasons—maybe because he grew tired of all the foot dragging and bureaucracy. If not for that particular afternoon, he would never have ended up in the States. At least not as a private detective in Florida.

And then there would have been no Ann in his life. Or the sor-row that they weren't able to have children. And the way that had brought them closer together.

His life would have been completely different.

As he now wound his way along the same curves in the road, his throat tightened painfully. By the time he reached Dalen down below, he was sobbing. He pulled over not far from the bridge where Knut had been found, leaned forward, and buried his head in his arms resting on the steering wheel.

It was not wholly Jørgen Homme's fault. His own cowardice had sent him off on a specific course. The fact that he'd given in and heeded the sheriff's cruel warning.

If you use the dog, it's the last thing you'll do in this job.

He could still hear so clearly how the man's voice had resonated in the farmyard that day. As if a filter had been removed—what usually made him sound like a decent human being. Suddenly it was gone, and Jørgen Homme stepped forward as the person he truly was—a ruthless man. He almost seemed to enjoy revealing this side of himself to his young deputy.

Finally Max had no more tears to shed. He wiped his face, put on his sunglasses, and got out of the car. Down by the riverbank, where Knut had been found, he began a methodical search. Not looking for anything in particular, just whatever he might find. Even though there was little chance the sheriff and his team had overlooked anything.

This time I'm not going to give up, he thought. This time the truth will come out. Cost what it may.

After half an hour he realized there was nothing more to find. When he made his way back up to the road, he saw that another car was now parked there. Jon Homme, in uniform, was standing next to the vehicle, regarding him with an inscrutable look on his face. At that moment only his big, icy-gray mustache distinguished him from his father.

"Out investigating?" he asked as Max approached.

"Just checking the temperature."

"Feel like going for a dive?"

"Dangerous place to swim, or so I've heard."

The sheriff laughed soundlessly. "Are you still staying out at the campground?"

Max hadn't mentioned where he was staying the last time they'd met. "No, I wasn't getting any sleep out there. By the way, where did you find Knut's car?"

"About the same spot where mine is now." Homme put on an apologetic expression. "I can understand why you can't let it go. He was an old colleague, and then he died right here, where the two of you used to work. I had the same thought—that it was strange he would show up here. But one thing I can say for sure: there was nothing to indicate that Knut Abrahamsen was murdered. Not the bruises on his knees or the cut on his lip. Not even the car key. Since you were once a police officer, you know this isn't a conclusion I've come to all on my own. It's mostly based on the work of the techs."

Max nodded. "You're right, of course. I don't think Knut was murdered either," he lied. "Not really. It's just so hard to let go of the past."

A hint of a smile appeared beneath the sheriff's mustache. "No need to apologize," he said. "I feel the same way."

Fourteen

A NARROW GRAVEL PATH led up to the yellow-painted seventies house at the edge of the forest just outside the center of Dalen. A simple Internet search had revealed that Tellev Sustugu still lived in Dalen. What surprised Max more was the fact that he hadn't died long ago.

An old Volvo station wagon was parked in a garage made from sheets of rusty corrugated iron. The car looked as if it hadn't been driven in a while. At any rate, there were no tire tracks visible in the tall grass covering the whole yard. On the porch, which was in urgent need of a good sweeping and restaining, stood a couple of straight-back chairs and a table with a Formica top that reminded Max of the furniture in his own family's kitchen back in the 1960s.

Instead of a doorbell there was a carved woodpecker attached to a string. When Max pulled on the string, the bird pecked at the door frame with a loud bang. He pulled the string several times without getting a response.

Just as he was about to head back to his car, a bare-chested elderly man wearing jeans came around the corner of the house. He had a big, white surgical scar down the middle of his suntanned torso. His black hair was smoothed back, lying so close to his skull that it looked as if a cow had been licking his head. Max recognized the man's face and his tough, sinewy build. He'd tangled with Sustugu a couple of times.

"Tellev?"

The man stopped a couple of meters away, giving him a suspicious look. "And who the hell are you?"

"My name is Max Fjellanger, and I was a deputy sheriff here for a couple of years back in the mid-eighties."

"Huh. Do the two of us have some unfinished business?"

"No, not at all. But Knut Abrahamsen, my colleague and friend from those days, jumped into the Tokke River last week. With his pockets full of stones."

"Oh shit," he muttered.

TELLEV SUSTUGU slurped up some of the piping hot coffee. "You and Abrahamsen were OK, as far as I recall. Just a couple of whippersnappers, but OK. Shame he died."

"I guess I should say thanks. I seem to remember that you and I met several times."

"Would have been impossible to avoid back then. But I settled down long ago. No more juice left in me. When I was young it was still the custom, if your boy was a troublemaker, to send him off to sea. That was supposed to straighten him out. In my case, it had the opposite effect. It just made me crave more fun. And more mischief."

He stretched his sinewy body and laughed. This was how Max remembered him, as someone who seemed to burn with an inner fire that had both fascinated and scared him. As if this was a man unwilling to accept any limitations.

"But it's one thing to make trouble when you're on shore leave in Singapore and you can get away with it. It's a whole different story when you do something bad in Dalen."

"So you got in trouble at a young age?" Max hadn't yet tasted his coffee. It was served black and smelled strong enough to curdle his stomach.

"You'd better fucking believe it," sneered Sustugu as he began rolling a cigarette from tobacco in a blue pouch. "You know how the girls were in the late fifties. . . . If you got a little too aggressive, they'd scream bloody murder. All I did was tug at a pair of panties. Attempted rape, they said. After that they never let up."

Bitterness was evident in the set of his lips. Max remembered an incident in the mid-eighties when a very young girl had accused Sustugu of attempted rape. The case was dismissed, as far as he recalled.

"Do you know whether Knut ever came up here to visit over the last few years?"

"No clue," replied Sustugu. "Besides, I wouldn't have recognized him anyway."

Max thought his answer came a little too fast.

Silence descended over them. He felt as if he were sitting with a ghost from the past. Yet he himself was actually the ghost, since he'd turned up here unannounced.

"I assume that you knew Jørgen Homme well," he said. "If not personally, then—how shall I put this?—professionally."

"I don't know how many times that old devil grabbed me by the scruff of the neck."

"Did you ever hear any rumors about him being corrupt?"

Sustugu burst out laughing, a brief, barking sort of laugh.

"Rumors? That guy was always seizing stolen property and fencing it. I know that from firsthand experience. And it must have made him a fortune. But you'll never get me to say a bad word about him in public. Are you still on the police force?"

Max held up his hands in denial. "No, not at all. I don't even live in Norway anymore. I just came back to revisit old territory after Knut died. His death stirred up some old memories for me. Why wouldn't you say anything about Homme in public? Are you scared?"

"Of course I'm scared," replied Sustugu at once.

"Scared of his son?"

"No, of the old man himself."

"But he's dead."

The former seaman, now marooned onshore, gave Max a long, calculating look. "Is he?" he said at last. "Let me tell you a story I once heard in prison. And don't ask me who I heard it from, because the guy's dead, and I can't even remember his name, but he was from somewhere up here in these parts. He told me about an old legend from Eidsborg that I never heard before or since. It went like this. The devil himself was going to get married, and one person on the guest list was Sheriff Homme. As you know, Homme was no nervous Nellie, so when the day came, he showed up in hell, wearing his best suit and ready to party. Over the course of the evening, all the guests got good and drunk, and it was well known that Homme turned real mean whenever he drank. And on this occasion he ended up in a fight with no less than the bridegroom. The devil wasn't the scaredy-cat type either, so it turned into a huge battle, and neither of them was willing to back down. Homme pulled a knife and stuck it into his opponent's ass. Then the devil went completely nuts, and the sheriff got scared and ran off. I don't remember how he managed to get back to Eidsborg, but he did. In the forest up above Homme's place, the devil caught up with him, and once again the sheriff fought with the Evil One. This time he won, and the bridegroom had to slink home with his tail between his legs. Then Homme noticed that the devil had dropped his wedding ring. He picked it up, but the ring evaporated in his hand. Afterward people said that nothing would grow in that spot on the ground where he'd found the ring. And they say a place like that still exists in the woods up above the Homme farm. I've never seen it personally, but . . . So maybe you'll understand now why I won't say anything against Jørgen Homme in public, even though he's been dead for years. That man was from another world."

Max had listened to this account with rising astonishment. "But how can it be an old legend when it's about a man I once worked for?"

"How the hell should I know?" said Sustugu, annoyed. "Maybe it has to do with the fact that the Homme family has been producing sheriffs for generations. And they've never been named anything but Jon and Jørgen, as far as I know. Wouldn't surprise me if it's the same man every time. What if the devil's ring didn't evaporate after all? What if the sheriff kept it and became immortal?"

Max picked up his cup and took a sip of coffee, mostly for the sake of appearances. It tasted like something that might have been served at the devil's wedding.

Fifteen

AFTER VISITING TELLEV SUSTUGU, Max headed back to the museum. The modern building had been built as an extension of the old one. Even though the old timbered structures individually looked modest and small, Max thought that together they seemed almost belligerent. Like when someone loudly insists on the value of something that looks unassuming. But that's the way things were around here; he remembered that from when he used to live in the area. The old was always shoved to the foreground, and anything new was met with skepticism. Including new people.

A short distance away, he saw the operations manager Johannes Liom and Pastor Julia Bergmann standing in front of the gray-timbered building, talking. He had nearly reached them before they became aware of his presence.

"So, you're still here?" remarked Liom.

"You can't get rid of me that easily."

Julia laughed. "You don't think we want to get rid of you, do you? On the contrary, we want people to come back. Like you're doing. You're actually the ideal visitor."

Max thought her smile was almost too sweet for a pastor. Her hair, which had been shaved at the nape of her neck, stretched forward like a long brushstroke over one eye. And again her hairdo seemed in sharp contrast to her somewhat old-fashioned attire. Her skirt reached to mid-calf, and her blouse was buttoned all the way up, even though it was blazing hot in the sunshine.

"Isn't he?" she said, turning to Johannes Liom.

Liom smiled slyly. "That remains to be seen."

In spite of their smiles and teasing tone of voice, Max thought he sensed a certain tension between the two. He had a feeling that it was because he'd interrupted their conversation. But no matter the reason, the tension cleared when a young man drove up in the same red pickup that Liom had been driving before. The young man stopped and rolled down the window. "Are you coming, or what?" he asked Johannes.

"This is Lars, my son."

Max shook hands and said hello through the open window.

Johannes went around and opened the passenger-side door. Before he got in, he looked at Julia over the roof of the truck. "We'll talk more about it some other time," he said.

She nodded, and Johannes got in next to his son. Then they headed toward the exit and drove off. Max was left standing there with the German pastor.

"I guess I'd better go too," she said.

As they were saying good-bye, Max remembered something that Henrik Thue had told him. "Is it true that they revived the Nikuls ritual a few years ago?" he asked.

Something in her face closed down the moment she heard the question. "That's what some of the locals claimed, at least," she said, sounding miffed.

"And?"

"Well, it had to do with a historical play. The idea was to create a special evening for the local residents. The Norwegian Directorate for Cultural Heritage gave us permission to use the statue, but the whole performance was just a dramatization, of course. Maybe it was my fault that things got out of hand. I played the role of the Catholic priest, you see. And that's actually quite comical, being that I'm a woman. But never mind! I walked along, chanting and singing in Latin. Doing my best. But a few people thought the line between drama and a Catholic mass ended up obscured. That's why the event was staged only twice."

Max thought about what Thue had said, that there was supposed to be a video of the performance. "So who exactly was opposed to the whole thing?"

"First and foremost, a majority of the church council. But Johannes was also against it, because he was worried about the statue. In fact, we were just discussing Nikuls when you arrived. I still think we ought to be using the saint figure more actively. Not in connection with a church service, of course. We're Protestants, after all. But we could arrange a Nikuls Day at Midsummer. We could take the statue out and display it publicly. We could invite experts to give lectures about the saint and the history of the church. Things like that."

"What does Johannes say?"

"He doesn't want to do any of that. For the same reason that he was against the Nikuls dramatization. He's scared something will happen to the statue. We were both getting a little upset about the whole issue."

"How strange," said Max. "You'd think the museum's man would want to show off the statue and tell people about it, while the Protestant pastor would want to have as little as possible to do with the old saint image."

"In Eidsborg things aren't always the way they'd be in other places. That's something I've had to learn to accept."

Again she gave him that unpastorlike smile of hers. What was it she'd said about the deadly sins? *Like most people, I'm guilty of all seven.*

Sixteen

MAX WAS BACK IN BØ in time to eat dinner at the hotel. He went to bed early but, as happened so often, he had trouble falling asleep. Shortly after midnight he decided to take a walk over to the two churches that stood on a hill, dominating the center of Bø.

When he got to the top, he could barely distinguish the outline of the newer church against the night sky. The old church, on the other hand, was partially illuminated by a single spotlight, making it look as if the edifice were floating freely in the night, like something plucked right out of the Middle Ages.

Max walked through the dark, moving past the newer, wooden church and over to the old, whitewashed building. He placed the palm of his hand against the cool surface. He wondered which saint this church had been dedicated to. What sort of processions had taken place here before the Reformation?

The spotlight shining on the church was fastened to a tree on the side facing the center of town. He found a bench there and sat down. Below him the night train to Oslo came gliding into the station like a long, gleaming serpent in the dark.

He was searching for the big picture, something that would show him how all the details of this story related to everything else, but he still had a long way to go. What had brought Knut to Dalen? It was inconceivable that he went there to take his own life. At least, that couldn't be the only reason. Max had never told Knut about the incident with the tracking dog that Sheriff Homme had refused to let him use. According to his widow, Knut had left the police force before she met him. Their son looked to be about twenty, so Knut had been off the force for at least a couple of decades. Yet this was a man who had loved the job. And he'd been receiving disability benefits for a long time before he died. There could be many reasons for that, of course, but something in the way his widow had mentioned his receiving benefits told Max that it wasn't due to some simple and concrete cause. The phrase "nervous condition" seemed to be practically screaming at him. Nerves and defeat. Something to be ashamed of. Not some serious injury from an on-the-job accident, for instance. He was certain Knut's widow would have told him about that.

Early dismissal from the force. Nerves. Disability pension. And then one final, inexplicable trip to Dalen, where they found his body in the river with stones in his pockets.

On his way back from Eidsborg, Max had thought about the fire. It was too serious an incident for him to write it off as some boyish prank. And if it wasn't a prank, then the fire had to be considered a warning. That was how he needed to think of it.

But who was warning him? And for what reason?

The night train left the station down below, heading for Kristiansand and Stavanger, traveling through darkened rural areas and small towns where people lived ordinary lives, guarding their secrets.

Max got up from the bench and walked back past the old church. As soon as he was beyond the reach of the spotlight on the tree, he heard the sound of footsteps on gravel. When he turned around, he saw a figure standing next to the church wall in the same spot where he had just stood. Where had that person come from? Had this stranger been standing close by the whole time he'd been sitting on the bench?

Max walked as fast as he could through the dark, past the big wooden church. The whole time, he heard footsteps behind him. When he reached the road, he stopped abruptly. The other person took a couple of steps forward and then stopped too. Max thought he could hear the stranger breathing in the dark, but maybe that was just his imagination.

The road down to the center of town was narrow and dark,

with fields on either side. Behind him he heard the other person's footsteps, and again he stopped short. This time it took a moment before the person behind him did the same. At first the footsteps slowed, moving hesitantly. As if waiting for Max to start walking again. Then they stopped altogether.

Was someone making fun of him?

Max turned around. The other person was only a short distance away—maybe about fifteen meters—but it was too dark to see the stranger's face. He seemed to be wearing a hoodie or something similar, with the hood pulled up.

"What do you want?" called Max.

In the silence of the night, his voice sounded more like a nervous shout. But the other person simply stood there.

Max took a couple of steps closer. Still no reaction.

"I know who you are!" he yelled.

At that, the unknown person turned around and began walking quickly back the way he'd come. A violent rage surged inside Max, and he ran after the man, who instantly picked up the pace. It turned into an outright race up the long, dark slope, but Max wasn't as fit as the other man and had to watch as his pursuer—who had then become the pursued—disappeared into the dark.

Seventeen

MAX ATE HIS NORWEGIAN HOTEL BREAKFAST with pleasure. Through the windows he could see Breisås—the expansive, forest-covered ridge with rowhouses, single-family homes, and the apartment building where Tirill lived.

The young woman in charge of the breakfast buffet came over to him with her hands behind her back and a secretive smile. Her name was Mette, according to the tag pinned to her uniform. "How's your breakfast?" she asked.

"Excellent."

"A present arrived for you," she said and held it out toward him.

On the palm of her hand was a little square box, nicely wrapped and tied with a red ribbon. There was also a note with his name on it. Not handwritten, he observed.

"Who's it from?"

"We don't know. Someone left it at the reception desk."

She turned around and went back to her place at the other end of the dining room.

It didn't take long to open the package. Inside was a box from a jewelry shop in Skien, but when he opened it, he didn't find a ring on the dark blue velvet lining. At first he didn't understand what he was looking at: a shapeless, light brown lump smaller than the tip of his little finger. When he took the object out of the box, he could tell it was made of hard plastic. He also noticed that the surface on one side, which was more or less straight, felt slightly rough, as if it had been sliced off with a dull knife.

At that instant his brain made sense of the shape, and Max realized what it was: the severed head of a little plastic pig.

He glanced over at the tourists at the next table, but none of them seemed to have noticed what he'd just unwrapped. As discreetly as he could, he stuck the box with the pig's head in his pocket.

Then he phoned Tirill.

A SHORT TIME LATER they were sitting in her small yellow Fiat in the parking lot in front of the hotel. On the slope above, Max caught a glimpse of the spire on one of the two churches. The rest of the building was hidden behind green foliage.

"I don't have much time," Tirill said. "I can't just leave work on a moment's notice. So, what's this all about?"

"Someone followed me last night. Up near the churches. When I tried to make contact with him, he took off. It could have been just some local idiot. Is there someone around here known for doing things like that? A Peeping Tom? A guy who enjoys sneaking around?"

"Did you get a good look at him?"

"No, he was wearing a hoodie. Or at least he had something pulled over his head. Besides, it was dark."

"Do you think it could be the same man I've seen outside my apartment?"

"Maybe. In that case, he must have noticed that I paid you a visit. By the way, I have something to show you."

Max took out the little jewelry box. "This was dropped off at the reception desk sometime this morning or late last night. No one saw who left it. Somebody must have taken the opportunity to slip it behind the counter when no one was around. It was nicely wrapped, and there was a note with my name on it. Not handwritten. Always fun to get a present, don't you think?"

He opened the box.

Tirill plucked out the little lump of plastic to examine it more closely. "A pig's head?" she said in surprise. "What's that supposed to mean?"

"I have no idea, but I noticed that it's been chopped off the body. And a pig isn't exactly a compliment. It's a threat, and it applies to you too, if you continue with this."

"What do you mean?"

"That you don't need to get involved. I can handle this on my own."

"No!" she practically shouted. "I want to be on the team!" She seemed to be driven by something more than just a search for the truth.

"Why does this mean so much to you?"

It took a while for Tirill to reply.

"When I was ten, I wanted to be a fighter pilot," she said at last. "When I was twelve, I dreamed of being a fiddler. I had a print of *Music and Dance,* by Halfdan Egedius, hanging over my bed in my room. Do you know the painting? It's like a dark maelstrom that sucks you right in. Which is exactly what happens when a truly skilled fiddler plays. The other twelve-year-old girls didn't share my enthusiasm for the painting or for folk music. Eventually I devoted a large part of my energy—and I have a lot of energy—trying to be like kids my own age. I can't even count the number of evenings I spent riding in the backseat of a hot rod, cruising up and down Bøgata. I learned to talk like everybody else: about parties and who was sleeping with whom. On rare occasions I'd forget and talk about something that really interested me. Like a book or some strange custom or a superstition I'd heard about. Then the others would look at me as if I were a total stranger. And each time that happened, I knew it was the real Tirill they were seeing. Later, after tons of disappointments, I decided never to be anything other than myself again. It's better that way. This is who I am." She threw out her hands, as much as that was possible inside the small car. "All this. You and me, and the truth that for the time being escapes us."

Max didn't know what to say. What she'd recounted was already more than enough. Clearly she wasn't about to retreat.

"And besides, you can't do it alone," she added.

"That's where you're wrong. I'm used to working on my own. And I've actually worked for the police in Telemark, you know."

"But not in the mythic Telemark. That's where you'll have to work if you're going to solve this case. And you couldn't ask for a better guide than me."

Max wondered how the employees in his agency would react if they'd heard this conversation. He decided they would probably put it down to what the Americans called "Old World charm."

"We know that somebody was watching you after Cecilie Wiborg disappeared. Or rather, after you went to the police and said that her disappearance had to be connected to the Nikuls ritual in Eidsborg. And if it's the same person who followed me, we have to ask ourselves: Who might have an interest in both of us?"

"Someone who's concerned about both disappearances."

"Such as Jon Homme, for example," said Max. "We have to assume that he was involved to some extent in the investigation when Cecilie went missing. He would have at least interviewed people she'd talked to up there."

Tirill nodded. "Homme, of course. But I think there's somebody else."

Eighteen

A T THE SPOT WHERE A SURVEILLANCE CAMERA had recorded the last sighting of Cecilie Wiborg, Max took out the map Tirill had drawn for him. He looked around to make sure the terrain and the map agreed. Then he switched on the stopwatch function on his cell phone and began walking.

It had taken Cecilie approximately eight minutes from the time she passed by the camera until her phone was either turned off or stopped working. Seven minutes and ten seconds later, he found himself standing in front of a yellow-painted house with a large garden.

"And then fifty seconds after that," he muttered.

"Hello?" said a woman who must have been crouched down behind the shrubbery. He hadn't noticed anyone, at any rate.

She came out from the shrubbery and approached, a bit hesitantly, holding a pair of hedge clippers in her hand.

"Hi," Max greeted her with a wave. "Is this where Henrik Thue lives?"

Tirill was apparently right in assuming the professor might have reason to be interested in both disappearances.

"Henrik's at work. What's this about?"

"I talked to him yesterday about the Eidsborg stave church. I live in the States, and I'm just over here on a quick visit to the old country. My name is Max Fjellanger," he said, taking a step forward with his hand outstretched, giving the woman his most trustworthy smile.

He could see the moment when she decided that he was OK. She shifted the hedge clippers to her left hand and wiped her right hand on her pants before clasping his hand.

"Åse Enger Thue. You'll have to excuse the way I'm dressed."

She was wearing worn jeans, a faded T-shirt with the words New York City on the front, and a colorful scarf tied around her head.

"No apologies needed," he said appreciatively.

"Henrik mentioned that he was supposed to meet someone at the Good Neighbor. So that was you?"

"Yes. And now I just happened to be walking past, and . . ."

"But how did you know where we live?"

"I asked someone at the college."

Max Fjellanger was used to reading people between the lines, so to speak. In the case of Åse Enger Thue, he read the story of a woman who radiated warmth that was in keeping with the lush garden behind her.

In other words, a far different impression than her husband presented.

"I actually wanted to ask the professor some more questions about Eidsborg," he said a bit dejectedly. "But I guess I'll just give him a call."

The woman looked at him as she rocked back and forth on the balls of her feet. If she'd been chewing gum, she would have blown a bubble and popped it with a bang, thought Max. It was that kind of moment.

"I was just going to get myself some juice to drink," she said.

THE SOUND OF RUNNING WATER filled the enclosed garden. A fountain was surrounded by natural stones with inlaid ceramic tiles depicting dolphins and octopuses in the ancient Greek style. A white cat was stretched out on its back on the newly mowed grass. Max set his glass of juice back on the table and leaned down to pet the cat, which immediately began to purr.

"So, what kind of work do you do?" Åse asked, her head tilted to one side.

"I run a small business that my wife and I built together. Various types of consultant services, you might say. But I'm a widower now, so I've granted myself some time off to come to Norway and study the stave churches. It's something I've wanted to do for a long time."

"And naturally you called Henrik when you arrived here in Telemark."

He nodded.

"And that's why you're sitting here now."

"No, I'm sitting here because you made me an offer I couldn't refuse."

He wondered if she was blushing, but he couldn't be sure, since it was a hot day and she'd been working outside in the sun.

"The raspberry juice, you mean?"

"In Florida, we mostly serve iced tea and lemonade. And they're OK, but they'll never be as good as this," he said, looking at her.

A long moment passed. Their eyes were fixed on each other, as if glued there by the heat and the juice.

"So, what about you?" he asked finally.

"Me?"

"Do you know a lot about the Eidsborg stave church?"

She laughed, a brief resigned laugh. "I'm sure I've heard everything there is to know about that church. Plus a few things more. But do I remember any of it? No. My weakness is that I'm interested in people who are alive, people I can talk to, right here and now."

"Then you must think I'm pretty hopeless to come all the way from Florida just to study the stave churches."

"Oh no, not at all," she said earnestly. "They're lovely buildings, and if you've been away from Norway for so many years, well . . . It's just that . . ."

She sighed and took a sip of juice. The clinking of the ice cubes was the perfect accompaniment to the splashing of the fountain and the sedate buzzing of a bumblebee somewhere in the bushes.

"It's just that the human element is more important for you," Max finished her thought.

"Something like that."

He paused for a moment before asking, "Did you know Cecilie Wiborg?"

Her reaction was instantaneous, and this time she was definitely not blushing. Underneath the delicate flush that the sun and her work in the garden had lent to her cheeks, Åse Enger Thue's face had turned pale. "Why are you asking me that?"

"Someone happened to mention her name. Her disappearance must have made a deep impression on folks around here."

"That poor girl. The thought of what might have happened to her . . ."

"Did you know her?"

"No. I met her only once."

"Were you in Bø when she went missing?"

"I was visiting my sister in Skien. Spending a few days there. It's something I often do."

He recognized a certain inflection in her voice. "You and your husband don't have any children?" he asked.

"No, we don't."

Her answer came too quickly, and she spoke so easily that he knew at once there was nothing easy about this subject. Ann used to answer in the same way, as if it was nothing, and for that very reason everyone understood how much it had meant to her.

"My wife and I weren't able to have children," he said.

The curiosity that awoke in Åse's eyes was not of the greedy type but rather like a hand reaching out. This too he recognized from his life with Ann.

"Did the two of you eventually resign yourselves to the situation?" she asked, taking a big sip of juice in order to hide the fact that she was struggling with emotion.

"I suppose I did, in a way. But it was different for Ann. I think she was happy for the most part, but she always carried a sorrow deep inside."

Sitting across from Åse at the small patio table, he saw her eyes fill with tears.

"All grown-ups carry some sort of sorrow," he said. "Even if they don't always want to acknowledge it."

"So, what's your sorrow?" she asked, sniffling a bit.

"Before Ann died? Something from the past, something unfinished. It has stayed inside me like a black claw for all these years."

"Was that why you moved to the States?"

"Yup."

The white cat got up and rubbed against his leg. Max petted it behind the ears as he sweet-talked it. "They say that cats are able to sense people's sorrows," he remarked.

"Not Missy. She can curl up on my stomach and purr as if everything was right with the world." She crossed her arms under her breasts, which made them suddenly appear far more prominent than they had before.

"How has your husband dealt with it?"

Åse uttered a sound halfway between a laugh and a snort. "He has the Eidsborg stave church. And . . ." She paused for a moment. "His students."

"It must have been a shock for him when Cecilie Wiborg disappeared."

She closed her eyes and sat motionless for a long time as the hint of a smile came and went. At least it seemed like a long time to Max, who sat there not knowing whether to speak or not. As so often before, he chose to remain silent.

Finally she opened her eyes and stood up. "Excuse me," she said.

He studied her backside as she headed toward the house. He couldn't help himself, and no doubt she knew that. As soon as she disappeared from sight, he looked around with curiosity. The garden was well hidden from anyone looking in, though without blocking the view of Lifjell. There was something unreal about the mountain. It looked like a painted stage set as it loomed against the sky behind the house next door. Down here in the garden, on the other hand, there was a strong lilac scent, and not far away a yellowhammer was singing its "one-two-three-four-five-six-SEVEN!"

When Åse came back out, he made sure to keep his gaze polite.

"Here," she said, placing something on the table in front of him.

It was a photograph of a bikini-clad young woman reclining on a blanket outdoors. She was propped up on her left elbow, smiling at the photographer as she shaded her eyes with her right hand. It took a few seconds before he understood the connection. In the picture published in the newspaper, she'd had longer hair. And was wearing more clothing. Plus, that picture was not taken in Henrik Thue's garden. Max recognized the dolphins and octopuses on the wall in the background.

"Right there," said Åse, keeping her tone light as she pointed to the spot where the young woman had been lying. "Do you know who she is?"

He nodded.

"So, as you can imagine, her disappearance had a big effect on Henrik."

"Did the police question him?"

"Yes, but he didn't mention anything about this." She nodded at the photograph. "I discovered it one day when he'd forgotten his cell phone. Are you shocked? You shouldn't be. People in my situation tend to do these kinds of things. And anyone who carries on the way Henrik does would panic when he realized that he'd left home without his phone. Believe me, he came back ASAP. But not before I had time to find this picture on his cell and upload it onto my computer."

The close relationship between Cecilie Wiborg and the photographer was evident in her smile. Not to mention the fact that she was wearing a skimpy bikini that barely covered the most intimate parts of her body.

Max stuck his hand in his pants pocket and touched the severed plastic pig's head. "Well, I'm not shocked," he said. "But why did you print out the picture? And in such a big size?"

She laughed that brief, joyless laugh of hers. "I don't really know. Maybe so it would hurt even more. I'm good at that sort of thing. As I said, I met Cecilie only once. Quite a while before she disappeared. She came over to pick up some papers. At least that's what she said, but suddenly she remembered that a different teacher had the papers, so she left. And I knew why. It was on a Monday morning. That's when I'm usually teaching, but on that particular day I'd stayed home with a cold. And that same morning Henrik had rushed off to Oslo, because his father was seriously ill. The papers were just an excuse that she thought up on the spur of the moment. I'm positive that she had actually agreed to meet Henrik here while I was at work—that's probably what they usually did—but he'd forgotten to cancel. Which is so typical of him. He just never bothers with things like that."

She held out her hand, and Max gave the picture back to her.

"So that's how things are," she said. "Henrik has his students, and I have the garden. And my job. I teach high school English. But it's less than half-time."

It all sounded so dreary for someone of her age. She looked to be in her late thirties.

Then Åse smiled. "But right now I have a visitor," she said, looking pleased as she stretched like a cat.

Max realized he needed to think of something fast. He was a married man, after all. The fact that Ann was dead didn't alter that fact.

"My train goes in half an hour."

"You're leaving?" Her voice gave nothing away.

"I need to go to Oslo," he lied. He thanked her for the juice and stood up. Åse walked with him around the side of the house, back to the spot where they first spoke to each other.

"I'll be back," said Max.

"You'll find me in the garden, as long as it's not pouring down rain."

She looked exactly the same as before—wearing the same clothes and holding the hedge clippers in her hand. And yet now she was so much more.

Nineteen

BACK IN HIS HOTEL ROOM, Max remembered something Henrik Thue had said. There was supposedly a video from the reenactment of the Nikuls ritual.

It didn't take him long to find it on the Internet. At first he saw only the stave church, as filmed from outside on a beautiful summer evening. Close-ups of wildflowers reinforced the midsummer atmosphere. Then he heard voices singing. A monotone song. And a cloaked procession emerged from the church door. Leading the way was Pastor Julia Bergmann. Behind her walked four men carrying on their shoulders what looked like a palanquin. It was simply made and clearly of new construction. That made the contrast seem even greater when he looked at the old, dark saint statue on the palanquin.

Following Julia and the four men carrying the statue was a long line of people dressed in medieval garb. They looked suspiciously young—presumably amateur actors.

The song was subtitled in both Norwegian and Latin:

> *Nicholaus pontifex, nostrum est refugium / Bishop Nikolai is our refuge*
> *Clericis et laicis, sit sember remedium / For priests and lay folk, he must always be the savior*
> *Clericorum est amator, laicorum consolator / He loves the priests, he is the one who comforts the lay folk*

Omniumque conformator, in omne angusita / He is the one
who lends strength to all those in need
Nicholae, Nicholae prebe nobis gaudia / Nikolai, Nikolai,
grant us heavenly joy.

Several of the cloaked figures seemed to suffer some sort of fit, causing them to fall down and lie on the ground, flailing their arms and legs. Presumably they were meant to portray afflicted parishioners in need of healing. As the procession wound its way down toward Eidsborg Tarn, more people joined in, though they were not wearing costumes. Instead they had on jeans, leggings, shorts, and T-shirts. Many seemed just as caught up in the ritual as the cloaked actors depicting people from the Middle Ages.

When the procession reached the lake, Bergmann sprayed water on the congregation using an object that looked like a broom or brush. Not holy water but water taken directly from Eidsborg Tarn, as if it were cleansing or life giving. At that point only a couple of the cloaked youths remained in view. The others all looked like ordinary people from Eidsborg and Dalen, along with a few who might have been tourists. It was quite a crowd. People were waving their hands at the priest, motioning her to spray them with water. If they managed to catch a few drops, they rubbed the water on their faces.

The only sound Max heard was the song—with the same words repeated over and over: *Nicholaus pontifex, nostrum est refugium . . .* It was almost hypnotic. Then the whole ritual ended with a long, drawn-out *Aaaaaa-men!*

Max noticed that they didn't lower the saint statue into the water, as was apparently the custom in medieval times. No doubt they didn't want to risk damaging the old wooden statue.

Fascinated, he started the film over, and this time he made a point of studying the individual players. He was curious to see the facial expressions of those who at first were visible only at the edge of the picture but who in the end stood stretching out their hands for some drops of water from Eidsborg Tarn. Was it possible to see whether some change had occurred?

Suddenly something caught his attention. A movement, lasting only a second, at the very edge of the frame. Something happened, but it was difficult to see what it was, because it took place so fast, and besides, a number of other things happened at the same time. There was constant movement around the palanquin, as the cloaked young people sprawled on the grass.

Max played the relevant seconds again.

A man came up alongside the palanquin and grabbed hold of it. He seemed to be trying to pull it down, but the incident happened so fast that Max couldn't really tell what was going on.

Mesmerized, he replayed that scene several more times, without making any sense of it. Was that part of the dramatization? But the reaction of the men carrying the palanquin indicated it had not been anticipated.

Finally Max managed to freeze the picture in the middle of the action. Then he enlarged the view.

He saw an old man with a white beard standing there, stretching out his hands toward the palanquin. With one hand he had actually grabbed hold of the saint statue itself, as if he were trying to pull it out. And next to him, with one hand on the old man's arm, stood Åse Enger Thue.

Twenty

SATURDAY MORNING. Magnus was staying with his grandmother a little farther down the slope of Breisås. The silence greeted Tirill like a welcoming embrace when she went into the living room after she'd taken a shower and got dressed. A calm as soft as cotton.

Incredible that it should feel so luxurious just to have the place all to herself for a short while, but that's how it was. Being alone felt almost like the spa weekend she'd never been able to afford.

She made herself a cup of green tea and got out her usual chocolate croissant and fat-free yogurt. The two canceled each other out, or at least that's what she always told herself.

While she ate, she thought about Max Fjellanger. She couldn't really think of him as just plain Max. In her mind she called him by his full name, or else she used only his last name. He was tall and straight-backed, with a neatly trimmed beard that was starting to show a few streaks of gray. The blazer he wore, along with his highly polished shoes, gave the impression of someone a bit old-fashioned and proper.

Yet this was the man who had fulfilled the most unlikely of all her dreams. Well, actually, it wasn't even something she'd dreamed of, since it was way beyond what she could ever have imagined happening in her life. Instead she'd allowed herself to get lost in books, and in the homicide cases that occasionally showed up in the news. While in a secret place inside her she'd been Detective Vesterli.

And now that's what she was in real life. Of course, it was a

shame she couldn't tell anyone, but she realized there was no getting around that. If it got out that the two of them were interested
in the Wiborg case, the police would intervene and stop them, the
same way they'd done when she tried to help them in the weeks
after Cecilie disappeared.

Her cell phone was ringing. She'd left it on the kitchen table. She
smiled when she saw who was calling.

THEY HAD TO DRIVE through the Homme farmyard in order to reach
Tveit, which was a smaller farm next door. Tveit is the starting
point, Fjellanger had said. That was where Peter Schram was last
seen.

Near the barn ramp a man was pouring water into the tank of
a pesticide sprayer that was mounted on a tractor. They parked
right next to him and got out. He paused to watch calmly as the two
strangers approached.

"It's a fine day," said Fjellanger.

"Yes, it is."

"Are you Erlend Tveit?"

The man shook his head. He had on worn jeans, a plaid shirt,
and a faded Arsenal soccer cap.

"Could we possibly talk to him?"

"Erlend's dead. Who am I speaking to?"

"Max Fjellanger. And this is Tirill Vesterli."

"Knut Lars Ljosland," said the farmer, shaking hands with both
of them. "Erlend was my father-in-law."

"I don't know if you're aware of this, but in 1985 a young man
who lived here on the farm disappeared," said Fjellanger.

"Oh, right. A guy from Oslo."

"I helped with the search, and since we were in the neighbor-
hood, I thought I'd ask if anyone ever found out what happened to
him."

A blue station wagon pulled up to the farmhouse. The woman
who was driving got out and looked over at the three of them standing next to the tractor. Then she waved, though Knut Lars made no
move to wave back.

"That's Ingebjørg. My wife. She's from here, so I'm sure she remembers what happened."

INGEBJØRG LJOSLAND was tall and straight-backed with a strong jaw and big, gleaming white teeth. A female version of the Norwegian writer Tarjei Vesaas. She seemed to sail rather than walk through the room as she brought coffee and baked goods and all the requisite plates, cups, and spoons.

"Of course I remember Peter," she said, taking a small bite of a cookie before putting it back on her plate. She sat on the very edge of her chair, and Tirill noticed how she kept her knees pressed together, as if she were wearing a short skirt instead of long pants.

"He lived here for two summers. He was supposed to stay for three, but . . ."

"What exactly happened when he disappeared?" asked Fjellanger.

"Well, he went out for a hike. Just going up the slope, he told my father, whom he ran into as he was leaving. Apparently he also said, 'I'll be back soon.' When he wasn't back by nighttime, we thought he might have gone to a party. But the next day he still hadn't returned, so Pappa went down to Dalen to talk to the sheriff. And that's when the big search was launched."

"Party?" said Tirill. "This wasn't by chance on Midsummer Eve, was it?"

Ingebjørg nodded silently. Somewhere inside Tirill it was as if a key had turned in a lock. She glanced at Fjellanger, whose expression remained impassive.

"Do you remember Cecilie Wiborg?" he asked now.

"The student who disappeared? Sure. So terrible."

"Did you ever meet her?"

She gave him a puzzled look. "Why would I have met her?"

"She was working on a thesis that had something to do with the Nikuls ritual. So she must have come up here a few times."

Ingebjørg raised her hand to her mouth with an alarmed look. "I didn't know that."

"And she disappeared on Midsummer Eve," he added.

"So you think that . . . ?"

He shook his head. "It's doubtful there's a connection, since there's such a long time in between. But let's go back to when Schram went missing. There must have been a lot of talk afterward. He was studying the saint culture, and then he disappeared on the very night that is so central to the worship of Nikuls. What did people say?"

"What did they say? Hmm. That was so long ago. There was some whispering about the fact that he'd been spending a suspicious amount of time alone in the church. And it's true that he had, because he was writing his doctoral dissertation on Nikuls. I remember somebody saying he was trying to catch sight of the monk, but Peter didn't believe in things like that. He was . . . scientifically minded."

"The monk?" said Tirill. "Do you mean the ghost?"

Ingebjørg nodded. "I know it's stupid, but . . ." She suddenly looked embarrassed. "I don't think anybody really took the rumor seriously, but there was a lot of talk about a policeman who had something to do with what happened. A case of jealousy, or something like that. People said they'd been in love with the same girl. Personally, I never really believed a word of it, but there was a lot of talk about it at the time. I seem to recall that the policeman finally had to leave."

"A policeman?" said Max. His voice suddenly faltered. "That must have been Knut. If it was me, I would have heard the rumors. Back then I was a deputy sheriff here," he explained. "Have they ever found any trace of Schram?"

Ingebjørg took a deep breath and paused before exhaling. The little smile she wore seemed directed inward, to three decades in the past. Through the living room window Tirill saw that her husband was in the process of spraying pesticide out in the fields.

"No, we never got any answers about what happened to him. Unfortunately. I was a teenager, and I guess I was a little in love with him, even though he was married and was about to become a father for the first time. Oh, that's right. Good Lord. On top of everything else." Her face took on a pained look.

"So there's a widow?" Fjellanger asked.

"There was, at any rate. But that was years ago. She came here once, a short time after it happened."

"Do you remember her name?"

Ingebjørg paused to think. "No, but I got a letter from her many years later. I think it's still here somewhere, but I'll need time to find it, and I can't do it right now."

"Do you think you could possibly . . . ?" Fjellanger put on a pleading expression.

"Oh, sure. I could do that."

He got out the little black notebook he usually carried in his inside pocket and wrote down his phone number before tearing out the page.

"How would you describe Peter Schram?" asked Tirill as Ingebjørg put the piece of paper with Fjellanger's phone number on the sideboard behind her.

"He was very . . . Hmm, what should I say? He had such a serious air about him, which I really liked. He took life and the world very seriously. Especially his work. For instance, I remember that he once had a terrible argument with someone about his dissertation. At least, that's what I think it was about."

"Who did he argue with?" asked Tirill.

"Oh, it's too long ago for me to remember. But that's how he was. Very proud. Self-confident."

Tirill wondered how many times Ingebjørg had tried to figure out, as she was doing now, what had happened to the long-lost love of her youth.

"I still can't go for a hike in the woods here—when I'm out picking berries, for example—without looking for him. On the scree and in the mountain crevasses. Looking for bleached bones. But it seems like he was swallowed up by the earth. Or by something else."

"And you can't recall anything else about this argument?" asked Fjellanger.

"No. It was one night when I heard a terrible ruckus coming from the little timbered cabin that Peter had rented. I think they were fighting. At any rate, I heard something heavy fall on the floor. I don't know whether it was furniture or the people who were fighting, but it was awful. I was shocked, because I had the impression that Peter was a calm and quiet man."

Her expression turned pensive. Tirill felt like she could almost see the thoughts moving inside the woman's head, like tiny little animals crawling around in there.

"I remember now. He was arguing with a young boy who used to visit him. That's right. The boy couldn't have been more than fifteen or sixteen, but he was totally obsessed with Peter and the work he was doing. Later he wrote a book about stave churches. I think his name was Fredrik something. Or was it Henrik?"

"Henrik Thue?" said Fjellanger in surprise.

"Yes, that's it."

"And Peter Schram argued with him?"

She nodded and took another bite of her cookie, then put it back on the plate.

"About his dissertation?" asked Tirill.

"At least I think that was it. Maybe Henrik had been snooping through his papers. He was just a boy, you know, but he came here from Oslo to spend the summers, and he was always hanging around Peter. But after that terrible fight, I don't think he ever came back."

Tirill glanced at Max Fjellanger, who gave her an almost imperceptible nod.

Twenty-One

A LITTLE LATER they were sitting in the museum café eating pea soup and surrounded by Japanese tourists.

"Both Peter Schram and Cecilie Wiborg disappeared on Midsummer Eve," said Tirill. "The most important night for the Nikuls cult. And Henrik Thue knew both of them."

"Plus he lied to me about Schram when I talked to him," said Max. He said he barely even remembered hearing about him. And what about the rumor that Knut had something to do with Schram's disappearance? That was totally new to me. Why would Jørgen Homme start that sort of rumor? If it originated with him, that is."

Tirill had plenty of other questions. For example: Why had Åse Enger Thue shown Fjellanger the photo of Cecilie Wiborg taken in their garden? Or: How strongly was he attracted to Åse? And was it affecting his judgment? There was something about the way he'd talked about Professor Thue's wife that had made Tirill suspicious.

After eating more of the soup, she decided to change the topic. "Have you seen the house gods they have here?"

Fjellanger nodded.

"My family had one up until the eighteenth century," she said. "It was called the Pork King. A wooden figure that they smeared with lard and other delicacies whenever there was a feast. At Christmastime, for instance. According to local legend, these ancestors of mine weren't exactly the most devoted of churchgoers, and finally some God-fearing neighbors decided they'd had enough of their idolatrous ways. They stormed into the house and took the house god over to another farm, where they chopped it into little pieces. When they used the chips in their stove, the smell of roast pork supposedly spread all over Bø."

Tirill sat there staring at the glass wall of the museum, holding the soup spoon in her hand.

"The Pork King?" chuckled Max.

"Go ahead and make fun of it. I'm sure he wasn't much of a god, compared to many others, but he was ours."

"I didn't mean to make fun," he said. "So, what did people use house gods like that for?"

"They were a kind of talisman, associated with a specific farm and the family that lived there. I suppose the intention was for them to protect the household against misfortunes and misdeeds, plus to ensure good harvests and the birth of lots of children. As Christianity gradually took hold, they became more like family heirlooms. Yet people continued to treat them with great respect. For example, it's said that they used to bathe the Pork King in the tub before Christmas. And only the mistress of the farm was allowed to do this. Even the farmer was not allowed to be present."

A man with a carefully waxed mustache came over to their table. "Welcome back," he said, shaking hands with Max. Then he greeted Tirill, introducing himself as Johannes Liom, the operations manager of the museum.

"Are you interested in house gods?" she asked him.

"Of course I am!"

"Have you ever heard of the Pork King from Bø?"

"I think I once saw him at the water park."

"No. I'm talking about a house god."

Liom shook his head, so Tirill told him the whole story about her ancestors' personal pork-smelling idol. As she talked, she studied Liom's reactions. It was as if the story came alive in him, and his expression kept changing.

"Wonderful," he said, impressed as she finished her tale. "Around here we know for certain that there were house gods on various farms up to the late 1800s, but it's probably a tradition that continued in secret even into the next century. What a shame that the Pork King was destroyed, or we could have added him to our collection here."

"Could I ask you something?" said Tirill.

"Ask away."

"Does Sheriff Jon Homme have any siblings?"

"He's an only child. Why?"

"It's just that I read somewhere that Jørgen was close to forty when Jon was born. In the 1950s that must have been awfully late to be a father for the first time."

"Jon's parents married young—I think they were both around twenty, which was perfectly normal back then—but they didn't have any kids until more than two decades had passed. That's when Jon came along."

"That must have been quite a surprise," said Tirill.

Liom gave her a wry smile. "Yup. I'd think it was."

"So he was a spoiled kid?"

"And fat, or so I've heard. A *real* little pork king."

He seemed pleased at getting her to laugh.

"So listen here," he said. "Will the two of you be in Eidsborg for a few more hours? I'd like to invite you over for coffee and cake."

"I have nothing planned for today," said Tirill. "My mother is babysitting my son."

"Great! I'll meet you guys back here in forty-five minutes."

And with that—after giving Tirill a wink—he left.

"Looks like you've got yourself an admirer," said Max.

Tirill rolled her eyes.

Twenty-Two

THEY FOLLOWED THE RED PICKUP through the Homme and Tveit farmyards. On the other side Johannes Liom turned onto a road that wasn't marked with any sign, merely a solitary mailbox. After a couple of hundred meters he turned in and stopped in front of a white two-story house.

"Welcome to Casa Liom," he said.

Besides the house and garage, there were also a red-painted outbuilding and an old playhouse that was partially overgrown with raspberry bushes and nettles. In the front yard were a jeep, a camouflage-painted all-terrain vehicle, and a wood chipper, which a young man with blond hair and ear protectors was operating with a steady hand. Next to him was a huge pile of gleaming birchwood, freshly chopped.

The sound of splintering wood greeted them as they climbed out of the car. The young man, whom Max recognized as Johannes's son, didn't stop even to say hello.

Johannes motioned for Max and Tirill to follow him inside the house.

The ceiling and walls of the living room were covered with knotty-pine paneling that had darkened considerably since it was first put up. Everywhere Max looked, black knots in the wood stared back at him. On the coffee table stood a bowl painted in the decorative rosemaling style, and on either side of the fireplace stood impressively large log chairs, also painted with rosemaling. Otherwise the room was dominated by graphic art with local motifs, such as timbered buildings and forest landscapes. A bookcase covered one entire wall and looked as if it held close to a thousand books.

Before going to the kitchen, Johannes invited Tirill and Max to have a seat. Instead they both went over to the bookcase to admire his collection. There seemed to be a lot of reference books about museum operations and related topics. Whole shelves were devoted to history, both local and from elsewhere. There was not as much literature, though Max did see the collected works of the classic Norwegian author Bjørnstjerne Bjørnson, as well as books by Leo Tolstoy and Fyodor Dostoyevsky, Tarjei Vesaas and Aasmund Olavsson Vinje.

"Not exactly a modernist," he murmured.

Johannes soon had the table set as nicely as any experienced housewife would have done. Max guessed he was either divorced or a widower, and no doubt had been for a long time.

"We had coffee over at the Tveit farm too," said Tirill.

"Oh? Do you know Ingebjørg and Knut Lars?"

"No," said Max. "We were just there to have a little chat about the disappearance of Peter Schram. And about Knut Abrahamsen. Do you remember me telling you about him the last time we met?"

"The man who was found in the river? Sure. An old colleague of yours, right?"

"And, more importantly, my friend. There are still a few minor details that haven't been cleared up."

"So it wasn't suicide after all?"

"Personally, I'm not really convinced. It turns out that Knut was accused of having something to do with Peter Schram's disappearance. Not by the police, just some rumor that was circulating. But what if Schram was actually the victim of foul play, and the person or persons responsible then tried to pin his disappearance on Knut? That might mean that somebody up here had a motive for offing him. If Knut discovered the truth, I mean."

While Max was talking, he paid close attention to Johannes's changing expression. His face was just as animated as when Tirill was telling him about the house god, but this time his reaction was more difficult to interpret.

"By the way, did you ever meet Cecilie Wiborg?"

"Oh. Sure. But only once, though we talked for a long time about Nikuls and the stave church. Cecilie was very knowledgeable, with a passionate interest in the subject. A great girl."

"And that was your only contact with her?"

"I answered a few e-mails from her, about the thesis she was writing. Why are you so interested?"

"I'm not that interested. I just think it's odd that both Cecilie and Peter were researching the Nikuls ritual, and they both disappeared on Midsummer Eve."

Johannes nodded. "I've wondered about that myself. But Cecilie disappeared in Bø, didn't she? And besides . . . there's thirty years between the two events."

Max was about to say something more, but at that instant a door opened somewhere in the house, and slow footsteps could be heard coming down the stairs from the second floor.

"My father," said Johannes apologetically before he got up and went out to the hall.

Tirill and Max looked at each other as they listened to the father and son talking. Johannes said something about "visitors from Bø," but then the two men stepped outside, and it was no longer possible to hear what they were saying. Tirill quickly devoured a big piece of cake. Max looked at her in astonishment but didn't say a word.

After a moment the door opened and Johannes came back in, followed by a gaunt old man. Max thought there was something familiar about him but couldn't put his finger on why. No doubt he'd talked to the man in connection with his work when he spent those two years up here, so long ago.

"This is my father, Gunstein," said Johannes. "Max knew the man who drowned in the river," he explained to his father.

"Oh? Was he out there fishing?"

"I don't know," said Max.

"Probably was," the old man concluded. "Did you know that the trout in Lake Bandak and the Tokke River are descended from the sea trout that swam around in these parts ten thousand years ago? After the Ice Age, there was a fjord that extended all the way up to where Dalen is today. When the sea retreated, some of the sea trout were left in the freshwater lake, and I guess they thrived. In any case, they're the ancestors of the creatures weighing fifteen kilos or more that you can find down there today. A unique breed, genetically unlike any other trout we know of. Fish from the Ice Age."

"You and your fish," said Johannes, sounding resigned. Then he turned to his guests. "I completely forgot that I have to drive my father over to a meeting of retirees in Dalen. I'm really sorry. It was nice you could drop by."

They thanked him for the coffee and cake and then said goodbye. Max cast one last glance at the old man as they were leaving, but he still couldn't remember where he'd seen him before.

Twenty-Three

HENRIK THUE LEANED BACK IN HIS OFFICE CHAIR and clasped his hands behind his head. If he was nervous, it didn't show.

"So, how's it going with your article?" he asked.

"It's coming along," said Max, who had just sat down on a simple steel-pipe chair.

It had been impossible to tell from Thue's voice on the phone whether he was surprised or not, but he'd agreed to meet with Max again.

"I keep finding that the more I work with the material, the more impenetrable it seems."

"Not an unknown phenomenon," said the professor with a smile.

"And I thought maybe you could help me to figure out a few things that are still puzzling me."

"I'll try." Thue took off his glasses and began polishing the lenses with a royal-blue cloth. Max looked around discreetly. A person's office could say a lot about how that particular individual wanted to be regarded. And that was always something worth knowing. Thue's office gave the impression of control and balance, evident in everything from his desk, with its thin metal legs and the surface of icy-blue glass, to the only decoration on the wall—a black-and-white print of the Eidsborg stave church. "So, what don't you understand?"

Max threw out his hands to indicate there were plenty of choices. "Where should I start? Didn't you say something last time about Eidsborg Tarn possibly being the center of some kind of fertility cult in pagan days?"

"That's one theory, yes."

"And didn't people also believe that the Nikuls statue could cure infertile women?"

"That's right, but it's typical to pray to a saint figure for something like that. Asking to be granted a child. People still do that today, in the Catholic world."

"Was your doctoral dissertation about these sorts of things?"

"Not primarily. It was about Nikuls as a genius loci."

Max gave him a baffled look, even though he was well aware of what the term meant.

But he knew that experts liked to spout their knowledge.

"'Genius loci' is Latin for 'guardian spirit,'" Thue explained. "It's something that people in antiquity would have interpreted literally. Scattered throughout the Roman Empire were countless shrines dedicated to local gods and spirits. Usually they served a protective function and were connected to one specific place. It was this sort of god or spirit that they meant by 'genius loci.' Today the term is used more loosely to describe the characteristic atmosphere or mood of a place, and it doesn't usually refer to any kind of supernatural being. But Eidsborg is one of the rare places where the old and the new meanings of the term coincide. There can be no doubt that Nikuls has functioned as a genius loci in the traditional sense. The saint statue was connected to the area's very survival, plain and simple—first and foremost through good harvests and the birth of children. Yet anyone who is asked to describe the unique qualities of Eidsborg today will immediately start telling the story of the stave church and the worship of Nikuls."

The historian sat up straight and cast a glance out the window at the sunny morning in Bø. This was what Max wanted. To lull him into a false sense of security.

"Was there anything else?" asked Thue distractedly.

"Why did you lie to me about Peter Schram?"

Thue closed his eyes and sat still for a few seconds. It was impossible to read anything into his expression. Then he opened his eyes and looked at Max, his gaze unwavering. "Because I don't like to talk about it. Peter Schram was a friend of mine. More than that.

He was my mentor, the one who welcomed me into the academic world when I was hardly more than a pimply kid. I have to admit that I've never recovered from the loss."

Max let a few moments pass before he asked the next question. "What was it the two of you argued about?"

"As far as I remember, we never argued."

"But you were both involved in a terrible argument shortly before he disappeared. In fact, it wasn't just an argument. It was a fight. At the Tveit farm in Eidsborg. In the cabin that he'd rented. I have witnesses."

Thue's expression hardened. His gaze turned stern and unreadable. "Witnesses? What exactly are you up to?"

Max didn't deign to answer the question. This whole performance was about putting pressure on the professor. Then they'd see what came out of it.

"What about Cecilie Wiborg?" he asked now. "Have you recovered from losing her?"

The color of Thue's face changed from a discreet summertime tan to a light pink in a matter of seconds.

"Both of them were writing about the same subject, in which a special ritual on Midsummer Eve plays a central role, and both disappeared on that very night," Max went on. "With thirty years in between. Don't you think that's a little too big of a coincidence?"

"What else could it be?"

"That's precisely what I'm wondering."

Thue slowly shook his head, as if it would be fruitless to go on.

Max stood up and thanked the professor. He was already on his way out the door when he heard Thue say something behind him.

"A word of friendly advice: don't let your article get so big that it buries you."

Twenty-Four

MAX WENT STRAIGHT FROM HIS MEETING with Thue to the library, but this time Tirill wasn't sitting behind the counter.

"She's in her office," said the young girl, nodding toward a door.

Max entered a narrow hallway lined with several doors. One of them had a nameplate that said Tirill Vesterli. He knocked and received a quick "Come in!" in response.

The piles of books and papers on the desk were so big that Tirill had to roll her chair back a little before she could see who her visitor was.

"Detective Fjellanger," she said mildly.

"At your service."

She swept a newspaper off a chair and invited him to sit down.

What you see is what you get. That was the only message to glean from this office. The walls were almost entirely covered with a cheerful mixture of children's drawings, postcards, and photographs, including one picture that he recognized from Tirill's apartment, where it hung in a frame in the living room. Here, the photo of her doppelgänger was tacked up on a corkboard. The similarity between Tirill and her great-great-grandmother was so striking that he had to stop himself from staring.

He noticed that she was looking at him with a slight smile on her face.

"It's totally unreal," said Max.

"Don't be ridiculous!" she exclaimed. "What's real involves so many different things that there's hardly a need for anything unreal."

Maybe she was right. Maybe there was something like that behind all of this.

Max told her about the conversation he'd just had with Henrik Thue. He also mentioned the poorly disguised threat the professor had issued at the end.

"We need to go on the offensive!" she said angrily when he was done. "Do you think we could force him to talk?"

"How would we do that?"

"We could use the photograph. The one his wife showed you of Cecilie Wiborg in their garden. Maybe we could threaten to take it to the police."

"I have no intention of stealing any photographs from Åse Enger Thue."

"But we don't need the actual picture to put pressure on him," said Tirill. "Can't you see that? All you have to do is give him one of your business cards and say you're working for the Wiborg family. Then tell him that you've come across a picture of Cecilie in his garden. He'll pretend he doesn't know what you're talking about, and he'll probably ask to see the photo. Then you just say that you saw it on someone's cell phone. You can describe it in detail, can't you? The way she's lying on the ground. The decorations on the wall. All of that. So he'll realize you actually did see the photo."

"That sort of approach could be potentially life threatening," Max objected. "Not only for us but also for his wife, who showed me the picture."

"No, I think he'll panic and start talking."

"I don't know about that." Max shook his head. "What if he killed Cecilie? What would he have to lose by getting rid of us?"

Tirill sighed with annoyance. "OK, maybe it's dangerous, but the situation is already dangerous."

Max realized this was an accurate analysis. "All right, but I'm not going back to his office right now. Let's leave him in suspense for a few days."

Tirill picked up her phone and looked at the display. "I have to go," she said. "I'm leaving early today."

"Plans for the evening?" For a moment he considered inviting her out to dinner.

"Yes," she replied, giving him a secretive look.

Twenty-Five

SHE'D SEEN THIS LANDSCAPE slip past outside the train window countless times before. Yet she never grew tired of allowing her eyes to bob and dip along with the slowly undulating shapes.

The train rushed past large nurseries in Akkerhaugen. On the other side of Lake Norsjø, she saw the Ryntveit farms, idyllically situated with a beautiful view of the lake. In the forest above the farms, a simple iron cross marked the place where Knut Ryntveit and Åste Gunnarsrud met for the last time. The Ryntveit murder case involved Knut, the male heir, who cut the throat of Åste, the pregnant servant girl, after making love to her one last time. Back then the case had stirred great interest far beyond the boundaries of Telemark. Today it was long forgotten in other parts of the country, but in the home district of the victim and killer, the case had settled into the collective memory. Numerous songs had been composed about the killing. Ballads about murder from central Telemark. Tirill had once stood next to the cross, trying to pick up some impression from the violent event that had occurred there in 1904. And she did sense something. She was sure about that. But it was impossible to grasp intellectually or with words. The connections between the landscape and the crime were subtle and intangible.

This sort of knowledge—embodied in everything from amateur ballads to the mighty, visionary ballad called *Draumkvedet,* or *The Dream Poem,* which originated in the late Middle Ages—enabled

101

Tirill to spin a complex network of connections between various places and times in Telemark.

Yet right now she was traveling away from her home district and would be for several hours.

SHE'D FOUND THE ADDRESS in the online Yellow Pages, but she gave the cabdriver an address a short distance away in order to avoid attracting attention to her visit. It was a marked house, after all—as if a hand from the Old Testament had painted a bloody cross above the door sometime during the previous summer.

When Tirill saw the sunlight flickering on the pavement beneath the leafy trees, she thought that Cecilie must have noticed the same thing on numerous occasions. Maybe the sight was even part of her earliest memories, something there from the very beginning, something she didn't really think about. Mamma's scent. Pappa's hand. The crack in the ceiling over her bed. The light on the sidewalk in the summertime, beneath the leafy trees lining the street.

The chiming of the doorbell sounded as if it came from deep inside a much bigger building. As Tirill stood listening to the echo, she was hoping nobody would be home. She hadn't discussed this with Fjellanger, because she didn't think he would have approved, given the investigation they had undertaken. If the parents suspected that someone was poking around in the case, they might decide to contact the police.

The door opened slightly, and a middle-aged woman with shoulder-length, ash-blond hair peered at Tirill. Her face was devoid of all expression.

"Are you a reporter?" the woman whispered, sounding suspicious.

"No, I'm from Telemark University College." Tirill took out her employee ID.

Mrs. Wiborg took the card and scrutinized what it said. "A librarian? What do you want?"

"This may sound stupid, but I knew Cecilie . . . and I just wanted to . . ." She gave Cecilie's mother a despondent look, noting to her surprise that the despondency was genuine.

"What do you want?" the woman repeated, but without hostility.
"Could we maybe . . . I just wondered if we could have a talk."

For several long seconds Mrs. Wiborg stared at her impassively. Then she took a step back and opened the door.

IN A DREAM, Tirill once found herself on the moon. She'd gone there as a member of an expedition, but when the others departed, they left her behind. Through the glass of her astronaut helmet, she'd looked at the blue planet Earth. A device on her wrist told her that she had eighteen minutes until her oxygen ran out, but there was no help to be had—everyone else was on the round blue disk in the sky. Her terror was all-encompassing, as if she were bathed in fear, but she couldn't even scream, because sound didn't carry in the void of space.

Fortunately she woke up before the oxygen was gone.

But Kathrine Wiborg was never going to wake up from her dream.

On the table just inside the living room door was a photograph of her daughter. Cecilie's face radiated youthful immortality.

"You can have a seat over there," the woman said, a quaver suddenly appearing in her voice. She thought she was about to have a talk with someone who had known her daughter. Someone she wasn't aware of until now. The prospect had to be both frightening and enticing.

Tirill sat down on the sofa and waited. Hanging on the walls were family photographs and a number of abstract paintings. One photo was clearly of Kathrine and her husband at a young age, with a little girl standing between them on a beach somewhere.

The girl looked like her mother. Tirill now regretted saying that she was a friend of Cecilie's, but it was too late to do anything about it. She was sitting on the same sofa where Cecilie must have sat. She must have stretched out here to listen to music, or maybe to make out with a boy at a home-alone party. And there was the TV she must have watched, with varying degrees of interest, along with her parents. The three of them probably watched movies with a bowl of snacks on the coffee table.

That was Cecilie's life, before somebody took it away from her in Telemark.

"Are you hungry?" asked Kathrine Wiborg as she came into the living room. "Can I get you something to drink?"

Tirill held up her hands and shook her head.

"OK," Mrs. Wiborg whispered almost inaudibly before sitting down in an armchair only a couple of meters away.

In the past she most likely would have insisted on serving refreshments, but she no longer had any patience for such trivialities. The silence in the room was like a heavy weight pressing on her chest. And Kathrine Wiborg made no attempt to speak. Tirill was the one who had sought her out, after all, and not the other way around.

"Cecilie and I . . . ," Tirill began, but the words died on her lips. "I won't claim that we were close friends," she tried again. Every word tasted like a piece of charred meat. "We met for drinks a few times. Not just the two of us, but with . . . some other students and employees. I liked her a lot. And when she disappeared, I couldn't really take it in. I read about it in the papers, but . . . It was as if they were talking about somebody else, not the Cecilie I knew. It's only lately I've realized that . . ."

She felt like spitting the words on the floor to get rid of the burned taste in her mouth. Then she could just tell the truth.

"That what?" Mrs. Wiborg said in a low voice.

"That she's really gone."

Neither of them spoke for a moment. Then Mrs. Wiborg raised her head and stared at her visitor. "My husband and I took part in the search that went on in Bø for several days. We looked through old hay sheds out in the fields. We looked inside junked cars and in all sorts of awful places. There were people everywhere; everyone was searching. But we didn't find a thing. Not a trace."

Behind her was a big picture window. The drapes were drawn, allowing only a few streaks of sunlight into the room.

"I hadn't talked to her in quite a while before she went missing," said Tirill. "And I was just wondering whether . . . Well, I wanted to ask you whether she was happy."

Something like a smile appeared on Kathrine's face, but it quickly vanished. "I think she was doing really well."

She spoke in the same low monotone, as if the slightest hint of emotion might suffocate her. "She came home the week before Midsummer. She seemed really excited. Almost as if she had a secret. At least that's what we've thought after the fact. But maybe it was just because she was so young."

Tirill felt her very presence was somehow offensive, since she still had the majority of her life ahead of her. "Did Cecilie ever mention Peter Schram?" Again that bitter taste of charred meat in her mouth.

"Schram?" Kathrine shook her head.

"He's just someone who was working with the same material," said Tirill. "Researching the saint worship in Eidsborg. I thought maybe—"

"No, I never asked her much about her work. Of course I should have, because then I would have known her a little better before she disappeared."

Kathrine sat motionless, staring straight ahead, until Tirill began to wonder whether she'd been forgotten. "Did she mention any of her friends or colleagues the last time she was home?"

Kathrine Wiborg looked as if she were trying to catch sight of someone out there in space. On the blue planet where all the others now were. Her eyes had taken on a shiny and faraway look. "There was something about a biologist."

"Oh?"

"Yes. Wasn't she working with some soil samples before she disappeared?"

"I don't know," said Tirill. "I thought she was a student in the humanities department."

"Hmm . . . I must be thinking of my niece, who's studying in England. She's going to be a landscape gardener."

"That sounds more likely."

Kathrine's gaze again retreated to the moon. Tirill knew she should try getting as much information as possible out of her now that she had the chance, but reality was becoming too insistent. Or maybe it was unreality.

"I'll always hold on to a tiny scrap of hope," Kathrine said suddenly. "Until they find her."

That was when Tirill knew she couldn't stand being there any longer. "I guess I should be going," she said.

"That's up to you," replied Kathrine without interest. "You're lucky, you know. Nothing is up to me anymore."

When Tirill was once again outside, staring at the flickering sunlight on the sidewalk, she thought that what she'd found out was more than enough.

Twenty-Six

MAX HAD CAREFULLY PREPARED what he was going to say to Henrik Thue, but he was still nervous when he knocked on the door. He'd never done anything like this before. Here he was, about to pressure a professor for information in the man's own office in the middle of a workday.

No one answered when he knocked, but luckily he didn't have to wait long before Thue showed up, carrying a bunch of papers in one hand. When he caught sight of Max, his face seemed to shut down.

"So, what do you want today?" he asked as he approached.

"Just some supplementary information," replied Max. "It won't take long."

Without a word Thue let him in. He pointed to the same chair where Max had sat on his previous visit. The professor then perched on a corner of his desk, possibly in an attempt to physically dominate the much taller Fjellanger. "What's this about?" he asked impatiently.

"A photograph."

A few seconds passed before Thue spoke. "What photograph?"

"A picture of Cecilie Wiborg."

Another pause.

"Are you asking me whether I have a picture of her?"

"No, I'm saying that both of us have a photo of her."

The professor looked confused, which pleased Max. Confusion was always a good thing.

"It's even the same one. She was a beautiful girl."

"Quit talking in circles."

"I'm referring to the picture you took of her in your garden. The one where she's wearing a bikini and lying on the ground in front of the fountain. It's easy to recognize the place because of the dolphins and octopuses."

The professor opened his mouth to speak, but changed his mind.

"So, what are you thinking of doing now?" asked Max. "Are you going to throw me out? Or maybe you'd like to call the police?"

Thue moved behind his desk and sat down, as if accepting that it was no longer possible to dominate Max, no matter how high up he sat.

"What happened on Midsummer Eve?"

"I don't know what you're talking about," Thue said.

Max took out a business card and placed it on the desk made of icy-blue glass. He stood up and went over to the door, but then turned back to look at Thue, who had picked up the card and was studying it.

"I'm going over to the sheriff's office," said Max. "I'm going to hand over a cell phone that has the picture of Cecilie in your garden. The bikini picture. I figure you'll be sitting in an interrogation room, talking to the criminal police, before the night is over. I'm sure they'd like to know why you never told them that you and Cecilie were having an affair."

Thue looked like a figure from Madame Tussauds's wax museum. And judging by the beads of sweat on his forehead and upper lip, the wax was on the verge of melting.

Max turned and pressed down on the door handle.

"Wait, wait, wait!" Thue cried frantically. Then he lowered his voice and whispered, "I loved Cecilie. I could never have done anything to harm her. Please leave me alone."

Now it was Max who went and perched on the edge of the desk. "I'm afraid I can't do that. If you refuse to cooperate, I won't be able to go any further in my investigation without asking the police for help. That's just how it is."

Thue slowly shook his head, as if trying to think of some way out of the situation. Finally he gave up. "I have a meeting in ten minutes. People are going to start showing up here any second."

Max didn't want to be interrupted by any intruders. "Come to my hotel room tonight at eight o'clock," he said. "And if you're not there . . ."

He raised his finger in warning, and the professor nodded compliantly.

Twenty-Seven

A T 8:20 THERE WAS A KNOCK ON THE DOOR. Thue seemed somber but composed, and he offered no explanation for his tardiness.

"By the way, I mentioned to the front-desk clerk that I was expecting you," said Max. "Just in case you happened to be planning anything . . . creative, so to speak," he said with a smile.

On the professor's face he saw an odd mixture of resignation and . . . what was it? Relief?

"If I tell you everything, exactly how it happened, do you promise not to report me to the police?" he said.

"That depends on what you tell me. I'll do whatever it takes to solve the case, but I promise to try and keep you out of it. So, what happened on Midsummer Eve last year?"

Thue took out his glasses case from the inside pocket of his blazer and began polishing his glasses with the royal-blue cloth.

"Cecilie had been pestering me for several days—it was a hell of a week—because she wanted me to drive her to Eidsborg on Midsummer Eve, but I didn't feel like it."

"Why not?"

"Because it was clear she just wanted me to drive her there. She didn't say anything about the two of us spending any time together. She wanted me to be her chauffeur, and that was all. But my wife was away, and that wasn't exactly how I pictured spending the evening."

"So Cecilie didn't have a car?"

"No. Lots of students don't. She came over to my house around

110

three in the afternoon. Did you see the picture taken by the surveillance camera? It was the last one ever taken of her. She was on her way to my house. It's a miracle that nobody saw us leaving Bø."

"So you drove her to Eidsborg?"

"Yes. Or rather, she told me to drop her off about a kilometer away, before we got there. Near a logging road. She said she was planning to spend Midsummer Night out there. I guess that was the whole point of the trip: to get as close as possible to what she was writing about. To take in the scent of the flowers and the dew on the grass on the night when they used to carry Nikuls around Eidsborg Tarn."

"But why didn't she want you to drive her all the way there?"

"I don't know. I just dropped her off. But first we agreed that she'd call me when she wanted me to come and get her the following day. That was the last time I saw Cecilie."

Henrik Thue's expression changed, but it was impossible to tell what he was thinking.

"What about her cell phone? It was either switched off or stopped working eight minutes after the surveillance photo was taken. I assume she turned it off when she reached your house. Is that right?"

"That's what she usually did when we were together. She didn't want to be disturbed. We lived in our own little bubble, and no one else was allowed in. At least that was true before she got pregnant."

He looked at Max, as if to check his reaction.

"Was it yours?"

Thue suddenly smiled.

"Why are you telling me this?" asked Max. "It wasn't something I needed to know."

"Because I want you to understand why I lied to the police. Do you really think they would have believed me if I said that I drove Cecilie to Eidsborg and dropped her off at that godforsaken place where nobody could see us? There were no witnesses to back up my story, but it's all true! And by the way, she was pregnant with my child," he added, purposely making himself sound stupid. "Can't you see that I was terrified? Thank God nobody at the college knew about our relationship. Nobody in her family either. She'd kept the whole affair secret. That's why the police mostly asked me about what sort of girl she was, and not much else. They asked me who her friends were. And did I know whether she had a boyfriend. Things like that. But that's all. I didn't hear from them again. Could I have a glass of water?"

Max went into the bathroom and filled a glass from the tap. "Here," he said, handing the glass to Thue, who emptied it with a couple of noisy gulps. "How did you react when she told you she was pregnant?"

"At first all I felt was a claustrophobic fear. But gradually it seemed more like a gift that had been dumped in my lap. Here was a young woman whom I loved, and who I thought loved me in return. And now a child . . . For me, who was never able to . . ." He sat still, staring dejectedly into space without finishing his sentence.

"Do you and your wife have children?" asked Max.

Thue shook his head.

"Are you not able to have any?"

"Åse can't. So you see, it was like being given a gift of life. A life I had started to realize I would never be able to experience. And suddenly there it was. Do you have any idea what I'm talking about?"

Max had a very good idea. He'd been there himself. The indifference of nature knew no bounds when it came to human beings.

"You must have been terrified that your wife would find out."

"She did find out. Only a few days later. Cecilie and I had an agreement to meet at my house on Monday afternoons. That's when Åse is teaching. But on that particular Monday she happened to stay home with a cold, and I'd received a call telling me that my father was seriously ill, so I rushed off to Oslo. With all the stressful news about his illness and the secret pregnancy, I forgot to tell Cecilie I'd be away. When she showed up at our house, Åse was the only one home. Wanting to provoke a divorce, Cecilie told her that she was pregnant with my child."

Max had heard a different and far less dramatic version of this encounter between Åse and Cecilie. He did his utmost to hide the surprise he felt. "So how did your wife react?"

"She called Cecilie a whore and threw her out. But when I got back from Oslo, it was as if her fury had completely gone."

"She didn't want a divorce?"

"All she said was that things would no doubt work out somehow."

Thue was fiddling with his glasses nonstop, which might be interpreted as a sign that he was lying. At least, that was often the case in movies and books. On a par with a suspect who frequently scratched his nose or whose eyes kept wandering. Experience had taught Max that things were different in real life, simply because reality was hopelessly chaotic—seven billion people simultaneously playing out the same game, in which life itself was at stake.

"You said that you thought Cecilie loved you," Max said now.

"Yes, but after a while I wasn't so sure. Toward the end she seemed so distant. I tried to tell myself that it was because of the pregnancy, but I actually had a feeling there was something she didn't want to share with me."

"When did you first notice this?"

"In the beginning I wasn't aware of it, but when I look back now, I think it started as early as April. Meaning before she got pregnant."

"Was there something in your relationship that might have caused her to withdraw?"

"What I noticed was that her thoughts were elsewhere. Do you know what I mean? As if she was no longer thinking about the world around her. Only about this other thing, whatever it was."

"How would you describe your relationship to pigs' heads?"

Thue frowned, giving Max a puzzled look. "I can't say I have any relationship to them," he said calmly. "What do you mean?"

Max studied him in silence for a moment before deciding that Thue wasn't bluffing. "The Tveit farm in Eidsborg," he said then. "Have you ever been there?"

"Years ago."

"But you lied when you claimed not to know Peter Schram."

"I've already explained why I did that. Why are you persisting in digging around in my past?"

"It's a widespread misconception that the past is past," said Max. "The truth is that it's never over. That's what you said the first time we met. I assume that applies to your own past as well."

Henrik Thue lowered his gaze, as if he were looking at something interesting right next to Max Fjellanger's polished shoes.

"Did you look through Schram's papers? Did you read something that you weren't meant to see? Was that why the two of you ended up fighting?"

Thue sighed with resignation. "You're on the wrong track again. As I told you before, I never had a fight with Peter Schram. And I don't know what any of this has to do with Cecilie's disappearance. On the other hand, I have to admit that I'm impressed with everything you've managed to find out. Earlier today you said that the fountain was recognizable in the picture I took of Cecilie. I didn't think much about it at the time, but afterward I wondered whether you'd been sneaking around in our garden."

"I'll do whatever is necessary to solve the case. And I know a lot more than you think. But there are still a number of things I'm wondering about. Like, for instance: Did Peter Schram really have some sort of accident while hiking in the woods? Or was he murdered?"

"I have no idea," said Thue and pointedly closed his eyes.

His face was drawn and he seemed exhausted, as if it had been a long time since he'd had a good night's sleep.

Twenty-Eight

THE GARDEN WAS FRAGRANT WITH LAVENDER and newly mowed grass. The only sounds came from the water splashing in the fountain and from the bees bathing in the nectar deep inside the blossoms. On the table where they'd sat before stood a glass containing some red liquid. Raspberry juice, Max thought. But Åse Enger Thue didn't seem to be home. He'd already made sure that her husband wasn't there by having Tirill call the professor to ask about a book he'd once borrowed and returned long ago. Thue had told her that he was in Oslo and wouldn't be able to come over to the library.

Max decided to go over to the porch and knock on the door. It was so bright out in the garden that it was hard to see anything inside the house. He pressed his forehead against the pane and peered through the glass as he raised his hands to shade his face on either side from the sun.

While he was standing there, a door opened inside the house, and Åse came into the room. She had a pink towel wrapped around her head like a turban. That was the only thing she had on. With no sign of embarrassment, she walked through the room the way someone does who is home alone and knows she won't be seen. The white areas of her body, normally hidden from the sun, seemed almost luminescent in the dim light of the room.

The sight sent a pleasant shock wave through Max. For a moment he thought she was looking right at him, and he waited for her to scream, but she continued on as if nothing had happened and vanished from his field of vision as unruffled as when she came in.

Breathing hard, he walked quickly back through the garden and headed for the road. When he was almost there, he heard the porch door open behind him. A few seconds later Åse appeared among the shrubbery, her wet hair smoothed back from her face.

"Hi!" she cried, waving.

"Oh, there you are," he said.

"Come on into the garden." She must have jumped into the shorts she was now wearing, a pair of worn-out denim cutoffs. Her white T-shirt also looked as if she'd thrown it on in haste. He couldn't understand how she'd been able to get dressed so fast after he'd just seen her naked.

"It's great to see you again," she said, giving him a big smile.

THE SCENT OF HER RECENTLY SHOWERED BODY blended with the fragrance of raspberry juice. He'd made up his mind to get her to say more about her encounter with Cecilie Wiborg. It was hard to believe her husband would lie about something like that. Why would he make up that sort of thing? And if he wasn't lying, that meant Åse was the one not telling the truth. That was the reason for his visit, or so he told himself.

But now Åse crossed her long legs. They were a golden brown almost all the way up, though at the edges of the ragged denim of her shorts, he caught a glimpse of white skin.

Did she realize he'd seen more?

"What kind of flowers are those?" he asked, just for something to say, as he pointed at the tall, intensely blue flowers that grew along the wall.

She turned languidly, looking in the direction he was pointing. "Delphiniums."

"Why does the Norwegian name translate as 'riding spurs'?"

"No idea," she replied without interest. "Maybe the blossoms look like spurs on a pair of riding boots."

"Do you ride?" The question just popped out of his mouth.

"Not often enough," she said, with the hint of a smile. "But by nature I'm a real horsewoman."

"It shows."

"Oh?" She looked at him in surprise.

"Well, horseback riding is good for . . . ," he began. "It gives you a great . . . a great . . ."

She left him hanging for a moment, his words flailing in the air, before she took mercy on him. "I need to go in and dry my hair, or it'll look like I've just got out of bed," she said.

After she left, he was finally able to breathe more easily. Ever since he'd seen her naked, his breathing had been quick and constricted, as if his lungs had shrunk to a fourth of their normal size.

After a few minutes she came back, her hair now dry. Max was pleased that she hadn't put on any more clothes. Right behind her came Missy, the cat.

"That's better," she said, ruffling her hair with her fingers. Then she smoothed it down again and pulled it back into a ponytail, fastening it with an elastic that she seemed to have conjured out of nowhere.

"Your garden is amazing," he said.

She sat down and peered up at him, like a sly shark studying tourists at the beach. "Did you get a chance to take a good look around?"

"I think I've seen quite a lot. Those beautiful delphiniums, for instance."

"Oh, right. So, do you ride?"

"It's been a long time, but I used to ride a lot in the States."

"Did you use cowboy spurs? The kind with little wheels and jagged edges?"

"I don't really remember," said Max. He wasn't quite sure what they were talking about.

"Have you ever thought about what it must feel like to the horse when those sharp edges get jabbed into her flanks?"

Max leaned down to pet Missy, who was lying at Åse's feet. Her naked right leg dangled in front of him. He couldn't recall the last time he'd seen anything so smooth. But he also noticed the ring that Ann had placed on his finger twenty-five years ago, and he straightened up.

"I don't know much about horses," he said. "But your garden is a sight for the gods."

"A garden has to be taken care of. Henrik takes care of the gods. Gods and saints. That's his thing. And students."

"Others' gardens?"

She laughed sadly. "When you can't trust the man you've married, who can you trust? In the end everything is just one big lie that you can never escape. Phone calls that have to be taken in other rooms. Text messages that make him smile. I can't remember the last time he smiled at anything *I* said or did. Except in a superior way, of course. There's been plenty of that. Superior smiles when the hysterical wife of the professor once again suspects that he's having an affair with one of his young students."

"Why do you put up with it?"

Åse shook her head. "Don't ask." The look she gave Max seemed to hold a trace of defiance. "When Cecilie disappeared, I was visiting my sister in Skien. I phoned Henrik, who claimed to be at home sitting on the porch and relaxing, but I know how the garden sounds on a summer evening. It's the same as now. Very quiet. Maybe an occasional car passing by on the road. But there was a different kind of background noise on the phone. A steady sound, like inside a car. Those are the sorts of things that fill my life."

Max leaned forward and placed his hand on her forearm. The touch sparked a fire inside him, and he couldn't resist the sun-warmed pathway of her arm, leading all the way up to her shoulder, as smooth and rounded as some sort of exotic fruit.

She removed his hand, but with such languor that it seemed more like a question than an answer.

"Sorry," he said, dizzy from how close she was.

She laughed soundlessly and took a sip of juice. "How long are you planning to be in Bø?"

"I don't know."

"You said you've come to Norway to study the stave churches, but there aren't any here. At least as far as I know. And believe me, I'd know. So why are you staying here?"

Since he couldn't tell her the truth, there was only one plausible thing he could say. "Because you're here."

"Oh, come on! It can't be that interesting to sit here listening to all my complaints."

"Because of you I feel like something is thawing inside me."

She frowned, looking surprised.

"Something has been frozen solid inside me for a long time. But we don't have to talk about that, if you don't want to."

"I do want to."

He took a deep breath and went on. "Actually, it feels more like my eyesight has been damaged. After my wife died—and before that too, while she was sick—I felt like I'd lost part of my sight. As if the world had somehow flattened out, or lost color. When I sit here with you, the world has all its colors and shapes back. That's why I've stayed."

He noticed with surprise how easy it was for him to lie and tell the truth in the same breath.

Åse had looked away as he spoke. Now she said, "That's the nicest thing anyone has ever said to me. But I'm married. . . ."

"So is your husband."

"Good point. But I'm not like my husband."

"You have a higher standard?"

"Everyone has a higher standard than Henrik."

"Then why—"

"Don't ask!" she interrupted him, and abruptly got to her feet.

She began pacing back and forth on the lawn as she held her face in her hands. "What a mess!" she murmured glumly. It sounded as if she were talking to herself.

Max stood up too and tried to take her arm, but she waved him away. "Do you want me to leave?" he asked.

She didn't answer. She didn't really seem to be paying attention to him anymore. Again he asked whether she would prefer him to leave. When she didn't reply, he headed out. The whole time, he was hoping that she'd call him back. When he came out onto the road, he heard the porch door close with a bang.

Twenty-Nine

MAX COULDN'T SLEEP, so he decided to take a walk. Yet as soon as he stepped out the front door of the hotel, he hesitated. For a moment he felt scared and vulnerable, but he pulled himself together and set off. He had no intention of letting some hooded figure frighten him.

Even so, he avoided going near the churches again. Instead, he took the path that passed through Elvjudalen, a parklike area between the hotel and the train station. He crossed Lortebekk—or Shit Creek, as Tirill told him it was called—by means of a small concrete bridge and then continued up the hill toward the station.

The long, deserted platform was bathed in a chilly light. It was past midnight, and it wouldn't be long before the night train arrived, but no passengers had shown up yet. The only people he saw were a few teenagers sitting in two parked cars over by the kiosk, now closed. They were talking to each other through the open car windows.

Max sat down on a bench. He let his gaze move along the train tracks until they disappeared in the dark. Maybe he'd already been here too long. The fact that he'd come over to the station at night to see the train arrive from Oslo seemed a clear indication that was true. Or maybe that was simply how he'd always been—a person who thrived best when surrounded by a vast silence.

In Florida he would sometimes get up in the middle of the night, without waking Ann. Then he'd get in the car and drive out of the city, looking for a completely deserted beach. And there he'd take a walk, with no destination in mind. He'd listen to the waves washing ashore and occasionally glance up at the stars. On those nights he often had the feeling that he could, at long last, breathe again. Yet he loved Ann.

That's just how I am, he concluded. A loner.

The night train arrived, but no one got on. Only two passengers got off, and they immediately moved away in opposite directions. Then the conductor blew his whistle, and shortly afterward the platform was once again completely deserted.

AS MAX STEPPED INSIDE HIS HOTEL ROOM and closed the door behind him, a dark-clad figure rushed at him and slammed him against the wall. He threw a punch but missed—his fist slid along the chest or stomach of the assailant. He managed to see that the man was wearing a dark hoodie, with the hood pulled well down over his forehead, but then a kick landed high up on his thigh, close to his groin, and as he doubled over he received a hard blow to his shoulder.

Max lowered his right arm and then delivered an upper cut that struck the assailant on the chin, as perfectly aimed as any knockout punch. The dark figure uttered a surprised groan and crashed to the floor.

For a moment Max stood still, gasping for breath. He noticed that his laptop was open on the desk.

Then he threw himself at the assailant, shoving him flat and sliding off his hood. The guy couldn't have been more than twenty. His eyes rolled around in their sockets, and it was impossible to make eye contact with him. Max's punch had knocked him senseless.

There was something familiar about the young face. The more Max stared at the guy, the more certain he was that he'd seen him before, and not long ago.

Then he suddenly realized who this guy was lying underneath him on the floor.

Thirty

A FEW MINUTES LATER Max was still breathing hard, but he'd at least managed to straighten his clothing.

Tycho Abrahamsen was slouched in an easy chair, scowling at him. Max thought about the kid's name. It sounded so old-fashioned.

"Why do you think I killed your father?" he asked now. "Knut was a good friend of mine."

"I'm sure that Pappa didn't commit suicide," said Tycho. "And then you suddenly show up at the funeral, claiming that you just happened to be in Norway at the moment."

There was something hard about the look of the young man's face. Max had noticed it at the funeral. A stony expression.

"I can prove that I didn't kill him," said Max. He reached for his laptop, which was still open and already switched on. With a few keystrokes he opened the e-mail showing his plane ticket.

"Take a look." He handed the laptop to the young man sitting in the chair. "I arrived in Norway the same day as the funeral. When I saw you there, I'd been in the country for only a few hours."

Tycho took his time studying the document. "You could have killed him and then gone back to the States first," he finally said.

"And then I flew to Norway again a few days later to attend the funeral?"

"I guess that's not very likely. But why did you lie?"

"Because I knew the truth would sound strange. Knut's funeral was the only reason I decided to come to Norway. I wanted to attend the funeral of a man I hadn't been in contact with for almost thirty years. My intention was just to show up and then go right back home."

"So why didn't you?" asked Tycho, handing the laptop back to Max.

"First I want to know how you got into my room."

"I'm staying on the same floor, two rooms down. I've been try-ing to keep an eye on you since you arrived. I was the one who fol-lowed you up by the churches. Tonight there was a new desk clerk on duty. So when I heard you go out, I waited a little while and then went down to the lobby to tell the clerk that the thermostat in my room had gone haywire and the place was like a sauna. When we reached the door of your room, I said I'd forgotten my key. I'd locked myself out. So the clerk went to get a key and opened the door. We decided the thermostat had turned off on its own, and everything was fine. So I said good night, and he left. Then I opened your laptop."

"But you spent too much time getting in here."

"Yeah."

"What were you hoping to find?"

"Notes or pictures on your computer. Something that might give me a clue about what happened to my father. So why didn't you go back home to the States?"

"Because your mother told me that he died in Dalen. And be-cause . . . Well, it's a long story."

"I've got time," said Tycho, rubbing his chin where Max had punched him.

WHEN MAX WAS DONE describing Peter Schram's disappearance and everything that had happened since he'd arrived in Norway, young Tycho shook his head in amazement. "You've got to be kidding me. A fire. A ghost. A decapitated pig. And Cecilie Wiborg. I guess it's my turn to talk. Let me start with Cecilie. Pappa was totally fixat-ed on the case. He was obsessed. He didn't tell Mamma anything, but after a while he let me in on what he was thinking. It all be-gan with the research that Cecilie was doing. Her work was barely mentioned in the newspapers, but there was enough for him to see a connection between her disappearance and Peter Schram's."

"So he still had that visceral instinct," said Max, mostly to himself.

"Uh-huh. And it was so strange for me to see that. I knew him as a sluggish kind of man who shuffled from room to room in his slippers. With a skimpy mustache and a cigarette in one hand. As if he'd been somehow crushed inside by what happened to him when he was on the police force."

"Are you talking about the rumor that he had something to do with Schram's disappearance?"

Tycho nodded.

"I didn't know anything about it until a couple of days ago," Max explained. "Someone said something that got me thinking along those lines. I wish Knut had phoned me, or sent me a letter about it sometime over the past decades."

"But don't you get it?" Tycho sounded surprised. "He could never be sure whether or not you were the one who'd spread the rumor. You left the force shortly after Schram disappeared, after all, and then you emigrated to the States. And he never heard from you again. Pappa thought that was highly suspicious. I did too. That's probably the main reason why I'm sitting here in this room right now. Along with the lie you told at the funeral, when you said you just happened to be in Norway. Plus the fact that Pappa died."

Max felt a twinge of pain somewhere inside, a spot that probably didn't exist and therefore could not be reached. Had Knut spent all these years harboring a suspicion that he'd been stabbed in the back by his good friend?

"So tell me, did Knut ever go to Dalen to try and find out about things?" he asked. "Before he died, I mean?"

"Yes, several times, but he never let me go with him."

"What do you think he did there?"

"I guess he must have talked to people. I'm not really sure. But in the end, the past caught up with him."

"It's a misconception that the past is past," said Max. "At least that's what Professor Henrik Thue claims."

"Cecilie's adviser. Though he was more than that, according to you."

"Definitely more than that. Did Knut know about their relationship?"

"I don't think so. He was more interested in your friend. The librarian. One of Pappa's former colleagues has a son who's also on the police force, and for a while he worked on the Wiborg case. It was through him that my father found out about a woman who claimed Cecilie's disappearance had something to do with Midsummer Eve and the old saint worship in Eidsborg. Pappa thought she either knew something that no one else knew, or else she was just a smart woman who could put two and two together. At any rate, he thought we should keep an eye on her. Find out what she was up to. Who she met, etcetera. That was my job. I didn't know her name or where she lived, only that she worked in the library at the college. So I went over there and asked if they had an employee who was particularly knowledgeable about crime cases. I figured that anyone who came up with that sort of theory about Cecilie's disappearance would also enjoy reading about crime. And I was right. The lady behind the counter left for a minute and then came back with Tirill Vesterli. I talked with her for a short time and quickly realized that I'd found the right person. After that, all I had to do was follow her to find out where she lived."

"So why did you stop spying on her?"

"Because it didn't produce anything of interest. She lives an incredibly boring life. She spends all her time at work or with her kid. The only exception was once when she went out with a friend and came home so shit-faced that she spent half the night trying to find the keyhole."

Max tried to picture Tirill in a drunken state.

She'd probably create quite a ruckus, he decided.

Thirty-One

MAX OPENED THE WINDOW and let the night into the small hotel room. The air smelled sweet and floral, evoking a memory of the hollow of Ann's throat.

Her soft skin. Her pulse.

"Is it conceivable that your father might actually have killed himself?" he asked with his back to the room.

"I guess you could say he was the right type to do something like that. He was a nervous person, and sometimes he suffered from depression. If this had happened a couple of years ago, I might have accepted the explanation for his death. But not after Cecilie Wiborg disappeared. It was like the investigation woke him up to a whole new life."

Max turned around to face Tycho. "The night after his funeral . . . Was that you outside Tirill's apartment?"

"Yes. It just seemed so strange that you would show up like you did. I wondered whether the two of you might be connected somehow."

For a moment Tycho Abrahamsen looked down, as if studying the toes of his shoes. Then he looked up at Max. "Did you know Pappa well?"

For a moment Max thought he sensed an emptiness in the young man. Maybe an emptiness left by someone who had never been there, meaning the Knut Abrahamsen that Max had known back in the 1980s. Before all the gossip and his slide downhill.

Max sat down. "We were both so young," he began. "Not much older than you are now. We knew each other from the police academy, and then we ended up working in the same sheriff district in Vest-Telemark. We went hunting and fishing, we took long hikes and camped out in tents. We were very different, but I liked him a lot. He was so determined and . . . strong."

The last word prompted an almost inaudible intake of breath from the son, who was slouched in his chair, looking like a teenager.

"Very different from me," Max went on. "My family expected me to have a military career. My father was an officer. When that didn't work out, the police force was an acceptable alternative. So I attended both officer training school and the police academy. My father's son, as you can see."

Another small sound escaped from the young man's lips. It was hard to tell whether he was laughing or crying.

"Ever since I could think for myself," Tycho now said, "I've hated the way my father acted. For me, he was the epitome of weakness. All that nervous smoking. And his shoulders were always slumped. Worst of all was the way he refused to change. But after Cecilie Wiborg disappeared . . ." He took a deep breath and then exhaled, his voice trembling as he said, "Now I'm wondering whether what I thought was weakness was actually strength."

"That could be," said Max. "My own father—in all his sternness—was a weak person. That's something I can clearly see now, after the fact. Maybe he wouldn't have been able to function at all outside the military system, where respect was associated with the number of stripes and stars on a person's epaulets. Yet when I was a boy, he seemed to me the strongest man in the world. Like a solid wall. I think that's how it is for lots of boys. We grow up with a father who is either too strong or too weak. And sometimes it's hard to tell the difference."

A toilet flushed in some nearby room. Otherwise there was complete silence in the Bø Hotel.

"So, what about you?" asked Tycho.

"I've been spared that particular problem. I don't have any kids." Max stood up and went over to the window to close it. "So Knut didn't tell you anything about what he'd been doing in Dalen? No names?"

Tycho shook his head apologetically. "The only thing I remember him saying was something about meeting again people he'd once arrested in 'the bad old days,' as he said. That's all."

Tellev Sustugu, thought Max. "What are you planning to do now?" he asked the boy.

"Find out who killed Pappa."

"I'm going to need some help in the near future. Do you think you could put a lid on it for a few more days? Right now it's important not to allow yourself to be ruled by emotions. I know that's easier said than done, but if we're going to find Knut's killer, or killers, you need to stay in the background. At least for the time being. Can I count on your help when the time comes?"

The young man nodded somberly.

Max didn't think they'd actually need Tycho's assistance, but he didn't want to have a revenge-seeking youth running around on his own in the midst of everything. The situation was complicated enough as it was. "Maybe you should go back home to your mother for a while. She needs you."

"You're probably right. But first there's something else you should know." Tycho took a deep breath, as if what he was going to say required an extra amount of oxygen.

Max sat down on the edge of the bed, right across from him. Their knees were almost touching.

"It happened on June 24, 1985, the day after Peter Schram went out on his last hike. Pappa and the sheriff were standing together in the parking lot behind the sheriff's office in Dalen. Pappa told me that you weren't there. It was just the two of them. Pappa noticed that the trunk of Sheriff Homme's car wasn't properly closed, and since he was standing nearest, he lifted the lid of the trunk in order to slam it closed. That's when the sheriff screamed and threw himself at my father. Pappa said he'd heard that sort of scream only once before. And that was when a little boy ran out in the road right in front of a car. The boy's father screamed just like Homme did. That's what Pappa said, anyway."

Tycho leaned forward and placed his forearms on his thighs as he looked Max in the eye.

"Why did Jørgen scream?" asked Max.

"Pappa managed to catch a glimpse of something inside the

trunk. A wooden figure that was partially hidden under a blanket. It looked like the figure of a person, but he couldn't see any details."

"A wooden figure?" said Max in surprise. "Why would that make the sheriff go through the roof like he did?"

"Well, that's the big question. Pappa thought there must have been something special about it. He said he sometimes wondered whether it might have been the saint statue from the church. But why would the sheriff be driving around with the statue in the trunk of his car?"

"Did your father say why he never mentioned this to me?" asked Max.

"He said he got really scared. The sheriff seemed totally out of control. As if he might do anything at all. And that's why Pappa never dared say a word about it. He said he'd never told anyone about it before."

Maybe that was the reason the sheriff had spread a rumor about Knut having something to do with Schram's disappearance, thought Max—to make him leave his job in Tokke municipality. And preferably to leave the police force altogether. He wanted to break Knut down and render him harmless as a witness.

And in that regard, he'd certainly succeeded.

Thirty-Two

I F THE RUNDOWN PLACE with its overgrown front yard and garage of rusty corrugated iron made any impression on Tirill, she didn't let it show. She merely waited, looking relaxed, as Max pulled the string that made the woodpecker slam its beak against the door frame.

After repeated pecking with no response, Max tried the door handle, but the door was locked. He went over to what looked like the living room window and tried to peer inside. The curtains were drawn, as if the sun were an enemy, though if he knew Sustugu, that was not a point of view he would have promoted.

"Tellev!" he shouted now. "It's Max Fjellanger. I just want to have a little talk with you."

He thought he saw movement through the slit between the curtains. And only seconds later he heard the key turn in the front-door lock.

"I must say you've changed your appearance," said Sustugu when he caught sight of Tirill standing there.

Max went over to join them. "She's my guide," he explained.

They introduced themselves, and Tellev held on to Tirill's hand just long enough that it was noticeable but not long enough to be uncomfortable.

"Could we come in?" asked Max.

"No." Sustugu didn't move from the doorway.

"OK. I'm just wondering what you and Knut Abrahamsen talked about when he was here."

"He wasn't here." Tellev was about to shut the door.

"Then I'm calling the police."

"What for?" was his scornful reply, which came a little too fast.

"To tell them about all the guns you have in the house."

"I don't have any guns."

"But the police don't know that. They'll search the whole place."

To underscore that he was serious, Max got out his cell phone and started to make the call.

Sustugu sighed and gave in.

ONCE AGAIN THEY SAT at the Formica table on the porch, but this time the host did not offer coffee. Which was just as well. He was barefoot, dressed in a pair of faded jeans and a T-shirt that said Absolut Vodka on the front. His slicked-back hair was so black that it had to be dyed. Max thought his whole appearance seemed strange for a man who was close to seventy.

"So Knut did come to see you?"

Tellev rolled himself a cigarette with practiced movements. He probably could have done it in his sleep. He lit the cigarette and took a deep drag. Then he released the smoke through his nostrils. "One day he was just standing there. I had no idea who he was until he explained. I hardly remembered him even then. But he remembered me, of course."

He took another drag on his cigarette and let the smoke pour out into the warm summer air. He tapped the ash into a cup that had clearly been used as an ashtray before.

"What did he want?" asked Max patiently.

Tirill showed no sign of wanting to take part in the conversation, which Max really appreciated. Tellev Sustugu was a ghost from his past.

"He wanted to talk about Cecilie Wiborg. But that wasn't something I wanted to do."

"Why not?"

Sustugu looked at Max as if the reason were obvious. "I'm a man who lives alone, and I keep to myself."

You're also someone who's been convicted of one rape and

accused of another, thought Max. He nodded that he understood. "When was this?"

"The night before they found him in the river," said Sustugu, speaking so low that his words were almost inaudible.

Max leaned across the scarred tabletop. "What time of night?"

"I'd just had dinner, so . . . around seven."

"That means you may have been the last person to see him alive."

"Hardly. More likely the second to last."

"So you don't think his death was suicide?"

The old rogue let his gaze wander over the village that he presumably both hated and loved, a community that definitely felt only hatred toward him. "If so, he must have had a complete breakdown after he was here, because he seemed perfectly normal."

"But people who are suicidal often seem normal," Tirill interjected.

Sustugu nodded. "Sure, I know that. But that man was in the middle of something. He seemed totally obsessed with it. And not about to give up."

"And by 'something' you mean investigating Cecilie Wiborg's disappearance?" said Max.

"Naw, not exactly. . . ."

"No?"

"Well, yes, but . . . I'm sure there was something else too. Something he didn't mention. He kept going on about an old missing-person case from years back. That guy from Oslo. Schram. Wasn't that his name? Seemed like he thought there was a connection between the two cases. But that can't be right. Cecilie Wiborg disappeared in Bø, after all, plus there must be almost thirty years between the two events."

Max saw no reason to tell him that, according to Henrik Thue, Cecilie had disappeared in Eidsborg. "Do you know anything about the case?" he asked. "About Peter Schram?"

"Nope. I had nothing to tell Abrahamsen. And that's all I have to say about his visit. He was here around seven on the night before they found his body, and as far as I'm concerned, I don't believe a word of it when they say he killed himself. But you can forget about making me say even a peep in a courtroom, if that's what you're thinking."

"But why? Are you still afraid of Jørgen Homme's ghost?"

Sustugu gave Max a stern look, as if he were joking about something sacred or dangerous. Or both. "No," he said finally. "I just want as little as possible to do with the police and the whole justice system. You might say I've had my fill of that sort of thing."

Max had a strong feeling there was more to it than that. A sly fox like Tellev Sustugu never showed all his cards unless he was forced to do so. "I don't believe you," he said as he once again got out his cell phone. "What's the number for the police, Tirill?"

"Zero, two, eight hundred."

Max tapped in the number, and when he heard the call go through, he held up the phone so Sustugu could hear it ringing. It didn't take long before a woman answered. Max pressed the phone to his ear and said, "I want to report a situation. . . ."

Sustugu grabbed the phone away from Max's face. "Hang up!" he barked in a hoarse voice. "I'll tell you what he said."

Max ended the call.

"I want to hear everything this time," he insisted. "If I think you're still holding out on me, I'll call the police back. I know exactly what to say to get them out here to turn your whole place upside down. And I'll personally stay on to make sure you can't hide anything you've got inside there."

Sustugu didn't look especially happy about that possibility.

"When Abrahamsen left here, he told me he needed to talk to his son. That's exactly what he said: 'Now I'm going to have a talk with his son.'"

"Who did he mean by 'his son'?"

"Jørgen Homme's son, of course."

"Oh my God . . . ," whispered Tirill.

Sustugu ground out his cigarette in the empty cup and stood up. Without saying good-bye, he headed for the door and disappeared inside the house. The last they heard from him was the sound of the key turning in the lock.

Thirty-Three

AS THEY DROVE THROUGH THE FRONT YARD of the Homme farm, the sheriff was nowhere in sight. He was probably at work. But it didn't matter, since they hadn't planned on talking to him. What would they say, anyway? That they knew Knut Abrahamsen had been on his way over to see Homme only hours before he was found dead? It was obvious that the sheriff would deny any such claim. The only thing they might have accomplished was to show him the most important card they now held. Under other circumstances, Max wouldn't have trusted any card dealt by Tellev Sustugu, but he was convinced that Tellev was genuinely scared. He was afraid of having his house searched, and he was also afraid of Sheriff Homme. Both the living and the dead sheriffs. For that reason, Max didn't think Sustugu would choose to involve Jon Homme if he was going to make up some story. His fear of having his house turned upside down must have been stronger than his fear of Homme. Max wished he knew what the old scoundrel was hiding.

At the Tveit property they parked the car and got out. It was very quiet except for the twittering of swallows flying at great speed in and out of the open barn door. Max and Tirill went over to the house and rang the bell several times, but with no response. As they stood there, Johannes Liom's son, Lars, drove past in the red pickup, tapping the bill of his cap in greeting.

As they were about to leave, the front door opened and Ingebjørg Ljosland stood there, her cheeks flushed. "Oh, it's you? How nice. I'm sorry it took me so long. I was . . . in the bath."

She gave them an apologetic smile, showing all her teeth.

THE LIVING ROOM AT TVEIT looked the same as before. The only difference was that Ingebjørg's husband wasn't around. Last time, he'd been driving the tractor out in the fields, spraying pesticide. But coffee and cakes and all the attendant requisites were once again on the coffee table.

Tirill launched right into a piece of chocolate cake.

"Please help yourselves," said Ingebjørg.

Not wanting to seem rude, Max accepted a cookie and took a minuscule bite, just as he'd seen Ingebjørg do before. He wasn't hungry at all.

"There's something I've been wondering about," he said. "Do you recall that a man was found dead in Dalen two weeks ago?"

"In the river, yes. It was awful."

"He was a colleague of mine, from long ago, back when I was a sheriff's deputy here in Tokke municipality. I might have mentioned that the last time we were here. And I'm convinced that he's the one you remember hearing folks talk about in connection with the disappearance of Peter Schram. The rumor he'd vanished because of a jealous lover, or something like that."

"How strange," she said.

"You can say that again. Now I'm wondering whether my colleague might have come over here to ask questions about what happened back then."

He could see that she was taking her time to consider what he'd said. "What did this man look like?"

"To tell you the truth, I don't really know. It's been thirty years since I last saw him."

"What was his name?"

"Knut Abrahamsen."

Her mouth fell open. "Knut Abrahamsen was the man who drowned?" she almost shouted. "I didn't even know that he'd been on the police force here. He said he was a relative of Peter's and just wanted to find out more about what really happened when he disappeared."

"So Knut did come here?"

"Yes, he did. I think it was in April. We were busy with the spring farmwork."

"He committed suicide. As an old colleague and friend of his, I'm just wondering whether he might have said anything that could explain why he chose to kill himself."

"That poor man," she said sympathetically. "No, he didn't say anything like that. Nothing at all. Mostly he asked about Peter's relationship with people around here. Who he knew, things like that."

"Nothing about the rumor that circulated back then, hinting that he had something to do with why Schram disappeared?"

"No, nothing about that. But he did ask about the monk. I was surprised he was so interested in a ghost."

"What did he want to know?"

"First and foremost, whether Peter had ever seen it. I told him truthfully that I had no idea. And then he asked me whether the ghost was still being seen. And it is. Not even a year ago, somebody claimed to have seen the monk again. Tourists, of course, but . . ."

"So who is this monk?" asked Tirill. Until now she had been preoccupied with eating cake.

"A monk from the Catholic era. Someone who was never able to let Nikuls go. People have seen him at night outside the church holding the statue wrapped in a blanket. A few times he's also been seen coming out of the building."

"Do you personally know anyone who has seen him?" asked Tirill.

"Several people. My father saw him coming out of the church carrying the statue in a blanket. He said he even heard the sound of the key turning when the ghost locked the door. So my father got hold of someone with a key, but when they went inside, they found Nikuls in his usual place."

Max wondered how common it was for ghosts to lock the door after themselves. The ones he'd read about in books were able to pass right through any door with no effort at all.

Thirty-Four

I T WAS EVENING by the time they were out on the highway again, heading for Bø. The sun, low in the sky, flooded the rugged landscape with a soft light that erased entire valleys. Tirill thought to herself that nothing was more beautiful than Telemark in the light of a summer evening.

"So, what do you really think about this ghost?" asked Fjellanger.

"Hmm . . . It's probably just an old legend."

"But it seems kind of strange for a ghost to wrap up the statue. I mean, how can anyone tell whether it's really Nikuls or not?"

Tirill was about to reply when she noticed an odd smell. She realized it had actually been with them for a while. She sniffed at the air.

"What is it?"

"Do you smell that?"

Now they both sniffed. He nodded.

"It almost seems like it's coming from the backseat," said Tirill, turning around.

What she saw sent fear racing through her body like ice water, completely paralyzing her.

"What is it?" asked Max, but she was unable to answer or move.

She couldn't even scream.

A severed head was lying on the backseat. One eye was half open, with ice crystals inside, and the upper lip was pulled back to show the teeth. A note was affixed to the forehead, with words printed in red. What she was seeing and smelling suddenly combined to conjure up a memory from her childhood of homemade Christmas cold cuts. The memory forced its way down her throat and all the way into her stomach. Then it rose up again. She desperately tried to turn toward the car door, but instead the vomit sprayed past Fjellanger's head and hit the windshield with great force.

He shouted with alarm and ducked.

Finally Tirill managed to find her voice. "A PIG'S HEAD!" she wailed. "A FUCKING PIG'S HEAD! A PIG'S HEAD, A PIG'S HEAD!"

Thirty-Five

IN FRONT OF THEM stood a timbered cabin with tarred planks and raspberry shrubs on the sod roof. Max thought it was a perfect location, some distance up the slope of Lifjell and only fifty meters from the winding road, but out of sight and with a view to the south, toward Lake Norsjø and the fruit orchards in Sauherad. It was Tirill who had decided they needed to find a hiding place. The cabin belonged to the family of a friend and wouldn't be used by the owners until Christmastime. Plus they wouldn't have to pay anything to stay there.

After they'd put away their things, they found two deck chairs and a small table, which they carried out to the front yard. A few white butterflies fluttered above the firewood stacked along one wall. Max had put on his Florida baseball cap, and Tirill was wearing a big straw hat.

"If I were you," he said, "I'd consider retreating now. I don't have any family, but you—"

"You're not me," she told him.

"You should think about your son."

She gripped his arm with a strength he didn't know she had. "Don't you talk about my son!" she snarled.

"OK."

"I'm always thinking about him." She loosened her grip. "Magnus does have a father, of course. The most important thing to know about the guy is that he has a Live Free or Die tattoo on his upper arm, and he lives with his mother. It's what *I* do that Magnus will remember. Maybe only subconsciously, but still. Whether I like it or not."

She let go of Max's arm. "I just don't want him to remember a lie," she went on. "That's why there's no question of me retreating. Do you get what I'm saying?"

"Sure," said Max with a nod.

He didn't really understand. Not fully, at any rate. But he realized it was useless trying to talk her out of it. He let his gaze rest on the flat blue surface of Lake Norsjø off in the distance. It would have been so nice to go for a swim. Naked and alone. He was afraid of getting cabin fever staying here in such cramped quarters with Tirill. And for how long? he wondered.

Until this whole thing was over.

From his wallet he took out the note that had been stuck on the pig's head with a nail. The brief message written with a red marker said, "Fear the Lord!" In the middle of the note was a hole left by the nail, which had been driven so deep into the pig's skull that Max hadn't been able to pull it out. He'd left the nail where it was when they got rid of the head.

"Why should we fear the Lord?" he asked.

"Because it says so in the Bible?"

"Do you fear him?"

"I'm not afraid of anything," said Tirill. She unfastened another button on her blouse and waved away some pesky flies. "With the possible exception of a pig's head that's suddenly staring at me from the backseat."

"Do you believe in God?"

"I believe there exist things that can't be seen," she said. "Probably a lot. Perhaps even more than what we actually do see."

He gave a snort, ending this venture into a theological discussion.

"Who could have done it?" she asked.

"Well, we didn't see the farmer anywhere."

"And Johannes Liom's son drove by."

"On the other hand, just about anybody could have come out from behind the barn and put the head inside the car without being seen," Max reasoned. "The perpetrator wouldn't have been in view for more than thirty seconds or so."

"It might have been a woman. Don't you think that's possible?"

"I don't know about that. A nail pounded into the skull of a severed pig's head, and the words 'Fear the Lord'? The perp might as well have left a footprint of a size 13 shoe," said Max.

"But why pigs' heads? First that tiny plastic one, and now this. And why the biblical reference?"

"Something to do with the stave church?" he suggested. "And Nikuls?"

Both shook their heads.

"Do you remember what we were talking about when you noticed the pig's head?" he asked Tirill.

"No, I don't."

"The ghost. From what Ingebjørg said, it sounds like the ghost is always seen with the statue wrapped in a blanket. Doesn't that seem strange?"

Tirill shrugged. "Ghosts are strange by nature. Aren't they?"

"But don't you remember what I told you? About what Knut saw in the trunk of the sheriff's car?"

"A wooden figure?"

"Partially hidden under a blanket. On the day after Peter Schram disappeared. The day after Midsummer Eve. A wooden figure."

They stared at each other, and Max could see they were thinking the same thing. "What if there's no ghost?" he said.

"Then what is it?"

Max opened his mouth to say the words, but she beat him to it. "A cult!"

"Yes!" He grabbed her wrist, because he felt as if everything was now becoming clear. "They go and get Nikuls from the church, because the old ritual is still being carried out. It probably never stopped."

"And that's why Cecilie Wiborg and Peter Schram disappeared," said Tirill. "Because they found out about the secret and had to be gotten rid of. The same thing probably happened to Knut Abrahamsen."

Max took off his baseball cap and ran his fingers through his gray, sweat-soaked hair before he put the cap back on. In his mind he took a step back, trying to get an overview of what they were discussing.

Then he shook his head. "Would they really kill somebody just to keep that sort of thing secret? We're not exactly talking about a Black Mass and sacrificing children here. It's the statue of a Catholic saint."

Tirill disagreed. "Just imagine if it's been going on for hundreds of years," she said. "Plus think about the isolated location and the whole history of the Nikuls ritual—what we already know about it. That would be a huge story in the media. And the people involved must realize that. The thought of being portrayed as backward hillbillies carrying a wooden figure around a lake in order to promote fertility and good crops—that can't be a very enticing idea. And it also has to do with their perception of the world. Their view may not extend beyond Eidsborg, but it's a world that still makes sense to them. In contrast to the chaos that greets us every time we turn on the TV or read a newspaper. Theirs is a story that is retold each year—maybe even more often than that, for all we know. A story that gives meaning to life. And think about the length of time these people have stuck together. Don't you think murders have been committed for far less important reasons?"

They sat in silence, staring straight ahead. For a long while the only sounds were the buzzing of insects and the faint roar of a plane high above.

Tirill cleared her throat. "There's one more thing," she said hesitantly.

Max had an idea what she meant. He'd thought about it himself, but hadn't wanted to say anything. Something in him resisted.

Thirty-Six

THE NEXT EVENING, a little before 10:00, Max strolled down Bøgata. Three young men were sitting on a bench, drinking out of brown beer bottles. One of them belched loudly as Max passed. Traffic was heavy in both directions. For long-haul trucks, which were plentiful, Bøgata was only a short hop from Highway 36. Part of the route between Grenland and Vestfold in the east and the Haugesund region in the west. For the local youths, with their furry dice dangling from the rearview mirror, the stretch between the roundabout and the high school formed a closed loop, where life was played out in all its complexities.

Max didn't feel comfortable in Bø. The town was small and claustrophobic, and he thought it looked like something that had accidentally fallen out of God's pocket.

He had phoned Åse to ask whether he could drop by. She told him that Henrik was attending a seminar in Oslo, and he was more welcome than he could imagine. That was a cryptic sort of thing to say, but he hoped it meant what he thought.

During the last few years before Ann got sick, they had made love about once a month. Afterward they'd had more urgent things to think about, and their sex life had ended. Not long before she died, Max realized that he'd simply stopped noticing women in the same way. He no longer eyed them with that male look of both admiration and lust. It wasn't something he missed. He merely registered with a distant sense of surprise that it was gone, and the only thing left to him was the usual way of seeing. A world that was banal, yet tolerable.

Åse Enger Thue had revived in him that former way of seeing. Yet he knew full well that she might be involved in the case he was investigating. Tirill was very aware of this too, and she'd told him point-blank that he should stay away from the woman.

When Max entered the garden, he saw Åse standing with her back to him as she arranged something on the table where they'd sat on the two previous occasions. She was wearing a knee-length dark skirt and a short-sleeved white blouse.

"Hi," he said cautiously, but not cautiously enough.

"My God!" she gasped, pressing her hand to her chest. "You scared me!"

Then her expression changed. "It's so nice you're here," she said with a smile.

Max went over to her. On the table stood a bottle of white wine and two glasses, along with some grapes, crackers, and cheese.

"Aren't you cold?" he asked, nodding at her bare feet. The grass already had a slight trace of evening dew.

"Not yet," she said, smiling again. "Have a seat."

As she poured wine into their glasses, he noticed that the bottle was only half full.

"You must think I'm totally crazy," she said after they'd clinked glasses and taken a sip of the wine.

"What do you mean?"

"Because of what I said, that you're more welcome than you could imagine. It's just that . . . I want you to be mine."

Whatever he chose to do or say right now, it would spoil the moment. So he said nothing as he stared at the fountain, where the water spouted up nonstop in a little column, only to fall back on itself. The dolphins and octopuses twined in antique elegance along the curving wall. The delphiniums were as tall and bright blue as before.

Max swallowed hard and looked at Åse. Her expression was somewhere between a plea and a command. Then he held up his left hand and waggled his fingers.

When she saw what he'd done, she grabbed his hand and pulled it down onto her lap. Hesitantly she ran her fingertip over the furrow on his ring finger, where he'd worn his wedding band. The narrow, bare strip was a dazzling white against the tanned skin of his hand.

"That's what twenty-five years looks like," he said, his voice husky.

THEY MADE IT only as far as the living room. She knelt on the sofa, her back swayed, as he took her from behind. "Fucking hell! Oh, fuck, fuck, fuck!" she shouted into the cushions. It didn't take long for him to be dangerously close to coming. With a great effort he managed to stop and stood there with only the tip of his dick inside her.

Åse quit swearing. It seemed as if she was listening with her whole body, from the top of her head to her buttocks.

"What is it?" she whispered.

"I just don't want to . . . not yet," he groaned through clenched teeth.

She moved a little, which almost made him come, but he managed to hold back.

"No, don't," he said. "Lie still. If you move, it'll be too much for me."

She turned her head so he could see her face in profile. There was something dreamy and yet triumphant about her smile. Slowly she began pushing her body backward, a couple of millimeters at a time, twisting herself onto him, almost as tightly as the now removed wedding band had sat on his finger. He wanted to protest, wanted to make it last, but he couldn't utter a word. For a few last seconds he teetered on the brink.

Then he fell.

Thirty-Seven

A BIRD WAS SINGING outside the open bedroom window. Next to
him slept Åse with her lips slightly parted. She looked younger now, as if sleep had taken her back to a time before everything
started getting complicated. He wanted to wake her but noticed
that he'd at least have to empty his bladder first. That was what had
woken him.

After pulling on his underwear, which lay on the floor, he went
out to the hall in search of the bathroom. He'd been in there once
during the night but couldn't remember where it was. The first door
he opened had stairs leading down to the basement. The second
door led to an office. The big picture of the Eidsborg stave church
on the wall indicated the room belonged to the master of the house.
Max went over to take a closer look at the photo, which had been
taken in the wintertime, with fresh snow on the trees and roof. The
tarred-brown building radiated a sort of inner warmth in the midst
of all the cold and whiteness.

Max paused to listen but didn't hear any sound coming from the
hall or bedroom. As quietly as he could, he pulled out the top drawer
of the desk. He saw envelopes, stamps, the program for something
called the Telemark Festival from a couple of years back, and a lot
of other miscellaneous things of no interest.

In the middle drawer he found a picture of Åse wearing a flow-
er garland on her head. The photo had apparently been taken outdoors a number of years ago. Next to the picture was a tiny bell, no

bigger than a thimble. It was attached to a ring, as if it was meant to be worn on a finger.

Something didn't seem right. He looked around the room and thought about Thue's office at the college. The way it had emanated control and balance. This room wasn't exactly messy, but it was not the same style at all.

Then he caught sight of something. On a chair in the corner was a stack of magazines. He grabbed the top one and looked at it. An issue of the gardening magazine *Norsk Hagetidend*.

This wasn't Henrik's office. It was Åse's!

Then he heard a door open. In a flash he put the magazine back, closed the desk drawer, and slipped out into the hall. Åse was naked, her hair ruffled from all the nighttime exertions.

"I can't find the bathroom," said Max.

She looked at him for a long moment, her face impassive, until she nodded toward the door marked with a heart.

THEY MADE LOVE SLOWLY, and then he fell asleep again. When he woke, she was lying next to him, propped up on one elbow and looking at him. He had a feeling that she'd been doing that for a while. Observing him. He was usually the one who preferred to be the observer.

"Hi," he said, his voice hoarse.

She didn't reply.

"Do you know what time it is?"

"Eight thirty. Which means I have to get up. I'm going to visit my sister."

Max slipped his hand under her left breast, feeling its weight.

"We don't have time," she said, removing his hand.

"Is something wrong?"

"I'm just feeling a little stressed," she said. "Is that so strange?"

"You mean . . . What do we do now?"

She nodded, looking worried.

"I thought we might repeat the same thing as many times as possible," he said.

Åse sat up, pulled her legs toward her, and wrapped her arms around them. Then she leaned her forehead on her knees and began gently rocking back and forth. Max didn't say anything more. The naked curve of her back was as blatantly dismissive as any words.

They must have sat like that for several minutes before she finally raised her head.

"If only you knew . . . ," she began, but then didn't finish the sentence.

"Knew what? Yesterday you said that you wanted me to be yours."

"Knew how I feel," she whispered. "Not that I'm jealous, because I'm really not, but it's the humiliation . . . The lies I pretend to believe. When I called Henrik on Midsummer Eve last year and he said he was at home, that wasn't the only thing he lied about."

Max thought she was acting like a defiant little girl refusing to do what she'd been told. "What else did he lie about?"

"He said he was alone. But his cell phone stayed on a few seconds after he thought he'd ended the call. That's when I heard a woman's voice."

"So he was with someone?"

"Uh-huh."

"Was it Cecilie Wiborg?"

"I'm not sure. Knowing Henrik, it could have been anyone. The point is that this is what my life is like. And I guess it makes him think I'm stupid. Actually, I think he despises me. And that's OK. At least it's one thing we have in common."

Max put his hand on her back. "You don't mean that."

"Don't I?"

He didn't know what to say. And it wouldn't do any good to ask. The woman next to him seemed as baffling as a Gordian knot.

Thirty-Eight

TIRILL VESTERLI WAS ALONE, driving west along the waters of Seljord as she listened to a CD with Per Anders Buen Garnås, one of Norway's best fiddlers. Not something Fjellanger would have liked, although they'd never actually talked about music. For all she knew, he might be a hard-core folk-music enthusiast. She tried to imagine that, but failed. He was probably more of a classical-music guy, if he liked any type of music at all. But when she thought about it, she couldn't recall anything he seemed to like.

Well, with the exception of Åse Enger Thue, apparently. And that worried Tirill. Because how much control did the middle-aged widower have over his emotions? And another thing: Wasn't he exploiting her? Åse had to be deeply unhappy with that philandering husband of hers, and suddenly a good-looking middle-aged man happens to appear, showering her with compliments and attention. Maybe she'd fallen in love with Fjellanger, while he, for his part, was using her to find out as much as possible about Henrik Thue. That had been a large part of his interest in her, at least before Thue recounted his version of what happened on Midsummer Eve last year. After that, Tirill's suspicions had focused more on Åse. But how could they be sure that Henrik was telling the truth?

They couldn't.

So now Tirill was on her way to Eidsborg and Dalen, because that was where she'd felt scared. And over the years she'd discovered that the best way to fight fear was to confront the source of that fear. Never run away. Never hide. Moving out to the cabin might well seem like running away, but she hadn't done it for her own sake. She did it to keep Magnus safe. She and Fjellanger seemed to attract danger, and that probably wouldn't change until this whole thing was over.

So she needed to spend as little time as possible with her son.

She'd told her mother that she'd met a man and wanted to have "a little quality time" with him. Could her mother babysit Magnus for a while? That had led to a humiliating conversation, but in the end her mother had agreed. Tirill couldn't tell her the truth. If she did, her mother would have instantly called the police. And then it would have been curtains for Detective Vesterli.

She had almost reached Eidsborg when she thought of the one thing Fjellanger actually did like.

The truth.

TIRILL STOOD OUTSIDE THE STAVE CHURCH, surrounded by Japanese tourists who were waiting to go in. She was standing there because she wanted to be seen. So that the person or persons who had used the pig's head to frighten her would know she was back. And that she wasn't afraid. Even though she was. Somewhere inside her was a dark seed of panic, waiting to be watered so it could sprout and bloom.

She noticed a couple of surveillance cameras, which were to be expected in a place like this. I wonder whether the ghost ever gets caught on video, she thought. Regardless, the images would undoubtedly never be seen, unless something out of the ordinary should happen, like a fire or a break-in. Then the police would review the videos from the relevant time period. Otherwise the images would be erased without anyone looking at them. And no one would ever know whether the ghost had appeared on film.

Among all the Japanese tourists she saw a face that looked familiar. She realized the woman must be the local pastor. Tirill recognized her from the pictures in the newspapers when the Nikuls reenactment took place. Right now the pastor was studying the crowd in front of her old church—because the Eidsborg stave church was more than just a tourist attraction; it was also a functioning parish church.

That can't be easy for her, thought Tirill.

It looked as if the pastor was filming the tourists with her cell phone. Maybe she wanted to send a video to a colleague to show what it was like to be a pastor up here.

Then Tirill remembered that the pastor was one of the people Fjellanger had talked to the first time he came here. She'd even given him a private tour of the church, and it sounded like that wasn't something she usually did. So why had she offered to show Fjellanger around?

Tirill went over to her. "Are you the pastor?"

"Yes, I am," said the woman, as she stopped filming.

"I'm a friend of Max Fjellanger."

"Oh, really? The guy from the States?"

Tirill could hear from the pastor's accent that she was not Norwegian. Probably either German or Austrian.

They shook hands and introduced themselves.

"Is Max still here?"

"Uh-huh. He hasn't gone back home yet," said Tirill.

She found Julia Bergmann's hairstyle annoying. Not because it was such an unusual style for a pastor, but because it seemed so assertive. As if it were some sort of declaration, announcing that here comes a pastor who isn't dull and conservative. Tirill knew she shouldn't be reacting this way, but she couldn't help it.

"Did you want to ask me something?" said Julia.

Tirill paused before replying. "Do you believe in ghosts?"

The pastor let a few seconds pass and then smiled. "No, it's not in keeping with my Christian faith."

"Then how do you explain that so many people have seen the monk?"

"How are ghosts explained in general? A vivid imagination, I assume. Do you believe in such things?"

"I'm actually quite open to the possibility," said Tirill. "But I don't believe in this particular ghost."

Julia Bergmann studied her for a long moment. At least it seemed like a long time to Tirill. "Why not?"

"Because ghosts aren't killers."

Julia gave a brief, nervous laugh. "What on earth do you mean by that?"

But Tirill merely smiled and began walking back toward the parking lot.

Thirty-Nine

S HE WAS SITTING IN THE MUSEUM CAFÉ with a glass of Farris mineral water in front of her, observing the other customers. She tried to figure out what they were talking about as she fiddled with the locket hanging around her neck. She could never help eavesdropping whenever she was out. She liked to guess what sort of relationships the various people had at nearby tables. Which of them were sweethearts. Which of them were siblings. It was like her mother always said: she was 50 percent busybody—good at sniffing out all sorts of things, but never passing on the information, thank God.

"Hey, if it isn't the house goddess herself," said a voice behind her.

Tirill turned around to see Johannes Liom standing there and giving her a crooked smile as he held a cup of steaming coffee. "Mind if I join you?"

Tirill invited him to have a seat. "Still on the job?" she asked. It was getting close to 6:00 p.m.

"Yup. They can't manage without me."

"What exactly do you do?"

"All kinds of strange things that you wouldn't even believe," he said with a wink.

At least his job didn't seem to be taking a toll on his energy or mood. Maybe he was the type who got charged up from his work.

"I've been thinking about something we talked about last time," he said. "The fact that Cecilie Wiborg and Peter Schram both disappeared on Midsummer Eve. That can't be a coincidence. What do you think?" He raised his eyebrows, making them look like two birds.

"It's hard to say," she told him.

And that was true. It was hard to know what she should say to anyone up here anymore until she found out who had tried to scare off both her and Fjellanger.

"But it does seem strange," she went on. "Don't you think Cecilie must have heard about Peter Schram?"

"Probably."

"But she never mentioned him to you?"

"No, we just talked shop. Mostly about the local resistance to the Reformation. That's what her thesis was about."

"Is that the main reason the ritual is interesting?" asked Tirill. "The fact that it continued for such a long time after it was banned? Personally, I think what's more exciting is the possible connection to the past and the even older, pagan ritual."

Johannes's smile seemed a bit patronizing. "Of course it's fascinating to imagine that long ago folks around here walked around Eidsborg Tarn carrying a pagan idol instead of Nikuls. A sort of fertility cult, maybe because the water of the lake was considered sacred, or something like that. Those sorts of speculations are always exciting, but if you shine a scientific light on them, they quickly crumble."

Tirill saw that Julia Bergmann was sitting at a table at the other end of the room. She hadn't noticed the pastor come in. Julia looked away when their eyes met, but there was no question she had been staring at Tirill and Johannes.

"I assume that a woman such as you has been inside the stave church before, but if you'd like to have a personal tour, we close in fifteen minutes. I'd be happy to show you around if you want."

Tirill wasn't sure whether he was putting a move on her or what. But he and his son were both potential candidates for the person who'd put the pig's head in the car, and she decided she needed to be cautious.

"I've been inside a few times," she said. "But thanks for the offer."

"So, what are you doing after we close?" he asked with an apologetic smile.

Tirill liked him, but not enough to bite. At least one of the four chambers of her heart remained unmoved. "Going back home to put my son to bed."

"Oh, I see. So you're a single mom?"

"Uh-huh. What about you? A single dad?"

"My wife took off when Lars was four. She was a city girl and didn't like being so isolated up here. She actually wanted all of us to move, but it's impossible to tear me away from this place."

"It's rare for the father to get custody in a divorce," said Tirill.

"I didn't. But Lars has always spent a lot of time with me, and a few years ago he moved back here."

"That must have made you happy."

"I'd always figured he would. Are you sure you wouldn't like a private tour of the church?"

Tirill feigned regret.

"OK. Well, I enjoyed talking to you," said Johannes as he stood up.

As soon as he was gone, Julia Bergmann came over to Tirill and sat down without asking permission.

She grabbed Tirill's wrist and held on tight. "I need to talk to you!" she whispered.

Forty

AT 7:30 SHE RANG THE BELL at Julia Bergmann's place in Dalen. The pastor had insisted that Tirill come over to hear what she wanted to say. Julia opened the door at once. Tirill had the impression that she'd been keeping an eye on the driveway. Julia had changed into a knee-length summer dress with a floral pattern, and she had obviously just taken a shower. Yet her hairdo was as sleek as ever.

"Come in," she said, practically pulling Tirill inside, as if urgently wanting to get her out of sight as fast as possible.

The single-family house was well kept, though it looked as if nothing much had been changed since it was built, probably sometime in the 1980s. For that reason it didn't really match Julia Bergmann's appearance. On the contrary, it seemed like a remarkable break from her personal style.

No doubt the house was owned by the municipality and was meant to serve as the residence for the local pastor.

"Would you like a glass of wine?" asked Julia.

"No, thanks. I'm driving."

"Would you mind if I have one?"

"Of course not."

"Is Farris OK?"

"Sure."

Julia invited her to have a seat on the sofa and then disappeared into the kitchen. Tirill was curious to see no sign of a husband or children. Maybe the pastor was single.

The art on the walls didn't seem to suit Julia either. Mostly various prints, but there were also a couple of oil paintings. The common denominator was that they all showed classic Telemark motifs. Timbered houses with sod roofs. Men sitting in horse-drawn carts on their way across an old stone bridge. Meadows filled with flowers in the light of a summer evening.

Maybe the art came with the house, thought Tirill.

One of the pictures surprised her. It showed a face that looked as if had been subjected to a torture rack, stretched out until the features were unrecognizable, although there was no doubt it was a face. The image was totally unlike any of the other artwork. Yet that was not the main thing that surprised her. The face had only one eye, and the head extended into what looked like a pointed gray hat.

"Is that . . . Odin?" Tirill asked the pastor when she came back with the wine and mineral water.

"What? Of course it's not Odin. It's just a . . . face. Kind of abstract."

But Tirill was convinced that Julia was mistaken. Or could it be that she didn't want to admit she had a picture of a pagan god on the wall?

"So, what did you want to talk to me about?" she asked now.

Julia poured wine for herself and filled a glass with Farris for her guest. "Max Fjellanger is some sort of private detective, isn't he?"

"What makes you think that?" asked Tirill.

"I Googled his name."

"Why?"

"Because he seems so out of place here. A man like that doesn't just show up for no reason. And I don't believe that he's simply interested in stave churches. He hardly asked me a single question during the brief tour I gave him. I had a clear sense that he has some ulterior motive. I'm right, aren't I?"

"If that's what you found out from Googling him, I guess you're right," replied Tirill.

It was impossible to see from Julia's expression whether she took that as confirmation or not. "How do you happen to know him?" the pastor asked.

"Is that why you invited me over?" asked Tirill. "To ask me about something that's none of your business?"

Julia smiled nervously. "Sorry. The reason I asked is that I need to know whether I can trust you."

"Well, that depends on what you want," said Tirill.

"I want to talk about a suspicion that I think we already share."

Tirill figured that something of potentially great importance was just within reach. At the same time, she wanted to be especially careful in her word choice. "As I said, that depends on what you want to tell me. But in general I'm a very trustworthy person. Is that good enough?"

The pastor took a sip of her wine, studying Tirill over the rim of her glass.

"Ghosts aren't killers," she said, setting the glass down.

"I already told you that. Is there anything else you want to say to me?"

"Yes. Maybe there are others who are."

Tirill felt like she was standing on a thin sheet of ice and under her feet was a bottomless pit. "Let's not talk in riddles. Who do you think is a killer?"

"Who do *you* think?" countered the pastor.

Annoyed, Tirill stood up. "Thanks for the Farris," she said. "But you're wasting my time."

Julia reached out to grab her forearm. "No, don't go!" she exclaimed. "Please. I'm so scared!"

Tirill sat down. "Then spit it out. Or else I'm leaving."

The pastor looked her in the eye. "I've seen the monk. It was three nights before Midsummer Eve last year. I'd been in Oslo for a conference and didn't get home until after midnight. When I drove through Eidsborg, I thought I saw something moving in the cemetery. But it was dark, and I was tired, so I figured it was just my imagination. When I got home and was about to go to bed, I couldn't get the idea out of my head. When you're dealing with an old stave church, you always worry that someone might set fire to it. Satanists, or whatever they call themselves. I know that hasn't happened in a long time, but the fear never goes away completely. So I ended up driving back to Eidsborg. I parked a short distance away from the church and went the rest of the way on foot. I have to admit I felt a little foolish, since I didn't really think anything was wrong. I was just playing the part of a hysterical female pastor.

But when I reached the gate in the cemetery wall, I saw someone wearing a cloak among the headstones. Since it was close to Midsummer, it wasn't completely dark outside. I knew at once that I was seeing the famous monk, because he was carrying something wrapped in a blanket. It wasn't easy to see in the dim light, but it might have been Nikuls. The size was about right.

"But two things convinced me that this monk figure was a live person and not a ghost. First, ghosts don't exist. And second, if they do exist, you most likely wouldn't hear twigs snapping under their feet when they walk. So I followed him at a distance until he disappeared into the woods. The way he climbed over the cemetery wall also told me that I wasn't dealing with some ethereal being. There was something clumsy about his whole manner."

Julia Bergmann let out a trembling breath. Tirill sat on the sofa, her back straight, as she listened intently to every word issuing from the pastor's lips. "We talked about whether it might be something like that," she said.

"You and Max Fjellanger?"

"Yes."

The pastor leaned across the coffee table and grabbed Tirill's hand. "That's what I thought when you said that line about ghosts not being killers. I knew he was a private detective, and I figured he was here because of Cecilie Wiborg. That's true, isn't it?"

"I can't answer that," replied Tirill, realizing she'd already said too much. "But what about the statue? I assume you checked to see if it was still inside the church."

"I don't actually have a key to the church. The sexton keeps the key. I didn't want to call him late at night to say I'd seen a ghost that wasn't a ghost. But around eight in the morning I went in, and there was Nikuls, in his usual place."

"Do you think somebody takes the statue out at night to use in some sort of ritual?"

"It's hard to see what else anyone would remove from the church."

"Did you see this person come out of the building?"

"No, I didn't. But other people have. When I drove past and thought I saw something in the cemetery, he must have been on his way to the church. By the time I came back, he'd already taken the statue and locked up after himself. I did check to make sure the door was locked."

"Have you told anyone else about all this?"

"Not a soul. I'm way too scared."

"Scared of what?"

"Only three days later Cecilie Wiborg disappeared. On Midsummer Eve. As you know, she was doing research that included the Nikuls ritual. Exactly like Peter Schram was doing thirty years earlier. Both of them were working on the same topic. The only thing I can't get to fit is the fact that Cecilie disappeared in Bø. But are the police really so sure about that? Just because she was last seen in Bø doesn't necessarily mean that something happened to her there. I think she must have been in Eidsborg that night. Don't you agree?"

Tirill didn't reply.

"So, was she?" Julia repeated impatiently.

This was information that Fjellanger had forced Henrik Thue to reveal, and she had no right to go behind his back to share it with anyone else, so she remained silent.

"I'll take that as a yes," said the pastor. "And I think we both know why they were killed."

"Take it however you want. I'm not saying a word. But I have to admit I wonder why you haven't gone to the police. There are video cameras at the church. It seems to me that the police would have been able to find out quickly whether someone had actually been inside the church, and whether the person in question removed anything. Then it wouldn't be just some stupid ghost story but a punishable offense."

Julia Bergmann smiled. "I was starting to wonder whether you were ever going to ask me about that," she said. "I certainly would have gone to the sheriff if it weren't for something that I haven't yet told you about. I was saving it up until you asked me this very question. On his way over to the cemetery, the monk stopped and knelt down. There, he unwrapped the statue. Well, I didn't actually see it, because he had his back to me, but that's clearly what he was doing. He unwrapped it and held it up."

"What do you mean?"

"He held it up as if he were showing it."

"To the dead?"

"To the Homme ancestors. At least, it was their headstone that he was kneeling next to. It's big and easy to recognize. So there he was, holding up the statue, as if he wanted to show them it was still there, or something like that. Maybe you can see now why I didn't feel compelled to go and see Sheriff Homme to ask him whether he could make sense of what happened."

Outside the window it was a completely ordinary summer evening. Cars and RVs drove by on the road below. Tourists, in pairs and in groups, strolled along the sidewalk. Tirill could hear them laughing and cheerfully conversing. "So, what are you planning to do about it?" she asked.

"Nothing," said Julia. "I don't dare."

"But you think I do?"

"The two of you," she said. "I think the two of you dare."

"I have to go now." Tirill got up. "Fjellanger doesn't even know that I'm here."

"I won't mention it if I see him again." She too stood up.

As Tirill was about to leave, she paused in front of the painting of the elongated head. "Are you sure that's not Odin?"

Julia Bergmann placed her left hand on Tirill's shoulder. "Never mind about that painting," she said. "You have other things to worry about. Be careful! And remember this: three nights before Midsummer Eve. I don't know why the date is important, but that's when I saw him."

As she stood on the front porch with the low evening sun shining in her eyes, Tirill had a horrible feeling that she'd made a mistake.

Forty-One

THE CABIN STILL SMELLED OF THE DINNER that Fjellanger had cooked for himself. It smelled good. Tirill's own dinner had consisted of a hot dog that she stopped to get in Seljord on her way home. Now she made herself a piece of toast, aware the whole time that he was watching her. But whenever she glanced in his direction, he had his nose buried in a book, either *The Spirit of the Place* or *The Eidsborg Stave Church*—copies of the two books by Henrik Thue that he'd managed to acquire.

"Have you read these?" Fjellanger asked when she was done eating.

"Sure. Both of them, a few years ago."

"He thinks the Eidsborg stave church was built on the site of a pagan temple."

"It was important to show that the old gods had been defeated," replied Tirill.

It was 10:30 at night, and still not completely dark. Outdoors there was a sort of half-light that clearly indicated Midsummer Eve was fast approaching.

"There's something I need to tell you."

"Why am I not surprised?" said Fjellanger. "I was wondering what you've been up to. Did you find out anything?"

She took a deep breath and then said it. "Julia Bergmann knows."

"What does she know?"

So Tirill told him about her meeting with the pastor, including as many details as possible. When she was finished, silence fell over the small room. She waited for his reprimand.

"It could be a trap," Fjellanger said at last. He seemed perfectly calm. "An attempt to lure us out there three nights before Midsummer Eve."

"Do you think she might be involved in whatever it is that happens on that night?"

"Basically anyone up there could be involved. And we don't know what goes on."

"How come you're not mad?" Tirill asked.

"Getting mad hardly ever creates new opportunities. And to be honest, I think it's good that you're starting to show some initiative."

Tirill wasn't sure whether that was an insult or a compliment. Hadn't she shown initiative before? Or was he just teasing her?

She decided to find out. "I showed initiative last week," she told him.

Fjellanger didn't reply but merely raised his eyebrows.

"I went to see Kathrine Wiborg. Though I didn't find out anything useful. Except for the fact that losing your only child . . . Well, it's not like I didn't know that before."

She noticed his jaw muscles tighten. He clearly wasn't happy to hear about what she'd done.

"Were you able to trick her into talking to you?" he asked.

"I convinced her that I used to know Cecilie."

"Good. But she couldn't tell you anything?"

"Not really."

"OK. I haven't just been lying around either. Well, actually that's exactly what I've been doing. Lying here on a blanket and reading. I dozed off. Dreamed a little too. It's not always necessary to do anything else to find out things. Sometimes it's enough just to relax. And suddenly a text message might appear, for example."

He gave her an expectant look. Tirill hated this sort of guessing game, yet she saw no alternative but to play along. Besides, she suspected he was doing this because he knew full well she hated it. Which meant he was still bent on teasing her.

"Who was it from?" she asked.

"Ingebjørg Ljosland at Tveit. Tomorrow I'm going to Oslo to meet with Vibeke Østbye."

"Who's that?"

"Formerly Vibeke Schram, Peter's widow. I found out that she'd remarried and now her name is Østbye. What if she has Schram's papers from Eidsborg? Because he must have put something in writing, don't you think? Or maybe she'll remember something important, even though it all happened a long time ago. So, what are your plans for tomorrow?"

"I have to go to work. Some of us have a job, you know. But right now it's past my bedtime."

As Tirill lay in bed, trying to sleep, she could still hear Julia Bergmann's words: *And remember this: three nights before Midsummer Eve.*

Forty-Two

MAX WAS SITTING IN AN OUTDOOR CAFÉ on Saint Olavs Plass in Oslo, with a double espresso and a bottle of Farris on the table. There was something liberating about being away from Bø, where he felt like everyone was always looking at him because he was a stranger.

Most of the café customers were a couple of decades younger than him. And a remarkable number of them had tattoos on their arms. When he left Norway, in 1986, hardly anyone was into tattoos except sailors. Back then tattoos were mostly images of sailing ships against a blood-red sunset or roses or the names of women. Now he had the impression that a whole generation—or even two—had decided to turn their bodies into art galleries.

Presumably the intent was to express individuality.

He had persuaded himself that whatever was threatening him and Tirill would have no effect beyond Telemark, that the farther away from the source he went, the weaker the threat became. But he realized it might be dangerous to think that way.

A woman had stopped nearby and was peering at everyone seated in the outdoor area. That had to be Vibeke. About fifty, with dark hair pinned up in a painstaking and slightly old-fashioned style. She wore a blouse and knee-length skirt. Her shoulder bag was small and elegant.

Max had e-mailed her a photo of himself, and now she caught

sight of him. She strode over to his table, looking determined. "Max Fjellanger?"

He stood up to greet her.

After they sat down, he handed her a business card.

"I've checked out who you are," she told him, sticking his card in her bag without even glancing at it.

Then she looked at him, her expression somber and inquiring. "How does a private detective from Florida end up interested in something that happened in Eidsborg in 1985?"

"Because of a different case I've been working on. Do you remember hearing about Cecilie Wiborg, who disappeared in Bø last year?"

She nodded.

"Cecilie was doing research on Eidsborg and the saint worship," Max told her. "She disappeared on Midsummer Eve. I thought it was strange that she and Peter were working on the same topic, and then they both disappeared on Midsummer Eve. The very night that was so important for Nikuls worshippers."

"Do you think that's why Peter was killed?" she asked.

"No, there's more. An old wooden figure was observed on the following day. . . . You see, I also got interested in the Wiborg case because of another matter. An old friend of mine died, and I decided to come to Norway to attend his funeral. It's a long story."

"I live right around the corner from here," she said.

A PIANO AND A LARGE, ORNATE MIRROR contributed to the air of a bygone era that permeated the apartment. Among the potted plants on the windowsill lay a black cat, basking in the warm sunlight shining through the glass. From the next-door apartment came the sound of laughter and the thudding bass of a stereo.

"What a strange, roundabout way of trying to find out what happened to Peter," said Vibeke when Max finished telling her about everything that had happened since he'd arrived in Norway.

"If the goal begins to move, it's important to move with it."

He liked her, and he said that mostly to impress her. Yet he also recognized there was something to what he'd just said. It was important to keep quiet and listen, not only to what other people were saying but also to what was going on inside yourself: the voices speaking, the images emerging, those semiconscious thoughts that might appear just as sleep was on the verge of erasing everything. If things began to shift and you tried to stand still with both feet planted on the ground, you would be knocked over.

If Vibeke was impressed, she showed no sign of it. "This wooden figure you mentioned, the one your colleague saw in the car . . . Do you think it was the saint statue?"

Max nodded.

"And now your colleague is dead?"

Again he nodded.

"Are you sure there's a connection between the three . . . murders? If that's what we're going to call them?"

"No, I'm not sure, but more and more is pointing in that direction."

He had decided to be honest with her, because she might be sitting on information that could solve the case.

"On the phone you said that you're getting close to figuring out who killed Peter."

"That's something I'll be able to tell you in a very short time. I promise you that. But in return, I need your help."

"Of course. By the way, do you happen to play the piano?" She nodded toward the black baby grand.

"Haven't played since the piano lessons I had as a child."

"That's too bad. I'm not great myself, so I always enjoy having visitors play for me. It makes the apartment come to life. But not many people play well, you know."

She hesitated a bit before going on. "Cecilie Wiborg, for instance, had good technique, but she didn't have much musical sensitivity when it came to playing the piano."

Forty-Three

ANNOYED, TIRILL TOSSED ASIDE the Swedish detective novel she was reading and got up from the sofa. It was impossible to concentrate when all she could think about was her son, Magnus. She had convinced herself that she even missed the way he fussed in the morning when she tried to get him dressed. But it was hard to tell when it would be safe for him to come back home.

She started writing a text to Fjellanger to find out how his meeting had gone with the widow, but then erased it. He was due to catch the night train, which arrived in Bø around 12:30, and she knew she wasn't going to be able to sleep until he was back. They'd talk when he got here.

Instead she called her mother. It turned out that she'd already put Magnus to bed, and she refused to wake him just so Tirill could hear her son's voice.

"It's important for him to get enough sleep," her mother admonished her.

The slightly chilly tone of her voice was no doubt due to the lie Tirill had told her about meeting a man and wanting to spend some "quality time" with him. She definitely regretted her choice of words.

"When do you think you'll be done . . . ?" Her mother left the question hanging in the air like a soiled sheet.

"I'm afraid it's going to be awhile."

"Well, I suppose you need to look out for your own needs too."

"Er . . ."

"Experience some intimacy, I mean," her mother added.

When Tirill was done with this mortifying conversation, she sat still and listened. The cabin was no more than fifty meters from the road, but considering how quiet it was, she could just as well have been in the middle of the Alaskan wilderness.

Actually, she liked silence. Certain kinds, at least. Like when she'd put Magnus to bed and could curl up on the sofa and pick up where she'd left off the previous night in the exciting mystery she was reading. It was even better if she heard no voices or music coming from the neighbors' apartments. Or the kind of silence that made people automatically lower their voices when they entered a church or museum. Or a library, for that matter. But the silence of nature, which was due primarily to the absence of any people, was not really Tirill's thing, even though she was a country girl.

In an effort not to dwell on how isolated she felt, she tried reading some more, but her mind kept wandering. She thought about the controversy surrounding the use of the statue in the historical reenactment. She pictured the monk kneeling to show Nikuls to the long-dead Homme ancestors. And she recalled the one-eyed face in the painting at the pastor's house.

She jumped when the wind caused a branch to scrape against the side of the cabin. A second later she remembered there was no wind. At least there hadn't been earlier in the evening.

An icy shiver passed through her as she took the few steps over to the door and opened it.

No one.

And not a trace of wind.

Forty-Four

CECILIE WIBORG CALLED ME to ask if she could possibly look through Peter's old papers from Eidsborg, if I still had them. And I did."

Vibeke Østbye poured piping hot tea into his cup. The scent that rose up reminded him of hay drying on a long rack.

"Did you give her access to the material?"

"She sat here one whole evening, reading and taking notes."

"But you didn't let her take the papers with her?"

"They have great sentimental value to me."

"What did you think when you heard that she had disappeared?"

"I didn't think anything," she said, slowly shaking her beautifully coiffed head. "I didn't dare."

"Did you consider going to the police?"

"They didn't believe me when Peter disappeared, so why should they believe me now?"

"What didn't they believe?"

"That Peter never would have gotten lost in the woods right across from the farm where he'd stayed for two whole summers. He took hikes in those woods almost every day. And he had an innate sense of direction. He always knew where he was. Besides . . . the police never said as much, but from what I understood, they thought suicide was a plausible explanation. That he'd drowned himself in the lake, or something like that. They dragged the lake, but found nothing. Of course they didn't! It's unthinkable that Peter would kill himself. He was a happy man. He was really looking forward to becoming a father. And his research was going so well. He talked about making a real breakthrough. Why would a person like that go into the woods and take his own life?"

Vibeke gave Max a desperate look, as pained as if her former husband had disappeared only last week. "I remarried a few years later."

"So Østbye is your present husband's last name?"

"No, it's my maiden name. I took it back after our divorce. The marriage didn't last long. Nobody could replace Peter. Do you really think he was killed because of the saint statue?"

"I think the Nikuls cult is still alive and well in Eidsborg, and that your husband found out about it."

"Maybe that's the breakthrough he meant. He didn't want to tell me what it was. All he said was that it was going to create a sensation. I thought he meant 'sensation' in an academic sense, but if what you're telling me is true, then it would have been a big deal in the newspapers. All the TV news shows would have covered the story. And yet . . . to kill someone because of . . ."

"The Nikuls figure in Eidsborg is not just any run-of-the-mill saint statue," said Max. "That seems clear because the saint worship continued long after the Reformation. Certain characteristics of the cult are also reminiscent of even older fertility rituals. Maybe it was merely a Christian adaptation of something that existed long before the arrival of Christianity. In that sense, you might say it's a matter of an entire worldview," he said, quoting Tirill.

Max could see that Vibeke accepted what was basically a foreign idea. She was an intelligent person, able to think beyond the boundaries that others had erected. Plus the mystery of her husband's disappearance must have stayed with her all these years, like a dark seed merely waiting to sprout and turn into a tree bearing new insight.

The black cat jumped down from the windowsill and onto the sofa where Max was sitting. It stretched the way only cats can do and then stared at him through narrowed eyes. When he scratched behind the cat's ears, it began purring loudly. "What's your cat's name?"

"Cleopatra. She likes you."

"The feeling's mutual."

They spent a few moments watching the cat, which soon curled up around his arm and gave him an affectionate nip. When Vibeke smiled, all the tension and guardedness in her face dissolved. "When my daughter was little, my women friends or members of my family and I could sit and look at her for hours. All of a sudden no words were necessary. She's moved away from home now. But whenever I have visitors and Cleopatra comes over to say hello, the same thing happens. What is it about children and cats?"

"I couldn't tell you. I don't have either. At least as far as I know," said Max.

"Maybe they offer us some sort of escape from ourselves."

"In that case, I really should get a cat."

Cleopatra rolled onto her back to show the gleaming black of her belly. "She wants to go home with you."

"I live in Florida."

"She wouldn't be allowed to leave this apartment anyway."

For a while they savored this escape from themselves. Then Max gently lifted the cat away.

"Did Cecilie say anything about what she'd read in your husband's papers?"

"Nothing specific. She just said how grateful she was and what a big help it had been. Things like that. Actually, she seemed totally obsessed, just like Peter was before he disappeared. As if she was also on the verge of a breakthrough."

"Does the name Henrik Thue mean anything to you?"

"No. Who's that?"

"Her academic adviser."

"I've never heard of him."

"He visited your husband during both of the summers he spent in Eidsborg."

She shrugged. "It's all so long ago. Was he one of Peter's fellow students?"

"No, Henrik was only a teenager at the time. Completely infatuated with Peter and the work he was doing. Spent a lot of time with him."

"As I said, it was so long ago."

"Did you ever visit Peter there?"

"No, during the first summer I didn't have time, and the next year I was pregnant."

"What about later on? Have you been to Eidsborg?"

"I went there to talk to the sheriff. I tried to explain that Peter couldn't possibly have killed himself. Or gotten lost. The sheriff treated me like a child. I haven't been back there since. And I have no intention of ever going there again."

"There's something I haven't told you," said Max now.

She looked at him attentively.

"I haven't told you that someone had what I think was the Nikuls statue in his possession on the morning after your husband disappeared."

"Who was it?"

"Sheriff Jørgen Homme. I think he was involved."

Vibeke raised her hand to her mouth. "That . . . that . . ."

"He was a real bastard, to be perfectly blunt," said Max. "And his son is the sheriff today."

A look of deep scorn mixed with anger slowly appeared on Vibeke's beautiful, middle-aged face. "He held my hand," she said with revulsion. "He told me there's a purpose behind everything, even though it may be hard to see it. As if he were a . . . pastor! I've never understood why it felt so disgusting when he did that. Now I get it."

She looked at Max, her expression dark and challenging. "You're going to tell the police about this, aren't you?"

"When I know enough. The most important thing you can do right now is to give me access to the same papers that Cecilie saw. I'm afraid I don't have time to sit here and take notes. You'll have to let me take the papers with me. I'll make copies and send the originals back to you."

She nodded.

"It's crucial that you don't say a word about this to anyone. Not even your daughter."

"Of course."

While Vibeke left to get the papers, Max looked around the living room. It gave him the feeling that time had stopped. Even though she had remarried and a small child had played here not so many years ago, it still felt as if death were present, as if something old were in the very air. Like in a museum, he thought. Or a church.

Forty-Five

TIRILL HAD ALMOST FALLEN ASLEEP when she heard the sound. Twigs snapping under the weight of something moving slowly and cautiously. She decided to risk getting out of bed and moved quietly over to the kitchenette. From there it was possible to peer out from under the low, transverse curtains without being seen. She glimpsed the outlines of bushes and trees, and the small shed that held tools and patio furniture. As she knelt on the floor, she felt fear rise inside her like a cold tide.

Was she overreacting? Was it simply some animal that she'd heard? As if in answer to the question, a figure slipped past the window and vanished. A person. She hardly dared breathe. Part of her wanted to rush to the door and run through the woods as far as she could go, all the while screaming her head off.

Quietly she rummaged in the bottom drawer below the counter and a moment later found what she was looking for. A good, old-fashioned rolling pin.

Not wanting the stranger to see her through the windows, she began crawling toward the front door. Then, in one swift movement, she stood up and pressed her back as tightly against the wall as she could, as if wanting to melt into the timbers. Next she reached for the key and turned it in the lock as quietly as possible. Even so, the metallic click sounded as if it might be heard all the way to Bø.

For a long time she stood there listening. She hadn't heard a sound from outside after catching sight of the person who had moved past the kitchen window. With one hand gripping the rolling pin, she used the other to pull open the door. She stayed hidden behind the door, like a woman waiting for her night-roaming husband in an old-style cartoon.

Nothing happened. She noticed only a slight breeze coming in through the open doorway. And the smell of the forest floor. Her fear hadn't diminished, but she no longer felt so vulnerable or so trapped—at the mercy of someone else's will.

Filled with a cold anger directed at anyone who tried to make her feel smaller than she was, Tirill slipped out into the night.

As she rounded the corner of the cabin, she almost collided with someone standing there, facing the other way. The person spun around and threw a punch, which struck the rolling pin and knocked it to the ground. Tirill tried to see where the rolling pin landed, but it was too dark. That brief moment of distraction was enough for the person to vanish, though maybe only a couple of meters away, invisible in the dark.

Tirill was shaking all over, from both anger and fear, but she refused to let fear win out.

"Who are you?" she called, facing the woods. But no one answered.

A sound made her whirl around, and the next second something struck her on the head. Suddenly she was lying on her stomach, with her face buried in leaves and heather.

She could hear the other person breathing hard, standing above her. And she could tell it was a man. Suddenly she felt a knee jab into the small of her back. Two hands began burrowing through her hair, trying to find her neck. Tirill realized he was going to strangle her. Terror gave her new strength. She managed to kick and flail her way free from the knee in her back, and then she turned over. A ski mask hid the man's face, which scared her even more. When she reached out to pull it off, she ended up ripping open his shirt instead. Buttons scattered all around.

Suddenly she felt a hand inside her T-shirt. The man pushed up her bra and grabbed hold of her breast.

"Shit!" she shouted and then managed to tear herself out of his painful grip and get up onto her knees. But a fist slammed into her forehead, right above her eye. A warm sensation raced through

Tirill's body, as if a chinook wind were blowing through her blood and nerves, and she toppled over onto the grass. She wanted to run, but all her strength was gone. The internal chinook had left her empty. Now he was sitting astride her stomach, shoving up her T-shirt. Oh my God, she thought, he's going to rape me! His hands had already found both breasts. Tirill struggled desperately as she lay there on the ground. Suddenly her hand touched the smooth round shape of the rolling pin. Without hesitating even a second, she grabbed it and swung it as hard as she could.

Forty-Six

ALL THE PASSENGERS IN THE NEARBY TRAIN SEATS were either watching movies on their laptops or had already fallen asleep. With a sense of being initiated into something old and rare, Max took out the brown envelope that Vibeke Østbye had given him and pulled out a stack of papers. They smelled like books that hadn't been opened in twenty years.

He saw at once that this was by no means a completed dissertation. "Fragmented" was probably the best word to describe what he was holding in his hands. There were even a number of pages of handwritten notes that might prove difficult to decipher. He was a little disappointed but then reminded himself that the last person to read these papers was Cecilie Wiborg. And Vibeke had said that she'd seemed excited afterward. The same way Peter had been before he vanished. As if both of them had been on the verge of a breakthrough.

Max began to read, in search of the breakthrough.

It didn't take long before he found something unexpected. Peter Schram's planned doctoral dissertation had concerned the Nikuls figure, viewed as a classic genius loci. Of course, it was possible that Henrik Thue's work was merely a natural continuation of what his friend and mentor had begun. Yet Max thought about the violent argument that Ingebjørg Ljosland had described, the fight between Peter Schram and the teenage Henrik Thue. Was there a connection between that incident and the doctoral degree that Thue received years later? Thue claimed that he didn't remember any such argument, but that hardly seemed plausible. Who would forget about a violent confrontation with his friend and mentor a short time before the latter disappeared without a trace?

When the train conductor came to tell him that Bø was the next station, Max had still not found what might explain why Peter and Cecilie, with an interval of almost thirty years between them, had both seemed so obsessed.

LIGHTS WERE ON IN THE CABIN, and the door stood open.

"Hi, honey, I'm home!" Max called in English as he stood on the threshold. But no one answered.

After checking to see that she hadn't fallen asleep with the front door wide open, he found a flashlight and went back outside.

"Tirill!"

The woods seem to swallow his voice. He let the flashlight beam play over the gray tree trunks, but there was nothing to see. Her car was parked over by the road, which meant she couldn't have driven down to Bø. It was almost impossible for him to do a real search, because it was so dark. He could see only a few meters ahead in the beam of the flashlight. He was scared that he'd suddenly catch sight of her lying on the forest floor, her body lifeless and bloody.

Who knew that they were staying here at the cabin? Hardly anyone except her mother. Could someone have followed her after work and found their hiding place? That was always possible, of course. What had happened here while he was away in Oslo?

"Tirill!" he yelled again. "It's Max!"

Several seconds passed, and then he heard a distant shout. "I'm here!"

She was alive!

"Where are you?" he called.

"Here!"

He began moving through the woods as he called her name at intervals, and each time she replied, "Here!" Soon he saw her in the beam of the flashlight. She approached hesitantly. There was blood on her face and T-shirt, and she was clutching a rolling pin. She looked ready to use it at any moment.

"Is he gone?"

"I think so," said Max, though he had no clue who she meant.

She stopped in front of him, as if she wasn't sure what would be the appropriate thing to do. Then she threw her arms around him and began sobbing. Max stroked her back and told her over and over that there was nothing to be scared of anymore.

Gradually she calmed down.

"Who was it?" he asked then, taking a step back.

"I have no idea. If I'd aimed better, he'd be dead now. But he got away before I managed to tear off the ski mask he was wearing."

"You're bleeding. . . ."

"It's nothing. Just a cut."

When they got back to the cabin and turned on more lights, he saw at once that she had a big gash above her left eyebrow. The cut was filled with dirt and debris from when she was lying on the ground. He ushered her into the bathroom and did the best he could to clean the wound with a rag and hot water.

"You need to see a doctor right away."

"But that means driving to Notodden."

"Doesn't matter. You're going to have a nasty scar unless you get that cut stitched up."

Forty-Seven

THE WAITING ROOM smelled of antiseptic mixed with the redolent fumes of liquor coming from the slumbering man sitting on the bench nearby. His head was slumped forward, and his greasy hair hid his eyes. He must have been Max's age, but his face told a story of years of drinking and general disregard for his own health. The bloodstained bandage on his right hand looked like it had been applied by a drunkard. He probably had no one else in his life except "the boys," a few broken-down men who were never going to help him with anything other than dying a little sooner.

Some people have no drive or ambition, thought Max. They sink like lead weights on a fishing line. The man with the bandage was a lead weight that hadn't yet touched bottom. But he'd already gone a long way down, to a place where daylight no longer reached. Soon the big fish that wait for everyone would appear and swallow him up.

Max glanced at the clock on the wall. The hands hadn't seemed to move since the last time he'd checked, but suddenly the second hand lurched to the right. So the clock wasn't broken after all.

Finally Tirill emerged. She had a bandage over her left eye. She seemed even more worn out than she had only a short time ago. Sniffing loudly, she headed for the door without looking at him.

"You're not catching a cold, are you?" he asked as they stepped outside and walked toward the parking lot.

"Nope."

She was still sniffing.

"Are you crying?"

"Uh-uh."

"Yes, you are. Don't worry, you're going to be just as beautiful as you were before."

"It's not that," she said.

"Then what is it?"

"I don't like being assaulted in the dark."

"Not many people do," said Max.

They both got into the car.

After driving down the steep winding road from the hospital, they crossed the airstrip and took the shortcut to Bø, across the forested and largely unpopulated Rejsemheia. A little light had begun to seep into the nighttime darkness. The road was narrow, with dense woods on either side, and bridges that were wide enough for only one car. At one time this had been familiar territory for Max, but after half a lifetime in Florida, which was as flat as a pancake, things no longer looked the same.

"Is there any point in staying at the cabin anymore?" he asked. "It seems like they know we're there."

Tirill took her time before replying. "At least it's a safe distance away from Magnus," she said then. "So I think we should stay."

That was an argument he found easy to accept. "How many stitches did you get?"

"Seven."

"A nice little zipper on your forehead."

The beams from their headlights swept over the dark spruce trees, which stood so close together they almost formed a wall. They saw a logging machine, like some strange prehistoric beast on a side road. And a beaver dam.

"Wait a minute!" Tirill exclaimed, slapping her thigh. "I knew I'd forgotten something!"

"What are you talking about?"

"The man had a big scar on his chest. When I ripped off the buttons on his shirt, I felt the scar under my fingertips. It was like a zipper on his bare chest."

Max knew that he'd recently seen a scar just like that.

"Do you know whether the sheriff or Johannes Liom has ever had heart surgery?" Tirill went on.

He didn't answer. What he was searching for was now very close: a big scar that went all the way down the brown chest. A yellow house. A rusty garage made of corrugated metal.

"I think it's time we phoned Tycho Abrahamsen," he said.

Forty-Eight

THE NEXT MORNING they were on their way to Dalen in Tycho's car, since none of the people implicated in the investigation had seen his vehicle before. Nor had they ever seen Tycho. An unfamiliar face was going to come in handy right now. Tirill was lying on the backseat, asleep. There was something almost unnatural about seeing her so exhausted, but she'd had a hard night. The bandage over her left eye was testimony to that. If Tellev Sustugu really was the perp—and Max thought he was—he was at least grateful the man hadn't raped her.

"This guy . . . ," said Tycho as he drove. "Do you think he's the one who killed my father?" This was at least the fifth time he'd asked the question since they'd started out.

"As I already told you, we don't know that," said Max. "But it's highly likely that he was the one who attacked Tirill. Let's not draw any hasty conclusions, OK?"

When they reached Eidsborg, Max ducked down so he wouldn't be seen through the car window as they passed through the area. He did the same thing when they drove through the center of Dalen.

A short time later they parked some distance from the driveway to Sustugu's house.

"Stick to the plan we made," Max told Tycho. "You've heard he knows a lot about antique folk art, and you're wondering whether he can tell you where to sell things like that. He might have his suspicions, but curiosity will probably win out."

"I'll text you guys when I think you can come in," said Tycho. Then he set off.

Max watched as Tycho hurried up the hill with his shoulders slightly hunched. His father had walked the same way.

Then he went back to the car to wake Tirill.

FIFTEEN MINUTES PASSED with no message from Tycho.

"Maybe we should go up and check on him," said Tirill.

Max nodded.

After closing the car doors as quietly as they could, they began jogging up the hill, keeping to the very edge of the road, where they were partially hidden by thickets and bushes.

The old Volvo station wagon was still in the garage, but now there were clear tire tracks in the high grass of the yard. Sustugu must have taken the car out for a drive since the last time they'd visited.

They paused behind a pile of old junk that was at least as tall as they were.

"What do you think they're doing?" whispered Tirill, her voice so low that Max could barely hear her.

"Maybe Tycho forgot to charge his phone," he said, though he didn't believe a word of it.

"What about sending him a text? Just a question mark, for instance?"

"Better not. A text might wreck things instead of helping."

He was silent for a moment as he assessed the distance from their hiding place to the house.

"I'm going to count to three," he said. "Then we run as quietly as we can across the yard."

Max whispered, "One, two, three," and they raced through the tall grass. When they reached the house, he pressed his ear to the front door but couldn't hear a sound from inside. Cautiously he placed his hand on the door handle and slowly moved it down, a few millimeters at a time so it wouldn't make a noise and warn Sustugu. When the handle was all the way down, he began pulling it toward him, but the door didn't budge.

"It's locked," he whispered in Tirill's ear.

"What do we do now?"

"Maybe there's another door."

They slipped around the side of the house, passing a paint-stained ladder that hung from hooks on the end of the gable, and then made their way around back. With their backs pressed against the wall, they approached a cellar door painted red. When they reached it, Max motioned for Tirill to stop. For a long moment he focused all his attention on listening for any sounds.

Then he repeated the same maneuvers with the door handle, moving as cautiously and quietly as before. This time the door opened. Down a tiny hallway he saw what must have been a living room at one time. There was a fireplace, at any rate, but the room was practically stuffed to the gills with all sorts of junk piled nearly to the ceiling. The light was on in the windowless room. He listened for voices or other sounds from the floor above, but heard nothing.

Slowly they made their way along the path that cut through all the junk. After a few more steps, Max stopped. Something had caught his eye amid the jumbled belongings. An old muzzle-loader gun that looked to be intact, with a ramrod fastened to the underside of the barrel and a hand-smithed cock shaped like the beautiful head of a wolf. A magnificent specimen of a gun. Etched into the stock were some ornate initials and the year 1776. It occurred to Max that not everything in this room was worthless trash. It was a dismal mixture of everything from yellowed newspapers and empty medicine bottles to chests painted in the rosemaling style and boxes containing silver jewelry meant to be worn with national costumes. There was also a profusion of tools and other items used on farms in the old days. Lots of things that he couldn't even identify.

Max took out his cell phone and snapped a few photos. "I can see why he didn't want the police in here. Looks like stolen goods to me."

He looked for something that he could use as a weapon to defend himself and decided on a heavy old hammer.

Holding the hammer, he pushed open the next door and found himself in a hallway. From there, a set of stairs led up to the first floor. A low hum came from a freezer, and some work clothes hung from hooks on the rough cellar wall.

Max motioned with his head to ask Tirill whether they should go up the stairs to the closed door at the top. She was wide awake now, and she nodded agreement. He didn't like the situation. If someone tore open that door, they would be extremely vulnerable standing on the narrow, steep stairs.

Cautiously they climbed the steps, which creaked under their feet.

"Quick now!" he whispered as he shoved open the door and they entered a hall.

With the hammer raised, he spun around, prepared for anything, but the house was deathly silent. In addition to the front door, he saw three other doors along the hallway. One of them had a big, wavy glass pane. He guessed it must lead to the living room.

When he glanced at Tirill, he saw that she was scared. And with good reason. No matter which door they chose, they'd be like sheep coming to the slaughter when they entered the room. Tellev Sustugu might be standing there with a gun, waiting for them.

Max slowly opened a door and then took two big strides into the room as he spun around, holding up the hammer. It was the kitchen, with an open door leading to what looked like a dining room, although it had clearly been used only as a storage space for clothes. There were piles of clothes on the table, chairs, and settee. No one was in the adjoining living room either, but one of the armchairs had been toppled over, and the contents of an ashtray had spilled onto the sofa.

"Oh no," gasped Tirill behind him.

When Max turned around, he saw her crouching down and staring at some small spots on the floor.

"It's blood," she whispered.

"Let's search the other rooms, just to make sure. But I don't think they're here anymore. Which means that Sustugu has Tycho in his control. Otherwise we would have heard from him by now."

They hurried to search the rest of the house. The bathroom was small and smelled bad. The next door led to a messy bedroom, but the last door was locked.

Max thought fast. Tycho Abrahamsen's life might be in danger, so they needed to find him ASAP. On the other hand, this might be their last chance to take a good look inside Sustugu's house. So far, no other room had been locked. Why this one?

He saw it was a modern, lightweight door made of some sort of synthetic material. So he handed the hammer to Tirill and moved to the other end of the hall to get a running start. Then he threw himself at the door, shoulder first. It flew open with a dry, ripping sound, and Max fell headlong into the room.

Forty-Nine

THE ROOM CONTAINED only a spartan iron-frame bed covered with a rumpled sheet the dull gray color of a well-used eraser. Next to the bed stood a large-size soda-pop bottle with a little clear liquid in the bottom.

"Oh my God," murmured Tirill.

She was staring at the pictures that covered every inch of the walls. It must have taken a long time to put together such an enormous montage. Some appeared to be several decades old, while others looked like they'd been cut out yesterday. All of them showed nude or skimpily clad women in demeaning situations. The biggest of them all—a grainy black-and-white photo that had to be more than a meter in height—showed a woman hanging from a gallows. Her clothes were bunched around her ankles, and her body bore signs of abuse. Max had absolutely no doubt that this was a photo of an actual hanging that had occurred somewhere in the world.

Several photos showed gynecological instruments in use. Others were of torture racks, crucified women, or women hanging upside down from chains, as if they were prey about to be butchered.

Max grabbed the soda bottle and sniffed at the liquid inside. "Moonshine . . ."

Tirill was still staring at the walls as she held the hammer in her hand. "Now I'm sure that he's the one who attacked me," she said.

"Oh?"

She nodded without saying anything more.

Max heard the sound of a car engine outside. He ran into the hall and unlocked the front door. With a roar, Sustugu's old station wagon backed out of the rusty garage, moving at full speed. It swerved violently from side to side before it slammed into some shrubbery and then stopped with only the front end still visible.

Max raced through the tall grass, past the garage and the huge pile of junk, and reached the car just as Tycho squeezed out of the driver's side door, holding his hands above his head. There was blood under his nose and on his T-shirt. Tellev Sustugu climbed out of the other side of the car, pointing a gun at Tycho. Both were standing in the dense birch thickets and could hardly move because of all the branches forming a tight latticework around them.

Sustugu suddenly noticed Max standing only a few meters away, and he aimed the gun at him instead. "Hands up!" he barked.

Those words sounded so out of place on such a lovely summer day with a whiff of manure in the air. They were clearly also out of place coming from Tellev Sustugu's lips. Maybe he was trying to imitate some actor he'd seen at the local movie theater in Dalen when he was a kid.

"Where's the dame?" he said now.

Max hadn't yet raised his hands. Judging from Tycho's apologetic expression, the young man had told Tellev everything.

"In the house," said Max.

"Go stand next to him," Sustugu told Tycho, waving the gun.

Tycho did as he was told.

"Now start walking toward the house," Sustugu commanded. "And you—put your hands up like I said!"

Instead Max began moving toward him.

"I'll shoot!" Sustugu shrieked.

Max grabbed hold of the gun, but Tellev refused to let go.

"I'll shoot!" he repeated, though it sounded more like the cry of a drowning man.

With a brusque motion Max wrested the gun away and then took a step back. "Not used to handling a weapon, I see," said Max, releasing the safety that had been on the whole time. "Now you can lead the way over to the house, and then we're going to have a nice, long chat."

SUSTUGU'S FACE TURNED AS GRAY as the sheets on his bachelor's bed when he saw Tirill standing in front of the photo montage. His thin, pale lips began to quiver, and he took several deep breaths, as if he was going to faint at the sight of a real, live woman in his secret room.

Max gave him a shove with the barrel of the gun, and he reluctantly took a few steps toward the splintered door, but then he stopped on the threshold, as if facing a glass wall that could not be breached.

"Inside!" said Max in a low voice, pressing the gun against the man's suntanned bare skin, slick with sweat.

Finally Sustugu allowed himself to be forced across the threshold and into the room, which until recently had been as hidden from the outside world as all his grotesque fantasies.

Tirill turned around. Max was surprised to see how calm and composed she seemed, her face expressing neither contempt nor anger.

For his part, Sustugu kept his eyes on the floor.

"Shall we start?" said Max, pushing him toward the bed.

"No, no, not here!" he cried. "I'd rather you shot me dead."

Max glanced at Tirill, who nodded.

"OK, let's go in the living room," said Max, and all four of them left the room, with their sweating, trembling host leading the way.

Max pushed him down into the armchair that was still upright, while Tycho picked up the toppled chair and sat down a safe distance away. Max sat on the sofa next to Tirill, who still seemed remarkably calm.

"It's my gun," said Tycho remorsefully. "Or rather, it's Pappa's gun."

"You should know that I'll shoot you before you even have time to stand up," Max told Sustugu. "And at this distance, I can't miss."

The coffee table was the only thing between them, and the gun was aimed at the man's midriff.

"Do you have any idea who we really are?"

"Private detectives?" the man whispered.

"That's true for my part. Eager young Tycho here is the son of Knut Abrahamsen. And this is special investigator Tirill Vesterli."

Tellev Sustugu had white crusts of spittle at the corners of his mouth, and he was breathing hard. Only now did Max notice that he hadn't moved his left arm at all. It hung limply, as if paralyzed. That must have been where Tirill hit him with the rolling pin.

"So now you're going to tell us everything we want to know. Absolutely everything," said Max. "If I have even the slightest suspicion that you're not telling the truth, we'll take a lot of interesting photographs and send the pictures to the police and a bunch of newspapers. You'll be famous."

Fifty

THE SMELL OF COW MANURE blended with the scent of suntan lotion from the lightly dressed tourists who were eager to immortalize this glorious summer day in the interior of Telemark. People everywhere were snapping pictures of what they were seeing: tunic-clad trolls, buildings with sod roofs, the Dalen Hotel with its carvings and dragon heads, and bowls painted with rosemaling that were displayed in the souvenir-shop windows. Credit cards were flying, and everyone agreed that nothing could match the authentic setting.

In a house just beyond the center of town sat four people behind heavy curtains, talking about death—the deaths of Knut Abrahamsen, Peter Schram, and Cecilie Wiborg.

Tellev Sustugu claimed that he knew about only two of the things they had asked him about: the pig's head in the car and the attack on Tirill last night, to which he confessed, his eyes lowered.

"And why should we believe you?" asked Max.

The man was the perfect candidate for kidnapping Cecilie and then killing her.

"You have to believe me! I'm telling you the truth!"

"Why did you put the pig's head in my car if you have nothing to do with any of this?"

"Someone forced me to do it."

"Who?"

"A stranger called me on the phone. Not long after you left here."

"And this person told you to find a pig's head and take it over to Tveit?" said Max sarcastically.

"Yes, as a matter of fact. And if I didn't . . ." Again he looked at the floor. "Certain things would come out."

"Like the fact that you have a locked room in your house with pictures of women being tortured or killed?"

He shook his head.

"Or all the antiquities in the cellar?"

"I was told to pick up the pig's head from a Dumpster not far from here and to write "Fear the Lord!" And it was important to use a capital 'L' on 'Lord.'"

"And you simply agreed to do this?"

"Yes, because otherwise . . . I can't tell you why. That's the one thing I can't tell you."

Max glanced at Tirill, but she was apparently just as puzzled as he was. "So why did you attack me?" she asked.

This was the first time she'd spoken directly to Tellev Sustugu. She should be glad she didn't kill him with the rolling pin, thought Max.

"The phone rang. It was the same voice telling me there was a cabin in Bø, on the road up to Lifjell. I got a full description, about the driveway and everything. I was supposed to go over there and scare whoever was inside the cabin. And beat them up, if I got the chance."

Tycho shook his head.

"I don't believe any of this," said Max. "So let's get started taking photographs of your whole house. We'll start with the porn. Then we'll contact the police and the press."

He stood up and motioned for Sustugu to do the same.

"Wait! Don't do that! I have family. A brother who has kids and grandkids. I don't want to embarrass them. Please!" he begged.

"First you have to tell us why you agreed to do what the stranger wanted," said Max.

"Can I talk to you in private?" asked Sustugu meekly.

Again Max looked at Tirill, who nodded her consent.

"Lead the way," said Max, motioning with the gun. "Let's go to your hobby room."

This time Tellev offered no objection. He merely went inside the room and sat down on the filthy sheet covering the bed.

Max got out his phone and took a few pictures of the walls as he continued to aim the gun at Sustugu.

"Now it won't matter if you tear down all this nastiness," he said when he was done. "I've got photos. So, what were you going to tell me? Why did you do what the stranger told you to do?"

The man sitting on the bed buried his face in his hands. "I fucked a girl who was underage. It wasn't rape. She was more than willing. But she was underage. It went on for a couple of years. The woman who called me claimed she had an audio recording of the girl describing the whole affair. And she threatened to send the tape to the girl's family."

For a moment Max forgot all about the creepy room they were sitting in. "It was a woman?" he asked. "You're saying that a woman called you up and told you to do these things?"

"Yes."

"Why didn't you say that before?"

Sustugu looked up, staring straight into the muzzle of the gun. "Because . . . I don't know. You didn't ask."

"Exactly how long ago was it that you . . . er . . . fucked this girl?"

"Five years ago."

"Could it have been the girl who phoned you?"

"No. She jumped off a cliff into the gorge at Ravnejuv. Three hundred meters straight down. On the recording she apparently says that she's thinking of killing herself, because we fucked when she was so young. That's total bullshit, but it would be devastating for me if it ever got out. I'm telling you this only so that you'll believe me about the other things. I did what the woman wanted because I couldn't let this story get out."

"You wouldn't have needed to tell me this if you'd said from the start that the stranger on the phone was a woman. Nobody would make up something like that."

Tellev slumped even more.

"Who do you think it was?" Max asked.

"Maybe one of Tone's friends. Or just somebody who knew her and got hold of the recording. Maybe there really isn't any recording, but I couldn't risk it."

"How old was Tone when she died?"

Tellev bowed his head beneath the picture on the wall showing

a woman's vagina being forced wide open with a metal speculum.
"Fourteen."

"And you had sex with her for a couple of years?"

"Something like that."

"You were raping her?"

"No, no! Are you crazy? She was a little shy at first, but gradually
she . . . I'd sneak into her room and fuck her several times a night.
While her parents were home, drinking."

He shook his head at the memory. "She really liked me, you
know. She told me that her father wasn't very nice to her. But God
only knows what she might have said, considering her state of mind
before she jumped."

The pictures on the walls spoke all too clearly of the swamp that
was Tellev Sustugu's inner life. Max wondered if he'd ever brought
that young girl here.

◇◇◇

"HE'S TELLING THE TRUTH," Max said when they returned to the living room, where Tycho and Tirill were waiting.

"What do they have on him that's so terrible?" she asked.

"I promised not to say."

Sustugu sat down, taking a few trembling breaths. Max remained
standing. "But the interesting part is that it was a woman who called
and told him to do these things."

Tirill's eyes opened wide.

"How old do you think she was?" she asked Tellev.

"Hard to say. Definitely a grown-up, but not old," he replied
without looking at her.

For a while no one spoke. Max thought to himself that he needed
to have a talk with Åse.

"What do we do now?" asked Tycho finally.

Max looked at Sustugu. "We're going to leave you to your fantasies. You need to sit here quietly, with your hands on your lap, and
don't do a thing until that anonymous woman contacts you again.
Then, and only then, will you remember that the three of us even
exist. Understood?"

Sustugu nodded so earnestly that a lock of his black-dyed hair fell into this eyes, and he had to reach up to push it back.

Max signaled to Tycho and Tirill that it was time to leave.

Then he took a business card from his wallet and tossed it onto the coffee table in front of Sustugu. "That's my number. Call me if you hear from that woman again."

Tirill and Tycho stood up. Sustugu did too, as if he were about to see his guests to the door, as custom dictated.

Tirill paused and looked at him. "Just one thing before we go," she said.

He nodded and fixed his gaze on the toes of his shoes.

"What do you think is really going on?"

"I have no idea, but it's something way beyond me. And way too dangerous."

"OK, thanks," said Tirill politely. Then she punched him in the nose.

It sounded as if someone had snapped a tree branch over their knee. Tellev Sustugu toppled backward onto the coffee table, which collapsed with a bang.

"You know what that's for," Tirill told him.

Then she turned away and groaned in pain as she rubbed the knuckles of her right hand.

Fifty-One

TIRILL WAS SITTING ON THE FLOOR of the bedroom that had been hers as a child, watching Magnus sleep. She thought about all the dreams she'd had in this room as she'd waited for her life to begin. Her real life. Then one day, years after she'd moved out, she came to understand that her real life had begun long before. It just wasn't what she'd once dreamed it would be. What she'd imagined as comparable to the first step a tightrope walker takes on the taut line suspended over the abyss—both wonderful and frightening— but that wasn't how her life had turned out at all.

She studied the soft contours of her son's face resting on the pillow. It seemed to be drawing sustenance from his deep slumber. What would *his* real life look like when it caught up with him some day?

Tirill was not especially sentimental. At least she didn't think so. She had no illusions that her son's childhood would last forever, and she didn't weep over tiny shoes that had to be thrown out and replaced by larger ones. But after the horrible images she'd seen yesterday, she fervently wished that Magnus could remain in the innocent state in which he was now living. The world out there was undoubtedly filled with decent people and big surprises, but it also contained individuals like Tellev Sustugu. And many who were even worse. Those kinds of people repudiated the fundamental goodness that existed in her old childhood bedroom tonight. A mother's goodness. The unconditional protection that adults offered children.

What sort of dreams had Tellev had before he started to paint the inside of his head black? Or had it always been black from the very beginning? Was that even possible? No, thought Tirill. No, no, no. Not from the very beginning. For all she knew, Tellev's mother had sat the same way she was now sitting, watching her son as he slept. Pondering his future.

The only thing certain was that the little boy had ended up creating the room she'd seen yesterday. A room filled with abuse and death.

WHEN TIRILL WENT BACK TO THE LIVING ROOM, she found her mother watching a rerun of the TV show *The Luxury Trap*.

"People are crazy!" her mother exclaimed.

"What do you mean?"

"That young man is only twenty-two, and he's already bought twelve cars. And his wife took a trip with her girlfriends to the Mediterranean even though their bank account was completely empty. She put the whole trip on a new credit card. And neither of them has a steady job!"

She was practically shouting, as if it were Tirill's fault that these people were behaving so stupidly. Then she calmed down and muted the sound on the TV. "Is he asleep?"

"Yes, finally."

"I have to tell you, he was really excited when his mother suddenly showed up."

Tirill knew there was an underlying criticism in what her mother said, but she let it go. She was too worn out to fight. She sat down on the sofa.

"Are you sure you don't want to stay overnight? Stay here with Magnus?"

"I can't. But I'll sit with you for a while."

"Tirill, there's something I need to talk to you about. . . ."

"I know."

Magnus had instantly asked about the "ow-ow" his mother had, but she'd simply told him that she'd fallen off her bicycle. If the boy hadn't been present, her mother would have interrogated her long ago.

"Is it this man you've been seeing?" she began. "Has he been hitting you?"

"Do you really think I'd put up with someone hitting me?"

"No. That does seem a little strange. After all, you were the one who hit Asgeir. Not the other way around."

"That happened only once. And besides, you know what he did."

"Yes, but still . . ."

"And who he did it with. Lene Rudningen, for God's sake!"

"All right. . . ."

"He was probably the only guy left who hadn't dipped his wick in her."

"Tirill!" Her mother looked like a shocked little owl. She picked up her knitting but then put it down. "What exactly is going on?" she asked. "Is there even a man in the picture?"

"Yes, there is, Mamma. And we're staying at the cabin that belongs to Hallvard Kilane's family, just like I told you."

Tirill's mother gave her a skeptical look. She'd forgotten all about *The Luxury Trap* on TV, where the young couple were now seeing their irresponsible ways broadcast to the whole country, displayed as numbers printed on a chalkboard. The man grinned with embarrassment when he saw the amount he spent annually on cars.

"But why do you have bruises on your arms? And that bandage on your face? I want to know what you've got yourself mixed up in!"

Tirill sighed heavily. "I can't tell you. I'm sorry, but I can't. Someday I'll tell you the whole story. It's nothing like you think."

"Then what is it?" her mother insisted peevishly.

"It's . . . amazing."

Now it was her mother who sighed. Tirill knew that sound. It meant that her mother was done with the subject for the time being, but that didn't mean she wouldn't bring it up again.

Tirill tucked her legs under her and took a piece of Twist candy from the bowl on the coffee table. Right now it felt good to focus on what was familiar. Like her mother's sighs.

And *The Luxury Trap*.

"Could you turn up the sound?" she said.

Fifty-Two

T HE NEXT DAY AT WORK, Tirill made photocopies of Peter
Schram's papers, one set for herself and one set for Fjellanger.
Then she sat down to read. When a colleague knocked on the
door of her office, she pushed the papers aside and pretended to
be working on something on her computer. But as soon as she was
alone again, she went back to reading.

She'd been at it for quite a while when it felt like an electric cur-
rent suddenly passed through her body. She sat there motionless,
staring at the page with the handwritten note, which said, "Witzøe
writes that 'there is supposedly a circle on the forest floor near
the spring from which the Eidsborg stream issues. Within this circle nothing will grow. According to legend it's because the Devil
dropped his wedding ring at this spot.' In addition, the spring is said
to be 'bottomless.' Need to locate it as soon as the snow has melted
in upper Telemark. This could be the place."

The note was dated December 19, 1984.

"Could be the place"? What did Schram mean by that?

Tirill couldn't rid herself of the feeling that this note had something to do with what his widow had said about his being on the
verge of a breakthrough right before he disappeared. Because of
the way he'd worded the note, it seemed to be extremely important.

Then it occurred to her that Cecilie Wiborg must have seen this
note as well, when she went to visit Vibeke Østbye. Cecilie probably knew about Pastor Peder Witzøe, who wrote a topographical

account of upper Telemark in the 1700s, a book that Schram had apparently used in his research.

She wondered what books Cecilie had made use of while she was working on her master's thesis, which she'd never had time to complete. Only Henrik Thue would know. But there was something Tirill could check without consulting him. She could find out which books Cecilie had borrowed from the library.

She pulled up Cecilie's account on the computer and began going through it. Cecilie had borrowed only reference books on history and religion. And folklore. All relevant topics for someone writing about the popular opposition to the Reformation, with a focus on the Eidsborg stave church and the Nikuls cult.

So she was surprised to see one book on an entirely different subject: *Ashes to Ashes: An Introduction to Soil Biology,* by Lisbeth Sæthre, who happened to be one of the college's own professors.

LISBETH SÆTHRE was a woman in her fifties who always looked as if she'd just learned a big secret. Tirill hadn't been to her office before, and she'd never talked to her outside the library. That was indicative of Tirill's position at the college—few actually knew her, but everyone knew who she was.

"Wow, what in heaven's name happened to you?" exclaimed Sæthre, looking as if she was having a hard time not blurting out something.

"Oh, it's nothing. Just fell off my bike. I wonder if you could help me out with something."

"I'll do my best," said the professor enthusiastically. "Have a seat."

Tirill sat down.

"Cecilie Wiborg . . . You know, the student who . . ."

The biologist nodded.

"Well, she borrowed a book that she never had a chance to return, and it hasn't been found," she lied. "The reason I'm asking you is that it was a copy of your book *Ashes to Ashes.* I thought it seemed strange, because Cecilie was working on a master's thesis about the Reformation in Vest-Telemark."

"I can tell you why," said Lisbeth. "She was very interested in examining the soil content at a certain location. So she came to me for help. I may have recommended my book to her, but I have no idea where it might have ended up."

"Was it the soil in her vegetable garden she wanted help with?"

Lisbeth shook her head. "No, it was a place in Eidsborg. She pestered me so much that I finally gave up and went there with her. It was quite a hike through the woods, I'll tell you that. The place was way up in the middle of nowhere, and I'm not exactly a mountain goat. I can't recall ever seeing anything like it."

"Was there a circle on the forest floor?"

The professor peered at Tirill in surprise over the rim of her glasses. "How did you know that?"

"Just a guess," said Tirill, swallowing hard as adrenaline coursed through her body.

"A circular depression on the ground," explained Professor Sæthre. "I think it was about thirty meters in diameter, but the path around it was no more than half a meter wide. And maybe ten centimeters deep."

"Was anything growing inside the circle?"

"A little vegetation, but not much. It looked like a path that was seldom used."

"Except that it was circular," whispered Tirill, mostly to herself.

Sæthre nodded eagerly, looking as if ready to burst. "The only way it could have been formed was through repeated wear," she said. "Maybe an animal track, even though animals rarely walk in circles."

"And did you explain that to Cecilie?"

"I took some samples, since she wanted me to analyze the soil. I also explained to her that it had to be due to wear. She got all . . . like this." Sæthre raised her arms above her head like a soccer player who just scored a goal. "She didn't say a word, but she was beaming, as if that meant everything to her. When I asked about her reaction, she just said she was feeling overworked and a little off balance. Then she started to cry."

Tirill suddenly felt like she was again very close to Cecilie, the way she'd felt when she sat on the sofa in the young woman's childhood home, talking to her mother.

"But she quickly pulled herself together," Sæthre hurried to say. "She took tons of pictures of the circle."

"Pictures? With a camera?"

"No, with her phone."

Which is missing, of course, thought Tirill.

"How did she seem otherwise, during your hike?"

"Strange. Overwrought. As if she were walking on air."

"What do you mean?" asked Tirill.

"Well, she was practically floating. I've thought a lot about it since she disappeared. There was something really odd about that girl."

"Am I right in guessing there was a spring near that spot?"

"Yes!" cried Lisbeth Sæthre. "I'd almost forgotten about that. Cecilie had brought along one of those little rod and reels—the kind they use for ice fishing, you know. She'd heard that the spring might be bottomless, but of course there's no such thing as a bottomless spring. At least, that's what I thought until she got out the rod and dropped the line with the lead weight into the water. I'll never forget the way we looked at each other as the reel spun around and around, letting out the line. It didn't stop until all of the line was out. It hung there, straight down, but it hadn't yet touched bottom. Cecilie claimed the line was sixty meters long, and I saw no reason not to believe her."

Tirill stared at the professor in astonishment. "How can that be?" she asked. "Like you said, there's no such thing as a bottomless spring."

The gleeful enthusiasm had vanished from Lisbeth Sæthre's face, replaced by a slightly evasive and uneasy expression. "I know. But sometimes the ground water can rise to the surface through extremely deep channels in the rock. That must be what happened up there. Way underneath the spring there might be a subterranean river, for example. That's actually not so unusual. But the length of that particular crevasse or tunnel, which ends in the spring, isn't exactly an everyday occurrence."

"Have you ever seen anything like it?" asked Tirill.

"No, I haven't. And you know what? While Cecilie was standing there with the whole fishing line unwound—sixty meters, straight down—I suddenly had a feeling that something might bite. I've even dreamed about that happening. Suddenly the rod arcs, and we know that something is down there. It's not a particularly happy dream, I'll tell you that."

Tirill thought the biologist looked as if she'd visibly aged in just the past few minutes.

Fifty-Three

BEHIND HER TIRILL COULD HEAR FJELLANGER huffing and puffing. A private detective in Florida, she thought. What exactly did that sort of job involve? Ambling along white-sand beaches and spying on unfaithful wives wearing bikinis? Or sitting in a car and waiting for somebody to come out of a sleazy motel while he stuffed himself with doughnuts or whatever it was detectives ate?

"Let's take a break," he said, breathing hard.

"OK," she replied and sat down on a rock.

He waded past the blueberry bushes to sit down beside her. "I've been doing almost nothing but office work for the past few years," he told her apologetically.

"Is it big, this detective agency of yours?"

"Big enough to eat up nearly all my time as soon as I get near the place," he said.

"So are you glad to be here?"

He didn't answer at once, merely sat there looking down at the valley below. Between several pine trees they could just barely make out the museum, with sunlight reflecting off the big picture windows of the café. Light also shone on all the cars that were still parked outside, even though it was almost closing time. It was nearly impossible to see the stave church from so far away, though, as it was almost the same color as the tree trunks.

"Yes and no," he said at last. "I'm glad to be doing something other than office work, but sad because I wouldn't have come here if Ann were still alive. So I guess the answer is mostly no. Unfortunately."

Tirill looked at Fjellanger's hands resting on his knees. "I noticed you're not wearing your wedding ring anymore."

"I'm fully aware of that, but thanks for telling me."

"Are you sure you're a hundred percent in control of the situation?" she asked.

Max sat quietly, looking as if he were carefully considering his word choice. "I'm sure that I'm in control of the part that is important to the investigation," he then replied calmly.

His answer was not entirely satisfactory, but she chose to let it go.

"Do you think we're making a mistake by not tipping off the police about the perfect suspect in the Wiborg case?" he asked. "I mean, if it turns out that Tellev Sustugu is actually the perpetrator, then the two of us will have made a real mess of things by not notifying the authorities."

Tirill had been thinking along the same lines. "If we're to believe Henrik Thue, then Cecilie Wiborg was last seen a kilometer outside of Eidsborg," she said. "And there's a man living in Dalen, a short car ride away, who has a room filled with pictures of women being tortured. The police wouldn't hesitate to bring him in if they knew that Cecilie disappeared in Eidsborg and not in Bø."

"But I don't think he had anything to do with Nikuls and all the rest of it. And I'm convinced that Cecilie's disappearance is connected to that."

Tirill nodded. "So let's see if we can find the circle," she said and got up.

THEY FOUND THE STREAM and followed it up the slope. After a while it disappeared, exactly as Lisbeth Sæthre had described. The last they saw of it, the water was bubbling out between two large rocks. From there they were supposed to proceed about a hundred meters, straight ahead. But how good was the professor at recalling the distance from when she'd been here with Cecilie?

And what exactly did she mean by "straight ahead"?

It turned out to be more difficult than they'd imagined. In the early summer evening, with all sorts of insects buzzing around their heads, Tirill and Max literally crawled their way forward, keeping an eye out for a depression in the forest floor that was approximately ten centimeters deep and a half meter wide.

Max was the one who finally found it. He was farther up the slope, hidden by some bushes, and Tirill started running through the almost knee high heather to join him. When she caught sight of him, he was down on all fours, pushing aside the heather.

She had to go very close before she saw it too. "Are you sure it's not just an old path?"

"I'm pretty sure it's not," Max said. "Plus it matches the professor's description. About ten centimeters deep and hard to find. This is the place where the devil dropped his wedding ring. But we should probably confirm that we're right. If you start off behind me and move in the opposite direction, we should meet before long—if it's a circle, that is."

Tirill knelt down and started off. Slowly they crept away from each other as they followed the faint track. Every time she looked up, she saw the same patch of blue sky. Not so much as a bird or a white trail left by a plane. Underneath she felt the same sunken groove, and all around were the same swarms of insects that she inevitably stirred up from the heather and grass, and which inevitably did their best to suck at her blood.

The spot where they'd started was next to a marsh, and the circle continued out into the marsh, where it crossed a small stream and then passed through the heather to the other side of the marsh. As she crawled along, Tirill could see Max's head and back. He too was moving through the marshy grass and into the woods on the other side.

Finally they met among the heather and pines. Still on all fours, they raised their heads to look at each other. The track—if that's what it was—formed an almost perfect circle, bisected by marsh.

"Oh my God," panted Tirill, spitting out insects.

"We found it," gasped Fjellanger.

"The middle seems to be in the marsh, right about where the grass is a little darker. That's probably where the spring is," she said.

Fjellanger took out his cell phone and began snapping photographs as Tirill spread the heather away from the circle so it could be documented.

Together they walked over to the edge of the marsh and out to the place where the grass was a little higher and thicker. Just as they'd thought, they found hidden in the grass a perfectly round pool, maybe one and a half meters across.

Like a big black eye.

Next to the spring, and also more or less hidden by the grass, was a good-sized flat rock.

"Flat rocks are meant to be sat on," said Tirill. She sat down as Fjellanger took pictures of the spring and rock.

He leaned down and dipped his hand in the water. "It's ice cold. Let's follow the stream and find out where it goes. It's bound to disappear somewhere, since it shows up again farther down the slope."

Tirill followed, and soon they reached the edge of the marsh, where the water became a stream between moss-covered rocks. After they had walked several meters down the slope, they came to a spot where the stream disappeared. The water simply fell down a dark hole.

The sound it made was hollow and subterranean.

"The stream runs into Eidsborg Tarn," said Tirill pensively. "The spring is the place where the water in the tarn first rises to the surface."

Fifty-Four

THEY LAY ON THEIR BACKS in the heather next to each other. The air, warm from the sun, quivered above the forest floor, and all around swarmed midges and tiny flies.

"Do you think they've carried Nikuls around the spring so many times that they've left a visible path?" asked Max.

"What else could it be from? That must be what Cecilie decided too. And that's why she reacted the way she did when Lisbeth Sæthre told her the circle had to be the result of repeated wear. Cecilie stretched her arms high in the air like a soccer player after making a goal. She must have done that because she realized the same thing we did: the Nikuls worship continued up here. It might still be going on even today."

"That sounds unbelievable," he protested.

"If the circle is due to wear, then we're talking about either animals or human beings. And I can't really picture a moose or a badger walking in circles in the same spot for hundreds of years. Since we happen to be in an area known for an old religious practice that involves walking around the same lake year after year, and this practice was gradually suppressed, or whatever it was that happened to it . . . Well, what we're talking about now seems the most plausible explanation. As far as I can see, there really aren't any others."

"But the book that Schram mentions in his research was published in 1722," said Fjellanger. "At that time they were still carrying the statue around Eidsborg Tarn at Midsummer. Why would they do the same thing so far away, up here in the woods? And keep in mind that by that time, the ritual had already become a legend. In other words, the circle must have existed a long time before the book was written."

For a while the only sound was the buzzing of insects.

"What if two different rituals existed?" Tirill said. "One carried out in full view of the public, though over the objections of the church. And the other a deep secret, carried out by only a few participants."

"But not both on Midsummer Eve?"

"Or maybe the second one took place only after the statue was put back inside the church."

"What would be the point of all that?" Max asked.

"Maybe something connected with the original ritual, with the way it was performed when Norway was Catholic, wasn't allowed to continue after the Reformation. The few descriptions we have are based on oral accounts and clearly have to do with the ritual at the lake during its last phase, in the 1700s. We have no idea how it was performed during the Middle Ages. Maybe the Lutheran pastors agreed to a modified version."

"While at the same time the ritual performed up here in secret was given the full treatment?" Fjellanger speculated.

"Something like that. And if the ritual has continued to the present day, it's most likely performed in that secret version."

"And then Peter Schram happened to stick his nose in the wasp's nest, on Midsummer Eve, of all nights. That must be why the sheriff had the statue in the trunk of his car the following day. They hadn't yet had a chance to put it back inside the church. No wonder he was so stressed."

They looked at each other and shook their heads.

It's like plunging through floorboards and falling into a dark cellar, thought Tirill. But in a house that's not supposed to have a cellar.

Fifty-Five

THE POSTS HOLDING UP the old double storage shed seemed to smolder in the light of the low evening sun, which made the Homme farm look like a royal estate in a folktale. Even Elvis the elkhound seemed pleased with the state of things. But that lasted only until Max and Tirill got out of their car. Then the dog reared up on his hind legs and began throwing himself at them. Each leap was abruptly halted midway, when the chair tightened and yanked the poor animal back. But he refused to give up. His fur stood on end all along his back, and his bared teeth reminded Max of a wolf.

When Jon Homme came striding across the yard, the dog whimpered and curled up under the big tree, then lay there looking up at his master with a mixture of hatred and boundless adoration.

They had decided to show the sheriff they refused to be scared off.

"So, it's you again," Homme said in a chilly tone of voice as he shook hands with Max. "Didn't expect to see you again. And you've brought a lady with you this time."

"Tirill Vesterli. She's my guide."

Homme's gaze swept over Tirill, looking her up and down. "What's this all about?"

"The same thing as before," said Max.

The sheriff set his hands on his hips and looked up at the night sky above Eidsborg. Then he shook his head in resignation. "I guess you'd better come over to the porch and have a seat."

While they sat down, he went inside to get coffee and "some refreshments." Max guessed he'd serve the same kind of cookies he'd offered last time.

Below the farm was Eidsborg Tarn, as round and shiny as a mirror. Once upon a time it might have been a sacred lake—so many centuries ago that the human view of the world would have been radically different from Max Fjellanger's view. For him, it was a given that the earth was round and moved in an orbit around the sun. Just as much a given as that God did not exist. Only nature existed, and the human being was part of nature. But not just some ordinary part, because it was in the human being that nature, after billions of years, became aware of itself. Finally nature was in a position to meet its own eye and say, "There is a tarn whose surface is gleaming with light." For Max, this was greater than any quote he'd ever heard from the Bible.

Yet he and the people who had lived in pre-Christian Eidsborg did have one thing in common. It was their conviction that they actually knew how the world made sense. Realizing this, Max was suddenly no longer so sure of his own version.

"Without food and drink . . . ," said Jon Homme as he carefully set a tray with cookies and mugs of coffee on the table. "You'll have to excuse the simple refreshments, but my wife is away at a meeting."

Apparently he had decided to treat them with courtesy.

"So you're still wondering whether it was suicide or not?" Homme asked.

"How sure are your feelings that it was?" asked Max.

"I don't usually rely much on feelings when it comes to something like that," replied the sheriff calmly. "The tech team concluded that Knut Abrahamsen took his own life. But I suppose there will always be a possibility, theoretically speaking, that he could have been murdered."

Max wondered why he was lying. According to Tellev Sustugu, Knut had been on his way to see Homme on the evening before he was found dead. Max saw no reason to doubt Sustugu, who basically seemed terrified of the whole Homme clan—both living and dead.

"So you're saying the possibility that Knut was murdered is only theoretical?"

"He was found in the river with his pockets full of stones. The autopsy determined that drowning was the cause of death. And there were no signs of a struggle. The bruises on his knees and the cut on his lip were completely consistent with his falling on his way down to the river in the dark."

"But maybe he was pushed in," said Max.

"With his pockets full of stones?"

"Maybe they were put there afterward."

"It's possible. In theory."

"But not really credible in practice?"

"We looked into the matter and found no reason to surmise that he was killed."

"What about his car key that was found in the river and not on his body?"

"Are you still going on about that?" asked Homme, exasperated.

"Yes. And something else has recently come to light. I've been told there was a rumor that went around years ago up here. People said Knut had something to do with the disappearance of Peter Schram. Which means someone in the area had a motive for killing Knut."

Jon Homme's eyes abruptly took on an alert and watchful look. "I don't really follow you."

"I'm talking about the person or persons who were actually behind Schram's disappearance."

The sheriff held up both hands. "Now wait a minute! The person or persons behind his disappearance? Peter Schram fell down a crevasse. Or he drowned."

"Do you think the same thing happened to Cecilie Wiborg?" asked Tirill. This was the first time she'd spoken since they'd sat down, and Homme was clearly surprised.

"Cecilie disappeared in Bø. I don't know, but . . . Of course she might have drowned, but the police did a thorough search, both in the Bø River and in other places."

"Did the police search for her here?" Tirill went on.

"No. Why would they do that?"

"She was writing a thesis that included research on the Nikuls ritual."

"Well, of course we cooperated fully with the sheriff's office in Bø. And with Kripos, the National Criminal Investigation Service.

We interviewed people she'd been in contact with. But it was never considered relevant to do any kind of search in this area, since she actually disappeared in Bø."

Max was starting to feel the effect of all the coffee on his bladder. He cleared his throat. "Excuse me, but I wonder if I could use your bathroom."

"Through the living room and out to the hall. Second door on your left," said the sheriff, sounding grumpy.

In the big, dimly lit living room, a wall clock painted in the rosemaling style hacked out each second with the worn, mechanical sound of gears turning. The air smelled the same as the farmhouses of his childhood in Evje back in the 1960s—a somewhat sweet blend of apples, milk, and animal odors.

Max paused to peer at the family photos on the wall. One of them seemed to be of a young Jørgen Homme and his wife with a plump little Jon between them, evidently on a hike in the woods.

He went over to an old-fashioned sideboard on which more photographs were displayed. These were dominated by hunting motifs. A big bull moose that had bit the dust, brought down by hunters wearing old-fashioned clothing made of the coarse, thick wool called wadmal. One showed an English setter holding a grouse in its jaws. Another was of a hunting party posed with a mountain bear on the barn ramp of the Homme farm.

Then Max's gaze was drawn to a photo hanging apart from all the others on the wall. Something that felt like a cold wind raced down the hot and sweaty nape of his neck. It was a picture of Jon Homme with his arm around his father's shoulders. Even though it must have been taken toward the end of the senior Homme's life, Max recognized the old sheriff, though he probably wouldn't have if he wasn't standing next to his son. That was no doubt why he hadn't recognized him in the video of the Nikuls reenactment. Now he realized that the old man who had grabbed the saint statue was Jørgen Homme.

And Åse Enger Thue had been there too, placing her hand on his forearm, as if she wanted to stop him.

Or help him.

Fifty-Six

NEITHER OF THEM had said a word for a long time as they pored over Henrik Thue's books and Peter Schram's papers. It was barely a week until Midsummer, and they both knew they'd have to do something then. But they hadn't yet discussed what that might be. So far it was merely a big, threatening darkness up ahead.

"Do you think Åse is the woman Sustugu talked to on the phone?" asked Tirill.

"She's the strongest candidate, at any rate. Who else could it be? Julia Bergmann? But she's a Lutheran pastor. Ingebjørg Ljosland over at Tveit? I don't know. . . . She seemed genuinely upset about losing Schram. That said, she's the one who specifically pointed to Henrik Thue with her story about his arguing with Schram. And I'm surprised Thue would deny having a fight like that, when he was willing to tell us about everything else."

"I think it's because he plagiarized Schram's doctoral dissertation. Parts of "Eidsborg—A Sacred Place" are taken practically word for word from Schram's work. I happen to think that Ingebjørg was telling the truth about their fight. And if that's the case, then we're left with the pastor and Åse."

"Or someone we've never heard about," Max interjected.

It was time for him to relieve himself. "I'm going out to get some fresh air," he said.

Tirill gave him an embarrassed look. "Do you think you could get some fresh air a little farther away from the cabin? It's starting to smell."

Max didn't know what to say to that, so he simply left. This time he walked a short distance into the woods before stopping.

As he stood there, the spray of his urine darkening the leaves of a raspberry bush, he heard the ping of an arriving text message. He finished up, careful to shake off so as not to get any drops on his pants. Then he took out his cell phone and looked at the display.

Can you come over tonight? Henrik is away.

He didn't tell Tirill, merely reassuring her that he'd gotten fresh air way off in the woods. Then he said he needed to go for a drive. He was starting to get cabin fever. Tirill raised her eyes from Schram's papers only long enough to wave at him. Then she dove back into the old materials from 1985.

Fifty-Seven

FIRST HE LOOKED FOR HER in the garden, but no one was there. He saw only a solitary empty glass on the table. Then he went over to the porch. In the back of his mind, he still had the image of her walking naked through the living room. Again it was hard to see inside, because it was so light outdoors. Max rapped his knuckle against the glass and waited. No response. He tried to open the French doors, but they were locked. He knocked again—harder this time—but it did no good.

Annoyed, he went around the side of the house to the front entrance, which he'd never used before. He leaned on the doorbell, then waited, getting more and more irritated. She'd sent him a text saying he should come over! When he grabbed the door handle, he found the door unlocked. Should he go in? It didn't feel right. He rang the bell again, but no one came.

Hesitantly he opened the door and stepped into the entryway. He'd been here before, but he had a bad feeling about this. The house was much too quiet.

From where he stood he could see only part of the living room, but it appeared to be empty. Sensing that something was terribly wrong, he reluctantly went in and looked around. At first he didn't notice anything special, and he was just about to leave when he saw it. Sticking up above the back of one of the armchairs, which was turned away from him, were several tufts of blond hair.

"Åse?" he said cautiously.

No reaction.

"Åse?" His voice sounded hollow and strange.

Max took a deep breath, walked over to the chair, and moved around to the front of it.

Åse was sitting there with her lips slightly parted, staring blankly straight ahead. Her clenched hands rested on her lap. In one hand she held a piece of paper that had text printed on it.

Slowly he leaned toward her.

"Traitor!" she said. It was only a whisper, but Max flinched.

"Didn't you hear me ringing the bell?" he asked.

"Traitor . . . ," she repeated, the word barely audible, her gaze still rigidly fixed, as if she'd somehow gotten trapped in her own thoughts.

"What are you talking about?"

Trembling, Åse held out the piece of paper. Max brusquely snatched it out of her hand. She had scared him, and that made him mad.

"What's this?"

"Don't you recognize it?"

He looked closer at the paper and saw that it was a printout from his company's website.

"Ah. I see. I run a detective agency. Didn't I tell you that? What of it?"

Finally she looked up at him. Her eyes were red from crying. "I checked it out on the Internet, because I refused to believe it," she said. "But he was actually telling the truth."

"Who?"

"Henrik. He just left. I told him I wanted a divorce."

"What did he tell you?"

She gave him a scornful look, as if he didn't even deserve an answer. And maybe he didn't. "About the way you coerced him, using the picture I showed you. And about how you got him to tell you what happened on Midsummer Eve. You're a private detective working for Cecilie Wiborg's family, and the whole time you've been trying to find out whether Henrik kidnapped Cecilie and then killed her. I've never felt so used in all my life! If I'd known about all this in the beginning, I never would have shown you that photograph."

"So why did you show it to me?" asked Max.

"Can't you figure that out?" she said sadly. "The same reason I told you about Henrik's being unfaithful to me. About all the text messages that had to be answered in secret. The female voices in the background whenever I talked to him on the phone. It was because I wanted you to understand my situation. I was saying, See, here's a young girl practically naked in my garden, and my husband is the one taking the picture! What did you think it was all about? That I was trying to focus suspicion on Henrik?"

"The thought did occur to me."

"But why? Surely you didn't think that I . . ."

Max threw out his hands. "Well . . . you lied to me."

Åse gave him a puzzled look.

"About the time when you met Cecilie Wiborg. You didn't tell me that she was pregnant and your husband was the father."

"But that's not lying. Why would I tell you something like that?"

Suddenly Max found it very difficult to come up with a good answer.

"Can't you see how humiliating it was to hear that fertile young girl telling me about the child she was carrying? Henrik's child. The one I should have had. The one I wanted more than anything. Don't you understand anything?"

"I do understand," he said, reaching out to touch her cheek, but she pushed his hand away.

"Why didn't you tell me that you were present at the first Nikuls reenactment that took place a few years ago?" he asked her now.

Again she gave him that look of incomprehension. "Because I didn't know I was being interviewed by a detective—that's why. And besides, it was too embarrassing. That was my desperate attempt to get pregnant. It may seem ridiculous, but Henrik was away, and I knew that in the old days Nikuls was believed to have the power to make a barren woman fertile. So I decided to take part in the ancient ritual. As you can see, it didn't help. It wasn't any better than all the other methods I've tried. But I never told anyone about being there. Not even Henrik. How come you know about it?"

"I caught a glimpse of you in the video that was made of the evening. You're on screen for only a few seconds."

Åse laughed in disbelief. "And here I was, about to give up everything for you," she said.

When Max heard that, he realized he'd ruined something wonderful. "To be honest, there wasn't really much for you to give up," he said coldly, in an effort to hide his disappointment. "A husband who's notoriously unfaithful, and . . ."

She stared at him for so long that he started to feel uncomfortable and had to look away.

"Do you want to know why I didn't leave him long ago?"

"I've been wondering about that."

"I don't know what the rules are in the States, but here in Norway you have to be married if you want to adopt a child. These days it's not even good enough to be in a long-term relationship. So you have to give up any thought of divorce while you're in line to adopt. And Henrik and I have been on the list for several years now. It's a horribly slow process, but we could have done it. So that's how much I was willing to give up for you—my last possibility of having a child. And then it turns out this was all part of your investigation. Now I'll just have to learn to live my life differently—as someone who will never be a mother. And I never want to see you again. Henrik, in spite of everything, is just a man who thinks with his dick. The world is filled with men like him. But you . . ."

She studied him, as if looking for something deep in his eyes.

Something that probably doesn't exist, thought Max.

Fifty-Eight

MAX WAS MOWING THE GRASS in front of the cabin, using a short-handled scythe, a so-called *stuttorv*. It probably wasn't necessary, but he wasn't doing the chore to be helpful. He was doing it in order to keep all thought of Åse at arm's length. Every time he swung the scythe, it was as if he were mowing down his thoughts along with the grass. Thoughts of what might have been if only he'd met her under different circumstances. The blade of the scythe was strong and sharp and cut right through them.

When he turned slightly, he had a view all the way out to Lake Norsjø, glittering with sunlight. With the timbered cabin in the background, this could have been the ideal vacation for a returning middle-aged Norwegian wanting to experience a breath of old Norway, the way he remembered it from his childhood. But that was not what Max Fjellanger wanted. He wanted to see someone arrested for the murder of Knut Abrahamsen.

That was still the most important thing, he decided with some surprise as he stopped working. Regardless of the saint statue, ghost stories, and old disappearances, for him it was Knut who mattered most. The problem was that the truth was hidden somewhere among all those other things.

He wiped his brow with his handkerchief. When he stuffed it back in his pocket, he touched the ring that he'd put there before coming out to mow the grass. He'd been sitting at the table in the cabin, holding in his hand the simple gold band that Ann had put on his finger twenty-five years ago. He couldn't decide whether to wear it again or not. So he put it in his pocket and then came outside.

Now Max took out the ring and looked at it. He held it between his thumb and index finger to study the inscription inside: *Now and forever*. He couldn't recall the last time he'd seen those three words. Which wasn't surprising, since he never used to take off the ring. It was only after he met Åse that he'd decided to do so.

Yet he hadn't hesitated to exploit her. What's wrong with me? he thought. But he knew the answer: the truth was a stronger lodestar for him than love—if it even was love that he'd felt for Åse. In order to find out what had happened to Knut—and to Cecilie and Peter—he'd been willing to go behind her back. Maybe it was the same when I was with Ann, he thought now. When it came right down to it, the truth had always mattered most to him. Yet that hadn't been a problem with Ann, since the two of them had spent every day hunting for the truth.

A surprising coldness filled his heart as he acknowledged that he was glad they'd never had children. The realization was surprising, because he'd always shared Ann's desire to be a parent. At least that's what he'd thought. But maybe that wasn't the case, after all. Maybe this was who he was. A man who was able to turn away from what many regarded as the greatest thing in life, in order to search for a truth about something that was generally thought to be of lesser value. He did this because he knew something no one else knew. He knew that the truth, no matter what it happened to be about, was the greatest thing of all. Greater than God.

Max decided not to put the ring back on, but when he tried to stick it in his pocket again, he dropped it.

He squatted down and spread aside the grass where the ring had fallen. The grass was well over half a meter high, and so thick that it was hard to expose even a small patch of ground. The ring, which was both heavy and smooth, would have slid right down to the bottom. No matter how much he moved the grass aside or how far down he stuck his hand, he couldn't find the ring.

Something like panic began spreading upward from his stomach. Choosing not to wear the ring was one thing; it was a whole different matter to lose it.

At that instant he touched the smooth metal with the tip of his finger. He plucked the ring out of the tall grass, afraid he might lose it again.

When he stood up, he chose to put it back in his pocket. He wouldn't wear it again. That life was over.

But searching for the ring had given him an idea.

Fifty-Nine

MAKING THEIR WAY up the rough, pine-covered slopes that seemed to be trembling in the heat, he was glad the metal detector he'd bought didn't weigh much more than a kilo. Silently he cursed the nearly knee-high heather they had to plow through, the insects that kept biting him, and the dust that made his whole body itch. But the prospect of using the detector to find the devil's wedding ring gave him the energy to continue on.

When they finally reached the spot, it was impossible to make out the circle without going down on all fours to look for it.

"We should have marked it somehow," he said.

"No, it's good we didn't. This way nobody knows we've been here," said Tirill, who was crawling through the heather a few meters away.

"Here it is!" she shouted.

Max got to his feet and picked up the metal detector. Then he went over to Tirill, who had spread the heather aside so he could see the circle. In one hand she held the little garden trowel that Max had bought at the Felleskjøpet feed store.

Right at the edge of the marsh, the detector emitted a beep, but the ground was so hard that it was difficult to dig. Finally Tirill man aged to pry loose a clump of hard-packed dirt that sparked a signal when Max pointed the metal detector at it.

Tirill carefully began hacking at the clump with her trowel. After a moment she set the trowel down and picked up a little object.

"It's a coin," she said, holding it up between her thumb and index finger.

Max held out his hand, and she gave it to him. The coin was dark from being in the ground, making it impossible to decipher what it said with the naked eye. When Max got out a loupe and studied the magnified image, he recognized the coin from his childhood. It was a two-øre piece, with a black grouse on one side and the monogram of King Olav V on the other.

"A two-øre from 1963," he said, sticking it in his pocket.

Slowly they continued their search, moving into the marsh area, but nothing happened. As soon as they came to dry land again, they got another hit.

Tirill started digging. It was tough going, because the ground was so hard. Trampled underfoot for hundreds of years, thought Max.

Frustrated, she kept hacking at the ground.

"Be careful," he admonished her and received a furious look in reply.

Suddenly he heard the sound of metal striking metal. This time it had to be something bigger.

"There," she said, setting down the trowel.

"What is it?"

"I have no idea."

She picked up a clump of dirt the size of her fist. A slender pin was sticking out of it, and Max saw at once that it was made of metal. It looked old.

"This dirt is hard as rock," she said. "Let's go over there and see if we can open it up."

They sat down on a flat patch of ground, and Tirill continued to work at the clump. Cautiously she pried the tip of her trowel into the dirt. It turned out to be more efficient if she set it on the ground. After a few precise jabs, the clump split apart. Sticking out of one half was an object instantly recognizable as some sort of clasp.

Tirill threw that half of the clump against the ground, and it opened up. The object fell out with hardly any dirt left on it.

It was definitely a clasp, circular in shape. A pin stuck out a good distance beyond the circle and was presumably used to fasten the clasp to a cloak or some other garment. Max picked up the clasp, holding it carefully between his thumb and index finger.

All the details became remarkably clear when he studied them under the loupe. The clasp itself resembled the letter "c," which had almost become an "o" but not quite. Both ends were decoratively formed. When he looked closer, he uncharacteristically swore: "Damn!"

"What is it?"

He handed Tirill the loupe. She wiped the sweat from her eyes and leaned over their discovery. Max could tell the exact instant when she realized what she was holding in her hand.

"Jesus . . . ," she whispered and stared at him.

Then she turned back to take another look at the clasp that was not quite a closed circle. Each end of it was shaped like a dragon head.

FOR THE SECOND TIME IN TWO DAYS, Max and Tirill were lying on their backs in the heather, staring up at the blue summer sky. The buzzing of insects was the only sound in the hot, torpid afternoon. Actually it was evening by now, getting close to 6:00.

"How old do you think the clasp is?" asked Max.

"More than a thousand years. Or maybe not. That type of ornamentation was used well into the Christian era."

"Even after the Reformation?"

"I don't think so. But the style was really popular again from the late 1800s into the early twentieth century. It might be a replica from that earlier time period."

For a moment neither of them spoke. Again the only sound was the buzzing insects.

"You know what? Since we're here anyway, why don't we try searching the surrounding area?" said Max, sitting up. "Let's use the metal detector for a while longer. There are still several hours of daylight left."

IT WASN'T THAT EASY to use the metal detector when they didn't have a defined area to limit their search. Max made a few brief attempts, without results. Tirill went off on her own, clambering over a knoll right next to the marsh. The way she moved was not something a grown-up could ever learn. Only a childhood spent climbing on rocks could instill that sort of agility.

Max went over to the spring and stared down at the motionless black water. The thought of how deep it was caused a wave of fear to surge inside him, but he forced it back down and began using the metal detector to search around the edge.

Right next to the big slab of stone, he got a hit.

"Can you bring the trowel over here?" he called.

Tirill came over and squatted down beside him.

"There . . . right next to the stone," he told her.

It didn't take long before the trowel struck something hard. Tirill removed the last of the dirt with her hands and pulled up a small object.

"It's a knife," she concluded. "But the hilt has rotted away."

The blade was long and looked like the kind used more for a weapon than for a utilitarian purpose.

They sat down on the stone slab. Tirill cautiously pressed her thumb against the tip of the knife.

"I wonder what this was used for," she murmured.

Sixty

THE FOLLOWING DAY Max was sitting in the library in Dalen with a stack of books on local history on the table. Dalen and Eidsborg were centrally located in the area of Telemark that had produced a large part of Norway's treasure trove of folktales and legends. Many of the books contained these stories, but so far he hadn't found anything more about the devil's wedding ring. He did find a facsimile edition of Pastor Witzøe's topographical account from 1722—the same one that Peter Schram had referred to in his note. The book mentioned only briefly the supposed existence of a circle on the forest floor near a spring, and it was there that the devil had dropped his wedding ring. Nothing about the sheriff who had been invited to the wedding in hell. Tellev Sustugu claimed to have heard the legend in prison, from a man who had died long ago. But of course he could have been lying. It was impossible to know for sure where he'd heard the legend.

Another thought now occurred to Max. What if Tellev had made up the whole story about the sheriff and the wedding? He'd made it abundantly clear that he was afraid of Jørgen Homme. The legend could have been his way of trying to tell Max something without saying more than he should. Max had responded by questioning how an old legend could have anything to do with a sheriff for whom he'd personally worked. Sustugu was clearly annoyed by this reaction. Max hadn't thought about this before, but that part could have been something Tellev had made up on the fly, as a way of formulating his fear. What was it he'd said? *What if the devil's ring didn't evaporate after all? What if the sheriff kept it and became immortal?*

But what did that mean?

He looked up and spied a familiar hairstyle in between two bookshelves. Julia Bergmann gave him a hesitant smile. It looked like she'd been standing there, waiting for him to notice her. Max got up and went over to shake her hand. The pastor glanced around, as if to make sure no one was listening.

"How strange that I'd run into you right now," she said in a low voice. Her German pronunciation sounded so pleasant to his ears.

"Oh?"

"Uh-huh. . . ." She was about to say something else, but changed her mind.

According to Tirill, Julia had said she didn't dare follow up on her suspicion that the ghost in the church was anything but a ghost. Yet she'd also said that she hoped Max and Tirill would continue to investigate the matter. When she had spoken to Tirill, she emphasized that she had seen the ghost three nights before Midsummer. Was she trying to entice us to go to the stave church on that particular night? Max thought. It was only hours away.

That was probably why Julia was hesitating now. She couldn't know that Tirill had told him about their conversation.

"You're . . . a man of many talents, aren't you?" She gave him a searching glance from behind the wing of blond hair draped over one eye.

"If you say so."

"And presumably you're here in Telemark to make use of your talents. Among other things, you're trying to find out as much as possible about Knut Abrahamsen's death. Since he was your friend and colleague, I mean."

"How do you know that?"

For a moment she seemed at a loss for words. "Oh, er, Johannes Liom told me. The thing is . . ." Again she glanced around. "I know something about what happened on the night Abrahamsen drowned."

"What do you know?" he asked sharply.

"Please, not here. It's sensitive information. Could we go someplace more private?"

A FEW MINUTES LATER they were sitting in Max's rental car, in back of the library, where no one would see them.

"Did you know that the Catholic Church is not the only religion that offers confession?" she asked.

"Yes, I know that."

"Well, lots of people don't. It's one of the services of the Norwegian Church that isn't well publicized. But occasionally I hear confessions. In those situations, my pledge of confidentiality is absolutely binding. Even if it's in conflict with Norwegian law."

"Are you saying that you might be willing to make an exception?"

"I'm not about to reveal who told me this, since it occurred during a confession, but I feel strongly that you ought to know what I learned. It has to do with an old woman who is in the habit of waking in the middle of the night and going out, wearing only her nightgown. A couple of times, the police have had to step in. One fine day—or rather, one fine night—it may be the death of her, but everyone has to die sometime, and she's a very old woman. Sometimes this woman tells stories that not everyone believes. It could be that she mixes up the past and the present. I can't deny that, and you'll have to take it into consideration when you hear what she told me yesterday when she came to my office and asked me to hear her confession.

"She said that she'd gone out for a walk on the night Knut Abrahamsen drowned. As she was on her way toward the bridge, she caught sight of someone standing near the railing with one hand held out. As if he were blessing the water, she said. On the other side of the bridge, two cars were parked at the side of the road. It was night, but the sky was just starting to lighten. It's an hour when there's very little going on in Dalen, to put it mildly. Suddenly the other person caught sight of the woman, and he let go of something he must have been holding the whole time. That had to be why he was holding out his hand like that. The old woman said the object struck the water with a plop. That's all she saw, because she turned around and hurried back home as fast as she could go. Which probably wasn't that fast, but anyway."

Julia Bergmann turned to look at Max. "I thought this might be of interest to you," she said.

Max knew what the stranger had dropped into the water: Knut's car key. He wasn't sure why, but that had to be what the old woman saw. That's why the key was found in the river, and not on Knut's body. It was actually that detail—the sight of the person on the bridge dropping something into the river—that made him believe the woman's story.

"When she heard about Knut Abrahamsen, and how his car was found parked in the same spot where she'd seen the two cars, her conscience started to bother her. She realized she might have seen something connected to the drowning. Yesterday she couldn't stand it any longer, so she came to me to confess. She viewed it as a sin that she hadn't said anything, since a man had drowned on that night."

"But why didn't she go to the police instead of coming to you?" asked Max.

"Well, that's the thing . . . ," said Julia. It looked like she wasn't sure whether to say anything more.

"What is it?"

"She had a good reason for choosing a pastor over the police. Because this was no ordinary person on the bridge."

"No ordinary person? What do you mean?"

"It was the ghost."

Max sighed. "Clearly she was mistaken. Maybe the person was wearing a jacket with a hood."

"That's what I said too, but the old woman was insistent. As a young girl she once saw the ghost outside the church in Eidsborg. She never told anyone about that, because she didn't want to seem superstitious. But she told me it was the exact same figure she saw on the night that Abrahamsen died. The same long monk's robe with a pointed hood and wide sleeves. She was a hundred percent positive about that. It was the monk standing there, dropping something into the water."

Max leaned back against the headrest and closed his eyes. It was possible to track down murderers and get them convicted, but what could be done with a ghost?

Sixty-One

A T 3:00 TIRILL PACKED UP and left the library. On her way out, she passed Henrik Thue, who was talking with somebody from the administrative staff. He gave her a slight nod, and she nodded stiffly in return.

She found it physically painful to take the turn toward the cabin on Lifjell when she came to the roundabout. She missed Magnus more and more with every passing day. Her longing for her son sometimes took the form of a palpable absence close to her body, in the place where he should have been. Other times it was an aching sensation somewhere between her stomach and her heart.

But she wanted to finish what they'd started before she moved back to her apartment. She had decided to spend tonight inside the Eidsborg stave church. It was on this night last year that Julia Bergmann had seen the monk. Yet Tirill realized she'd have to do this without telling Fjellanger, who thought the pastor might be setting a trap for them.

It wouldn't do any good to hide someplace nearby in the hope of catching a glimpse of the ghost outside the church. If she did that, she knew what she would see. A cloaked figure carrying something wrapped in a blanket. But inside the church itself, whoever it was would have to turn on a light to see anything at night. If she was lucky, Tirill would then discover who it was.

One way or another, she'd find a way to get inside the church. The main thing was not to let on to Fjellanger what she was planning.

HE WAS SITTING in a deck chair outside the cabin, wearing the dark blue Florida baseball cap and writing in his little black notebook. When he heard Tirill approaching, he closed the book and stood up. He always did this when she came back from work. Stood up to greet her.

"How was your day?" he asked.

"Fine. But I miss Magnus," she said, plopping down in the chair that was now hers.

"I went to Dalen today," said Fjellanger. "And I ran into Julia Bergmann, who told me something she'd heard in confession."

"What?" exclaimed Tirill in surprise. "Is that allowed?"

"Hmm . . . Well, it's not illegal, though I don't think it happens very often. Even though she was careful to keep the person's identity anonymous."

"So, what did she tell you?"

As Fjellanger gave her a detailed account of the conversation he'd had with the pastor, Tirill felt her own conviction grow even stronger. The so-called monk was obviously at the center of everything. If she could find out who was wearing that hooded cloak, the case might really open up.

"At first I thought the detail about something being dropped into the water was proof the whole story was true," said Fjellanger. "Because it's totally consistent with the fact that Knut's car key wasn't found on his body. And I'm still positive that her description of the person dropping something over the railing is real. But the part about the ghost? I don't know. This is the second time in a matter of days that Julia has talked to us about the monk. First you and then me. I'm afraid that in both instances it's because she wants us to show up outside the Eidsborg stave church tonight. Of course, there might be a completely different reason. . . . I'm just not sure. But I know we shouldn't risk it," he said.

"I totally agree," said Tirill. "That would be insane."

Sixty-Two

MAKING STEEP DIVES, common swifts sliced through the sky-blue space above the stave church. The intense summer heat pressed the tar out through the pores of the wood and caused it to bubble on the exterior surface of the building.

It was almost six in the evening, but two buses were still parked out front. Some lightly clad Dutch tourists, undoubtedly the last visitors of the day, were on their way in, and those who had already taken the tour were snapping photographs of the church outside.

Careful not to draw attention, Tirill slipped in among those entering the building. As soon as they crossed the threshold, their voices dropped. Darkness hung heavily in all the corners, and the guide switched on a flashlight so they could see properly.

She hoped Fjellanger still thought she was on her way to visit Magnus at her mother's place. He wasn't happy when she told him where she was going. "But that's one reason we're staying out here in the cabin," he'd said. She knew full well what he meant. It was a matter of her son's safety, but she had to lie if she was going to carry out her plan. She had also lied to her mother when she persuaded her to trade cars for a day or two. She told her she needed a bigger vehicle so she could drive some things up to the cabin. In reality, she didn't want anybody to recognize her car if they saw it parked near the stave church.

As the evening wore on, Fjellanger was bound to figure out where she'd really gone, but by then it would be too late.

In the background Tirill heard the guide describing in English the Nikuls reenactment. "Some people in Eidsborg didn't approve of this modern use of the statue, and the play took place only twice," he was saying.

Still moving as quietly as possible—pretending to be a more or less invisible hanger-on with the Dutch group—Tirill sat down on a pew a short distance away from the others. When she was sure that no one was looking, she slipped off the pew and crouched down, listening. Nobody seemed to have noticed her little disappearing act.

Slowly, as if she were a cat sneaking up on prey, she proceeded to sink farther down onto the floor—one soundless paw at a time. The muscles in her arms and legs trembled, but she was in good physical condition. Soon she was stretched out on the cool, wide planks of the floor. There she lay, listening to the guide talking. After a moment she began squirming her way, centimeter by centimeter, underneath the pew, until she was hidden in the almost total darkness.

Now it was just a matter of making sure nobody noticed that one person was missing when they turned to leave. For several long moments she hardly dared breathe into the echoing church acoustics. At last the guide finished up his spiel, and then she heard the sound of many footsteps moving away.

After the tourists had left the church, she still wasn't sure whether the guide might have stayed behind. Maybe he needed to take care of certain things, since it was the last tour of the day. Tirill listened for any creaks coming from the old floorboards, but heard nothing.

A few minutes later she began to wonder whether this was really such a good idea. When the guide locked the door, she wouldn't be able to get out until someone opened it again in the morning. The first tour was at 10:00.

But before she could change her mind, she heard a key turn in the lock, making a sound that reminded her of dark dungeons in old movies.

WORRIED THAT SOMEONE MIGHT RETURN to do some cleaning or tidying up, she waited nearly two hours before she dared crawl out from under the pew.

Even though it was still a long time until sunset, the darkness inside the church made it hard to see many details in the room. So the first thing she did was search for a light switch, but she soon realized there weren't any. Of course not. She reminded herself that the guide had used a flashlight.

It was going to be a very dark night.

And a long one. Especially if nothing happened.

She went over to where Nikuls stood on a small plinth jutting out from the wall. She got out the little flashlight she'd brought along and shone the beam on the statue. His beard, painted gold, gleamed in the light. His bishop's cap cast a tall shadow on the wall behind him. Was this what Knut Abrahamsen had caught a glimpse of in the trunk of the sheriff's car?

Tirill reached out her hand to touch the statue. It felt smooth and slightly oily, as if from the hands of so many people hoping for help of some kind. The moment she moved the flashlight beam away from the saint, he disappeared into the shadows again, and she could make out only the outline of the statue.

Where would be the best hiding place inside the church if something was about to happen? It had to be somewhere she wouldn't be seen yet would be able to observe what went on. As far as she could tell, there was only one place that was suitable.

She went up the few steps leading to the pulpit and discovered there actually was one electric lamp in the church. It was there so the pastor would be able to see when she read her sermon.

Tirill switched it on. The light shone like an overturned bowl on the open Bible.

"Now the Lord had prepared a great fish to swallow Jonah," she read in a low voice. "And Jonah was in the belly of the fish three days and three nights."

Locked in as she was in the ancient building, she almost felt as if she too had been swallowed by a great fish. Suddenly she recalled what Gunstein Liom had said: that the giant trout in Lake Bandak and the Tokke River were a unique breed, descendants of the sea trout that had been trapped when the ice melted and the land rose. Fish from the Ice Age.

A little farther down on the page, she read, "Those who regard worthless idols forsake their own Mercy."

What did "Mercy" mean in this case? Compassion? Benevolence? Was that what happened to those who had secretly worshipped Nikuls? Had they lost their sense of mercy?

Tirill turned off the lamp and sat down on the floor of the pulpit. She didn't think anything would happen until after midnight. That was when Julia Bergmann had seen the monk. That was also when the old woman claimed to have seen the monk standing on the bridge, dropping something into the Tokke River. In general, between 2:00 and 4:00 in the morning would be the best time for anyone engaged in some sort of nefarious activity. During those hours everybody else was usually sound asleep.

If, that is, anyone actually decides to show up here at all, she thought. Maybe she'd just end up waiting inside the silent and empty stave church until the first group of tourists appeared at 10:00 in the morning.

She had nearly fifteen hours until then.

She sat on the floor of the pulpit for close to an hour, but finally realized it was pointless to spend the whole night in that spot. The space was much too cramped. Her knees and back were aching, and she was getting tired, but it wouldn't be a good idea to let down her guard.

Tirill left the pulpit and once again stood on the floor of the church. The sun was still bright outdoors, but there were only two small windows high up on the south wall of the nave and one that was even smaller in the choir. A pale light came through the biggest window to shine on the altar, while the nave, where the congregation usually sat, was very dark. She had to use her flashlight to see anything properly. From the walls the painted figures stared down into the room. Both women and men, some of them on horseback. Their clothing and hairstyles reminded Tirill of medieval ballads.

Above the entrance to the choir, the beam of her flashlight focused on the humble, gray crucifix, which she knew was as old as the building itself. The thought of all the parishioners who had sat here looking up at the cross over the past 750 years filled her with an inexplicable anxiety.

Their eyes. Their hopes and fears. It was as if they lived on in the old crucifix.

None of the pews was wide enough to use as a hiding place. She realized the floor was her best option, so she lay down in the center aisle. The rough, old floorboards weren't half bad as a resting place. For a moment she considered taking off her jacket to use as a pillow, but she was afraid she'd get cold. She'd just have to accept that her hair would get dirty. Besides, it wouldn't be wise to get too comfortable. She needed to stay awake.

Sixty-Three

WHEN SHE AWOKE, Tirill couldn't figure out where she was at first. She knew only that she wasn't at home, because it smelled different, and she was lying on something hard and cold. Then she remembered, and panic instantly set in. She sat up and fumbled around for the flashlight but couldn't find it. The church was pitch dark.

She dug her cell phone out of her pants pocket and touched the display.

Oh God, it was past 2:00 a.m.! In the pale light from her phone, she located the flashlight and switched it on. Then she turned off her phone completely. Holding the flashlight, she went up the narrow steps to the pulpit, which was otherwise reserved solely for the pastor's use.

Something came rushing at her at top speed. A piece of black night grazed her face like a gust of wind and then disappeared.

A bat.

For all she knew, there could be an entire colony of bats hanging from the overhead rafters during the daytime, but when night came, they let go and flew around inside the stave church. Flapping their way over the rows of pews, over the altar and baptismal font. Around the head of the saint statue. In and out of one or more small openings in the shingled roof. A nocturnal dance that no one ever saw.

Suddenly an avalanche of bats slid down from the rafters and began flying chaotically around the room.

"No, no, no," she whispered, reaching up to cover her head with her hands.

Then she noticed a different sound. Someone was unlocking the church door. A key scraped and rattled in the crude lock. Her heart began pounding so hard she felt sick.

She switched off her flashlight and crouched down in her hiding place. Slowly the church door opened, making a sound that seemed as old as the building itself, followed by a few moments of silence, as if somebody was standing in the opening, listening. Then the heavy door closed, making that same long, drawn-out creaking.

Huddled on the floor of the pulpit, Tirill could still see that a light had been switched on. Feeling as if every movement might release an explosion, she cautiously peered over the edge of the pulpit.

She was looking at a gray figure wearing a cloak with a pointed hood, the face hidden in the dark.

The monk.

But unlike most ghosts, he was holding a flashlight, and the floorboards creaked under his feet.

She had expected the monk to stop just inside the door, where Nikuls stood on his plinth, but he was already halfway up the center aisle. Tirill crouched back down, afraid of being seen, even though there was little chance of that unless he shone the flashlight directly at her. She tried to breathe as quietly as possible, though it seemed to her that each breath filled the entire space of the small church.

Even worse was the fact that the footsteps had now stopped only a couple of meters away.

For a brief moment all was quiet. Then a sharp, metallic click echoed off the walls of the empty church. A few seconds later she heard another, similar click. Followed by two more. Then came the sound of something heavy and hard falling onto the floor. A pew? She couldn't resist finding out. Once again she cautiously peered over the edge of the pulpit. The church was in total darkness except for the small space right below her, where the cloaked figure was shining the beam of his flashlight at the floor. Tirill barely managed to suppress a cry of alarm when she realized what had happened. The monk had removed one of the wide floorboards and toppled it over. That's what she'd heard. Now he was standing there, looking down into the opening. He didn't seem scared or on high alert.

There was something calm and serene about his whole figure. Tirill had the feeling he must have done this many times before.

Hardly daring to breathe, she watched as the man in the cloak stepped down into the opening. It looked as if he were sitting on something. Only his shoulders and the pointed hood remained visible. Then he disappeared completely.

Was he planning to lie under the church floor, like a vampire that goes into hiding as the sun comes up? No. She soon saw movement again. But she didn't dare continue spying on the monk, because the beam of his flashlight was now pointed almost straight up, and it might end up pointing at her head, which was sticking up over the edge of the pulpit.

Only when she heard the big floorboard fall into place did she dare risk peeking out again. The cloaked monk was on his knees, holding some sort of long tool that he stuck into the crack between the planks. He pushed and wiggled it until there was a loud click. Then he moved over and repeated the procedure. It had to be some kind of locking mechanism that required this strange-looking key, which was at least half a meter in length.

But that was not what caused Tirill's heart to pound even harder. Standing next to the man was an object that looked to be about a meter tall. It seemed to be the figure of a person, although no details were visible, since it was outside the flashlight beam.

When the monk finished locking the floorboard into place, he took out a blanket that he must have carried inside his cloak and wrapped it around the object. But just before the blanket went on, the flashlight beam lit up the object for a second. Tirill saw a dark wooden figure with a strange, pointed head. Then it was hidden away.

Now the ghost of the Eidsborg stave church did what he was known for doing. He picked up the figure wrapped in a blanket and carried it out of the church. When she heard the door being locked, Tirill sank onto the floor of the pulpit. She felt as if she'd been holding her breath the whole time the monk had been inside, and at last she was able to relax.

But it didn't take long before she left the pulpit and began inspecting the floor of the church. No matter how carefully she looked as she shone her flashlight on the cracks, she couldn't see anything out of the ordinary.

What she did find was the locket she always wore around her neck. The chain had broken, and it must have slipped off when she fell asleep on the floor. Tirill opened the locket and ran her fingertip over the tiny wisp of hair from her son.

Then she switched on her cell phone and sent a brief text message to Fjellanger.

Sixty-Four

MAX WAS STANDING A SHORT DISTANCE AWAY from the group of Germans waiting to go inside the stave church. They couldn't go in until the first group finished its tour and came out. Now he heard the guide speaking German as he thanked the participants, and then they all stepped outside. Among them he glimpsed the extraordinarily disheveled head of hair belonging to Tirill. Amazing that she managed to join the group without being noticed, he thought.

She squinted at the sunlight as if she'd been underground for days. Then she caught sight of Max. He got ready to say something funny, as a way of signaling that he wasn't mad. Of course he wasn't. She'd definitely taken a big risk, but she'd also come away with a big reward.

He gave her a friendly smile as she approached. "You look like somebody who's—"

"I have to pee!" Tirill snapped, striding right past him.

Max turned around to watch her go. Midway between the church and the museum, she set off running.

When she came back a few minutes later, she was in a better mood, and she'd also done something to her hair. It now looked more or less normal. Which meant like a meticulously styled coif that had exploded. Even with dark circles under her eyes and the seven stitches above her left eyebrow, she still looked good. All charged up and raring to go.

Given that they had each arrived by car and would have to drive back to Bø separately, they stood and talked for a while before leaving.

"What do you think it was?" asked Max, even though he'd already asked the same question on the phone a few hours ago.

And she gave him the same answer. "A god."

"You mean a house god?"

"I'm not sure. But it seems strange to store something like that in a church."

"The whole situation is strange, no matter what type of god it is. If it's a god at all, that is," he added.

"In any case, that little demon was not of this world. That much I can tell you."

THAT EVENING THEY SAT IN THE CABIN, each of them studying their respective copies of Peter Schram's research.

On the table lay the gun that Tycho Abrahamsen had brought with him to Dalen and Max had subsequently confiscated. Originally the gun had belonged to Knut. That may have been why Max found its presence so compelling. It seemed almost alive. As if his dead friend's representative were right there on the table.

Once again Max read about the concept of the genius loci. The spirit of the place. What he read was very similar to what he'd seen in Henrik Thue's books, but Schram and Thue differed on one point: whereas Thue only hinted at the possibility of an earlier fertility cult near Eidsborg Tarn, Schram seemed to have made that a central focus of his doctoral dissertation. It looked as if he thought Nikuls hadn't merely developed into a genius loci but had been one from the very first day, because he was part of an already established tradition. The men of the church allowed it to continue, with a light coating of Christianity, rather than lose the battle against the old ways. They had been willing to adapt.

What had Tirill actually seen in the night? Max wondered. What was that figure hidden under the floor of the ancient church?

Darkness began to fall as they kept reading, but neither of them took any notice. For the first time Max felt very close to the young

academic who had disappeared on June 23, 1985. Even his meeting with Peter's widow hadn't brought him this near. Although
the manuscript seemed somewhat chaotic, Schram's keen interest in his material was evident in every sentence. And it was not
just a matter of professional dedication on his part; it was a way
of viewing the world. A bold and expansive view that allowed for
what was small and local to be linked to the bigger picture, and vice
versa. For instance, Schram seemed to see a connection between
something the Roman historian Tacitus wrote and the deep love
the Eidsborg farmers felt toward their Nikuls. Tacitus recounted how tribes in the far north of Europe worshipped a goddess
they called Nerthus. He described, among other things, a ritual in
which the priests walked in a long procession carrying the idol and
then lowered it into a body of water to cleanse it, along with the
cart on which the figure had been conveyed and the clothing the
figure wore.

In Schram's opinion, this might explain the strange phenomenon of a saint figure being lowered into water to be cleansed, as
was done with Nikuls at Eidsborg Tarn—even though this was an
unusual custom when it came to saint figures.

Schram further wrote that Nerthus was a fertility goddess and
almost certainly a forerunner of the Nordic god Njord, who, even
though he was a male god, possessed many of the same traits.
Eventually Njord was ousted, so to speak, by his son Freyr—one
of the most popular gods in the Viking period—who was also a
fertility god.

"This is interesting stuff," Max said to Tirill, who seemed equally
engrossed. "By the way, don't you think it'd be a good idea to put
the groceries away?"

"Can't you do it?" she replied, indifferently.

Max got up, stretched his stiff muscles, and began putting away
the milk, juice, eggs, lunchmeat, and fruit in the fridge. Finally the
only thing left in the grocery bag was a box of tampons.

"Where do these go?" he asked.

"In the bathroom, of course," she said tersely before turning
back to the papers she was reading.

Max set the tampons on the shelf in the bathroom and went back
into the living room.

"Do you happen to know anything about Njord and Freyr?" he asked.

Tirill looked up at him. "Fertility gods. Father and son, if I'm not mistaken. Wait a sec and I'll do a search."

Max sat down next to her and watched as she pulled up an article about the Nordic gods on the Internet.

"As a fertility god, Freyr was depicted with an erect phallus," she read. "The ceremonies included songs and rites that offended the early Christians, who condemned the cult as obscene. The fertility cult was associated with both death and blood, against a backdrop of ritual sexual intercourse as part of a higher mysticism. The name Freyr means 'Lord.'"

She paused and looked at Max.

"Go on."

"In the animal world, Freyr is associated with the pig, because the boar Slidrugtanne pulled his cart. It was supposedly customary to . . . sacrifice pigs' heads to Freyr."

Tirill spoke these last words in a voice that was hardly more than air, but Max heard what she said.

A that moment a sudden gust of wind blew the curtains in from the window, and the fresh night smell of the forest floor burst into the small cabin.

"Fear the Lord," whispered Tirill.

Sixty-Five

ONE MORE DAY UNTIL MIDSUMMER.
Nobody had prepared Tirill for what she was about to do tomorrow night. At the same time, she felt as if her whole life had been one long preparation for this. She thought about all those evenings she'd spent as a teenager sitting in the backseat of a car, riding up and down Bøgata while she tried to be like everybody else who never gave a thought to life's limitations. The feeling she'd had in school of never being seen, yet everyone always seemed to be looking at her. The dreams she'd had, huddled under the covers, about breaching the speed of sound in a fighter jet roaring over Bø and causing a sonic boom that simultaneously shattered the windows in all the houses and hot rods. Or of being a green-eyed girl with a fiddle, someone who could cast a spell over any boy she liked, enticing them one by one into a waterfall with her music, as she waited for them in the warm torrent.

All these things had been ways in which she'd prepared herself for the unprecedented and groundbreaking events that would soon occur. She settled herself more comfortably on the floor by the bed and cautiously stroked her son's soft hair. His grandmother must have washed his hair earlier in the day. Maybe he didn't make as much of a fuss about it when she did it.

Having Magnus had been the most important preparation of all. She felt an unbreakable force of will rise up like a dragon inside her, spewing fire at those who wanted to do her harm. That same dragon

246

also spewed fire on behalf of Magnus, since his own personal dragon still had many years ahead to take shape.

"At least you can't say that your mother shies away from anything," she whispered, keeping her voice low so she wouldn't wake him.

Then she quietly left the bedroom that used to be hers.

Her mother was standing in the hall, looking exasperated. "I can't understand what happened to the key to the front door," she said.

"Isn't it always on the shelf?"

"Yes, and I know it was there a couple of hours ago. I haven't touched it since."

"Do you have a spare key?"

"Sure."

Tirill shrugged. "Magnus is asleep," she said. "I think I'll go for a walk."

HER CHILDHOOD HOME wasn't far from her own apartment, and maybe she should have gone over there to make sure everything was OK at her place, but the idea wasn't appealing. Instead, she headed off in the opposite direction, toward the center of town. As she took the pedestrian walkway over the railroad bridge, a freight train came thundering past, making the whole bridge shudder under her feet. She leaned over the railing and looked down as one train car after another disappeared below until the last one passed by and only the motionless track remained.

Three teenage boys were sitting at a worn table in front of the fast-food joint, looking as if they were up to no good. Tirill recognized one of them. The boy's father had been of the same ilk— operating on a wavelength which meant that most human utterances were interpreted as declarations of war. He probably hadn't changed. The man's son glared at Tirill as he spat in her direction.

It was strange what ended up being passed on from one generation to the next.

She walked all the way up to the two churches. There, she found the grave of her great-great-grandmother and read the name and dates etched into the headstone. How young she was when she died. Yet she'd managed to have one child: Tirill's great-grandfather. And that was all it took for Tirill to be standing here tonight.

This woman, who had long since been reduced to dust and bones in the earth beneath her feet, had looked exactly like her. Whenever the woman had looked in a mirror, she had unknowingly been looking at the face of her descendant. And whenever Tirill looked at herself, she saw her great-great-grandmother. A face that had traveled through time. Someday Tirill would also be buried here, not far from her ancestor. Where would the face they shared end up next? Would a future descendant see a photograph of Tirill Vesterli and feel as if she'd lived before?

Tirill stood up and looked out at this place she called home—an intricate network of interconnections linking both the living and the dead.

Sixty-Six

MIDSUMMER. The small, rocky hill close to the marsh seemed a natural lookout post. When Max and Tirill reached the top, they had an almost unobstructed view of the circle and the spring. But they were also on view, and they couldn't rule out the possibility that someone below might catch sight of them. So Max picked up the ax he'd brought and walked across the crag to a slender pine tree, which he chopped down. He dragged it over to their lookout spot and then went back to fell a birch. Behind these two small trees lying across the edge of the hill, they had a good observation post.

The ground was nice and warm right now, but after sundown it would cool off quickly and they'd be glad to have the ground cloths they'd brought.

"We need to put our phones on vibrate," he said.

"No, let's switch them off altogether," Tirill replied. "I don't trust them. They might still ring."

"OK. That sounds sensible."

As soon as they did that, the silence all around them seemed even more intense.

The sun was approaching the mountain ridges in the west, flooding the landscape with a final, soft light, illuminating the dust motes and tiny insects that filled the forest air.

In Florida, darkness came swiftly after sunset, deep blue and filled with the singing of cicadas—as if a hood had been pulled down over the world. Here, it happened almost imperceptibly. Even after the disk of the sun disappeared below the horizon, bright daylight remained.

Although not quite.

Something had crept into the light. Something gray rose up from the ground and seeped out of the rocks and tree trunks. The marshy gully below changed from a glittery silver in the green grass to a duller, almost straw color, while the spring—that round eye of water—was as dark as ever. The flat stone slab became even grayer.

Tirill yawned and glanced at the wristwatch she'd borrowed from her mother. Usually she relied on her phone to tell the time. "Ten past ten," she said. "I think we should take turns keeping watch."

"I agree. How long should each shift be?"

"A couple of hours, so we'll have time to take a nap in between."

"A nap?" he said in surprise.

"We should at least try," she replied. "Can you take the first watch? I'm feeling really tired at the moment."

"Sure. You can take over at midnight."

HE KEPT HIS GAZE focused on the marsh. Had he ever done this before? No, this was definitely a first. Marshes didn't usually do anything interesting, so there was no need to keep them under surveillance.

This wasn't exactly what he'd thought his life would be like when he pictured cutting back on his work hours. He'd imagined opening a small used bookshop in the Florida Keys, where he and Ann would have a glass of wine over lunch and look forward to all the years still ahead.

Instead he was sitting here in the woods somewhere in the interior of Telemark, with a strange woman sleeping next to him as he kept his eyes on a marsh.

Was anyone going to show up? No, he thought. What sort of crazy dream had he entered with his eyes wide open? A dream in which he seriously believed that people worshipped a god who had been dead and forgotten for a thousand years. What had happened to his ability to think rationally? What had happened to allowing the truth to be his lodestar?

But this was where the star had led them! And they *had* used their capacity for logical, critical thought.

Yet they'd ended up here.

NOTHING HAPPENED FOR THE NEXT TWO HOURS, except that more gray seeped up from the ground and out of the stones and tree trunks. Around midnight it began to feel dark, though it wasn't yet impenetrable. Max could still distinguish the marsh from the surrounding woods.

"Tirill?" he whispered.

She turned over at once. Maybe she hadn't been asleep at all. "My turn?"

"Yes."

They kept their voices low, as if someone might be listening from behind a tree trunk.

"I'll wake you up in two hours," she said.

WHEN SHE WHISPERED IN HIS EAR, Max thought at first that Ann had forgotten her keys and was standing outside their house in Sarasota, impatiently ringing the doorbell. He'd been dreaming about her, and he sat up feeling an emptiness inside, in the place where she was no more.

It hadn't grown much darker. He listened for voices, or snapping twigs. But nothing broke the silence, not even the sounds of frogs or nocturnal insects, which he was used to hearing.

After a long time with nothing happening, he allowed himself a glance at his watch. It was 2:30 in the morning. Soon after, he noticed the sky beginning to lighten. The shortest night of the year was already edging toward day.

A sound!

A sound amid the great silence of the forest—so brief that he couldn't tell what it was. Maybe something moving.

Holding his breath, he listened again.

And then he clearly heard the voice of a man.

Sixty-Seven

J UST TO BE SAFE, Max placed his hand over Tirill's mouth as he
whispered in her ear. "Someone's coming," he told her.

She didn't reply, just rolled over and looked at him, wide-eyed.

Max was stretched out next to her so that they were both hidden
behind the two trees he'd felled and dragged over. He got out his
camera and found a suitable spot between some branches where he
could stick his telephoto lens. As he adjusted the focus and tried to
get the marsh as sharp as possible in the viewfinder, he again heard
someone speaking. A man again. Closer now.

Was it simply someone who happened to be walking past?
Maybe they'd been celebrating Midsummer at a nearby cabin—or
somewhere outdoors, for that matter—and were now on their way
home in the wee hours of the morning.

Tirill suddenly burrowed her fingers into his upper arm, and
he glanced up from the camera. At first he didn't see anything, but
Tirill signaled with her eyes where he should look.

That's when he saw something among the pines below. Four people were heading toward the marsh and spring. Wearing long gray
cloaks with the pointed hoods pulled well down over their faces,
they looked like they'd stepped straight out of the past. The person
in front was carrying something wrapped in a blanket. It was impossible to say what it was, based on its shape. Another person was
clearly wearing a backpack, also wrapped in a blanket. The object
had to have some heft to it, because it stuck up above the person's

head. Slung over the shoulder of the third person was a black trash bag that clearly had something inside.

Max felt an urge to pinch himself, but Tirill had already done that for him. Her fingers were still gripping his upper arm so hard that it hurt, which meant he had to be awake.

It was almost 3:00 in the morning. A time of day when nearly everyone was asleep. Perfect for carrying out some secret activity.

He raised the light-sensitive digital camera to his eye again, looking for the people in the viewfinder. The lens passed over thickets and rocks, their outlines still blurred in the dim light, but finally he found them. Four gray figures, moving slowly but purposefully. As if whatever they were doing was important, yet there was no rush.

The person in front stopped and set down what he was carrying. It was still wrapped in a blanket. He said something to the others, but Max couldn't make out his words. Then the man reached inside the black trash bag and lifted something out, setting it on his shoulder before walking into the marsh while the other three stayed where they were. Suddenly Max realized what the man was carrying. Through the telephoto lens he could clearly make out the flat snout and big ears. Since the person's face was hidden by the hood, it almost looked as if a pig were walking along on two legs. Max steeled himself and then snapped a photo. In the great silence, it sounded like a musket shot, but the man below calmly continued walking.

When he reached the spring, he placed the pig's head on the big flat stone.

An altar!

Tirill cautiously tugged at the camera, and Max handed it to her.

The other three people had sat down on the heather among the pine trees. It was impossible to tell whether they were men or women, because the cloaks were so loose, hiding all shape, and the hoods hid their faces.

The figure out in the marsh now straightened up and paused for a moment next to the pig's head. Then he turned on his heel and went back to join the others. He moved at the same pace as before, unhurried and purposeful. Max was certain it was a man.

When he reached the others, he tore the blanket off what he'd been carrying when they arrived.

Even without the telephoto lens, Max could see what it was. A dark figure, probably carved out of wood, of a man kneeling. The head seemed strangely elongated and pointed, as if he were wearing a conical cap or helmet. There was no doubt in Max's mind that this was what Tirill had seen in the church. And what Knut had caught a glimpse of in the trunk of the sheriff's car. Nor was there any doubt it was a male god. The figure had an erection that was clearly visible, even from this distance.

"Oh my God," whispered Tirill.

"Is that what you saw in the church?"

"Yes."

"Let me have the camera."

Reluctantly she gave up the magnified view that the camera offered so Max could get a good look.

Now the man picked up the figure, holding it at waist height as he began walking. The three others followed, each with their hands on the shoulders of the person in front. They moved slowly, with measured and deliberate steps.

"They're walking around the circle," whispered Tirill.

Max and Tirill were finally witnessing with their own eyes how the legend of the devil's wedding ring had been born. Here was the answer that both Peter Schram and Cecilie Wiborg had been searching for.

This was the answer they most likely found, thought Max. And they paid for it with their lives.

As the cloaked figures crossed the narrow marsh, they began to sing. It wasn't possible to hear the words, but the tone sounded strange, as if it came from another world. And most likely it did. The words being sung down below probably stemmed from a time when people buried their dead in barrow mounds and longships sailed along the coast.

For a moment Max forgot to take any pictures, but as the procession turned back toward the marsh, he resumed snapping photos. After making their way around the whole circle, the procession started around again, but this time the song sounded different. Maybe new elements were added each time around. Max thought he heard a woman's voice, and after listening intently, he was almost positive that the group consisted of three men and one woman.

The man in front held out the carved figure the whole time they were walking. The phallus and pig's head indicated it was the figure of Freyr.

Max strained to recognize any of the voices, but the strange nature of the song made it impossible to place them in his own world.

The glow of the rising sun was visible above the mountain ridges to the east. As if in reply, mist had started rising up from the marsh. The hems of the cloaks had to be heavy with moisture. Still they sang in that strange monotone. There seemed to be more and more new verses. Max recalled the video he'd seen of the Nikuls reenactment. In both instances a wooden figure was carried around a body of water. In both instances a song was chanted. Yet here there was no hint of all the pomp and circumstance associated with the Catholic Church. No censers or colorful robes. Only cloaks as gray as the ground, and a song that sounded as if it had risen from the smell of cold marsh and the first light above the crowns of the pine trees.

The language reminded Max of Icelandic.

As the first rays of sunlight reached the spring, glinting off the water, they stopped singing. They exchanged a few words, but Max couldn't hear what was said, given that they were on the far side of the marsh, standing among the heather-covered tussocks. Still holding out the figure of the god, the leader moved out into the marsh. There, he lowered the figure halfway into the water and began splashing the god. This went on for about a minute. Then he lifted the figure out of the water, set it down, and went back to join the others.

Max was filled with a combination of nausea and awe as he looked down at the dark wooden figure sticking out of the grass, wrapped in the morning mist, with a pig's head nearby. Nausea at the thought that this bizarre drama was behind Knut's death—as well as the deaths of Peter Schram and Cecilie Wiborg. He was certain of that. Yet he also felt a sense of awe at seeing this wooden idol, more than a thousand years old. And at the incomprehensible fact that this ancient ritual had survived to the present day.

On the other side of the marsh, the four people were now standing close together, their hooded heads lowered, as they apparently spoke quietly.

After a moment one of them walked alone over to the wooden

god next to the spring. There, he stopped. Or was it a woman? Impossible to tell. The gray figure was turned away from Max and Tirill. Slowly the person's arms raised up, pointing like the hands of a clock to the numbers 2 and 10.

With a quick movement of the right hand, a crystal-clear tone rang through the air. Max remembered seeing a tiny bell fastened to a ring that looked like it would be worn on someone's finger. It had been lying in a drawer in Åse's office on the night they'd made love. So that had to be her, standing there down below, wearing a gray cloak that hid her face.

Max heard again the despair in her voice when she'd said, *"I've never felt so used in all my life!"* Yet she was the one who had been using him all along. She had probably known who he was from day one. She'd made a point of drawing him close, so she could find out what he was up to. At the same time, she'd tried to shift his suspicions toward her husband. And she'd done a good job of that.

Yet she was an overwhelming sight, standing there with her arms raised. Now she started to sing. Her whole being seemed to radiate love. Love toward what she was receiving and allowing to stream through her. Toward the rays of sunlight warming her and the mist wrapping around her like gossamer. Toward the forest with all its creatures. Toward the water in the spring, which never ceased coursing up from the underground depths. Standing there in the sun-pierced mist, she looked like a goddess.

But Max wasn't forgetting the fact that these people in their medieval garb were responsible for three deaths. They were the ones who had killed Knut. He stuck the gun into his waistband, making sure that his sweater hid the grip.

The song faded. Åse slowly lowered her arms and bowed her head as she stood before Freyr. The mist was so thick now that the lower half of her body was barely visible. The same was true of the dark wooden figure.

All of a sudden she seemed to sit down on the marshy ground, only to stand up again the next instant. What was she doing? Max stared so hard his eyes stung. Something had changed. Now she was gray only from her head to her waist. The lower part of her was whiter than the mist enshrouding her.

She had lifted up her cloak. And she had nothing on underneath!

At that moment Max realized what was about to happen. She crouched down with the god figure between her thighs. It was impossible to tell for certain whether she was touching the phallus, but that's what she seemed to be doing. Then she began to move, as if straddling a man. Slowly at first, until she was in the proper position, and then faster.

Max quickly took a few photos of the ritual intercourse playing out below in the marsh. Then he removed the memory card from the camera and stuck it in his pants pocket.

Åse's movements were getting faster. And wilder. The tiny bell rang nonstop. She uttered loud, gull-like screeches in time to the grinding motion of her pelvis. Faster and faster until her cries merged into one long, crystal-clear scream. It sounded as if the scream was rising up from the spring itself, getting louder until it shattered from inside and ended in a guttural moaning. Then she collapsed and lay in a motionless gray heap in the middle of the circle, the devil's wedding ring.

Max shifted his attention to the men standing among the trees. There were only two now. At that instant he heard the unmistakable sound of a dry twig snapping nearby under someone's foot. He spun around, fumbling to pull the gun out from under his sweater. But the cloaked figure shook his head in warning as he pointed a double-barreled shotgun at Max.

Sixty-Eight

HE'D FORGOTTEN to keep an eye on the other three. Apparently Tirill had forgotten too. And now they would have to pay the price. The man walking behind them didn't say a word as he aimed the shotgun at their backs. If he fired both barrels at once, he could undoubtedly shoot them both.

Åse had now joined the other two standing among the pines. Out in the marsh Freyr's pointed cap stuck up above the grass. The severed pig's head lying on the stone was an ominous symbol of what was to come.

Max cast a sidelong glance at Tirill. Her face was pale, her expression somber. He had no idea what was going on inside her head.

She should have done what he'd suggested and stopped while they were more or less ahead of the game. Now it was too late. The only thing she could do was pray to God that she'd get to see her son again.

Finally, after taking what seemed their last step—and no doubt it was—they reached the others. The man who had taken them captive handed the shotgun to one of his companions while he kept hold of Knut Abrahamsen's pistol. All of them stood with their heads slightly bowed, the hoods pulled forward.

Only a few meters away lay the black trash bag that had held the pig's head. There was something else there, hidden by a blanket. Probably the backpack that one of the participants had carried.

"Hi, Åse," said Max.

Tirill gave him a surprised look.

Åse Enger Thue pushed back her hood as the bell on her little finger rang. The face Max saw was the same one he had nearly fallen in love with, yet it was different. He was reminded of something, but he couldn't think what it was. Her expression was fixed and remote, as if she were not actually present. Even when he looked into her eyes, he couldn't make contact. It was as if she were looking inward instead of outward.

Her expression scared him more than the two guns aimed at him and Tirill.

"All right . . . ," said the man holding the shotgun, and he pushed back his hood as well.

The usual glint in Johannes Liom's eye had been replaced by a heavy seriousness. "The two of you showed up, right on cue."

The other cloaked figures now pushed back their hoods. Lars and Gunstein Liom. Johannes's son and father.

"Johannes . . . ," murmured Tirill.

"So, what's the deal with that locket?" he asked her. "Is there something inside it?"

"What?" whispered Tirill.

"Don't you realize I knew you were there the other night? In the church, I mean. You were so scared that I could hear you breathing. Well, I heard somebody breathing. And I wasn't quite sure what to do. But I was in luck. I saw a locket on the floor, and I knew who it belonged to. So then I knew who was hiding somewhere nearby. And there was something else I knew: that the two of you were never going to give up. If you'd figured out about the monk, then you'd soon figure out about the circle too. And clearly you have. We decided the simplest thing was to carry out the ritual, as usual, and then pull you in like two fish who swallowed the bait, hook and all, while Åse united heaven and earth. In my experience, at least, it's hard to concentrate on anything else when that is going on."

Now Max realized why he thought he'd seen Gunstein before. The man looked like Jørgen Homme. And his son Jon. The same nose and thick eyebrows. And something about the eyes too. Suddenly he remembered what Tellev Sustugu had said. That Knut was planning to talk to Jørgen Homme's son when he left Sustugu on that last night of his life.

He looked at Gunstein Liom. "You're Jørgen Homme's son."

The old man smiled. He seemed proud of the fact, more than anything else.

"That's how this whole thing fits together—am I right? These are matters that have been passed down through the Homme family. A family secret, if you will. That's why it has passed from the old sheriff to you, Gunstein, and onward to your descendants. You all have Homme blood. It took almost twenty years of marriage before Jørgen and his wife had their son Jon. But before that he must have fathered you illegitimately, and he initiated you into the secret. Maybe he also promised you the Homme farm. Jon probably doesn't know anything about all this. The poor man."

Out in the marsh Freyr was kneeling in the grass, wearing his strange-looking cap.

Max nodded at the figure. "What do you get out of all that?"

"Get out of it?" Johannes loosened the belt that held his cloak together. Underneath he wore his usual clothes, with a pair of handcuffs hanging out of his pants pocket. "Can't you picture anything that's not driven by egotism and self-fulfillment? Is that what we've come to? For time immemorial—presumably ever since the Christians drove us away from Eidsborg Tarn—this marsh has been the place where heaven and earth meet. The male and the female principle. Unlike the foolish talk about the body of Christ and the sacrament of the Eucharist, *this* is true. True in a very tangible sense. It is the actual meeting that keeps the world going. Here, there is no punishing god or bizarre rules to live by, originating in the deserts of the Middle East. Only what we see around us every day. The grass that grows, and the water that runs. The fish in the water and the reindeer on the mountain. The womb that receives the seed. The body that rots and becomes manure. The concrete ways in which the world makes sense. Freyr is an image of the world. Jesus is not an image of anything other than the bewilderment and decline of the human race. And it's not only at Midsummer that this ceremony takes place. It also happens at weddings and baptisms. And in connection with hunting. Especially in the past. Everything that has to do with fertility and harvest. If the ritual took place only at Midsummer, the circle wouldn't be as clear as it is. We've been walking here for over a thousand years."

"But if this is related to fertility, what is she doing here?" asked Max spitefully.

Åse spoke before Johannes could answer. "We have to take what we can get," she said. "Even an old barren creature like myself. If only you knew what it's like to fuck the whole world. To feel the sun and the rain bursting inside me. But you wouldn't know that, of course. Your performance wasn't exactly on the same level, and that's putting it mildly. But you thought you were a real stud, didn't you? I'm good at pretending."

Old Gunstein gave a coarse laugh.

"So you weren't visiting your sister in Skien after all, last year on Midsummer Eve?" said Max.

"Actually, I was," said Åse. "I was taking care of her dog while she went on a shopping trip to London. I just made a little detour during the night. The way I always do at Midsummer."

"And the whole scene at your house was just an act? When you said you felt like you were being used, and all that?"

"Henrik said there was something he needed to tell me. That's how I heard the whole story about a private detective working on the Cecilie Wiborg case. Good Lord, I knew who you were the first time I met you. Johannes phoned me the minute you showed up in Eidsborg. Stupid Henrik thought I didn't know anything about you. But I was actually surprised to hear how much he'd told you when you interrogated him. About Cecilie coming over and telling me she was pregnant. I knew that in your eyes this would put me in a whole new and more suspicious light. So I had to find some way to divert your attention. That was the reason for my little tantrum when I ended things with you. I was good, wasn't I?" Her voice sounded flat, and she still had that remote look in her eye.

"What do you think would happen if you stopped performing the ritual?" asked Tirill. "Do you think the world would end?"

Max noticed that she had her voice fully under control.

"No. Something much worse," replied Johannes. "We would be betraying a trust. We'd be the link that broke a chain reaching so far back in time that it's been lost in the dark of the past. No one who has gone before us ever betrayed the trust. No one. If they had, we wouldn't be standing here today."

"And that's why Knut had to die?" asked Max.

"He died because Cecilie died. And why do you think Cecilie died? Because Peter died. Everything started with Peter Schram. Somehow he managed to figure out that something went on here at Midsummer. It must have been because of that damn book by Pastor Witzøe. He mentions the wedding ring. The puzzle required a lot more pieces than that, but in the end Peter had put so many of them together that he decided to spend the night here, just like the two of you. And in the very same spot. Things might have gone very badly for us back then, but the sunrise saved us. The first rays lit up the crag. I was the one who saw it. Just a glimpse, but it was enough. Holding an ax, I crept up there to check. Out in the marsh my mother had sat down on Freyr. She always took off her cloak. She said that's how she liked it best, with the dew and the wind on her body. And up on the hill lay that long-haired four-eyes holding binoculars in one hand while he had his other hand in his pants. What do you think I should have done? Wait politely until he finished what he was doing? There was only one way that situation could end. I split his skull in half with the ax. Schram didn't even have time to turn around. Then we dragged his carcass down to the spring and dumped it in. He still had an erection when he disappeared. My mother had a good laugh over that." Johannes grinned as if it were a funny story.

"What about Cecilie?" asked Max.

"I wasn't telling the whole truth when I said we only talked shop," Johannes replied. "I quickly realized that she was onto something. And in Eidsborg, there's not much to be onto other than us. So I devoted time and cunning to win her trust. Cecilie had no doubt that the whole thing centered around the Homme family. She thought this had to be the case because ours is the only family that's been here since the Middle Ages. She was right about that, but of course she didn't know I was a member of the family. Eventually she told me her theory about the idol worship, as she called it. You might not believe this, but she actually asked me if I'd come up here with her that night. And I was more than willing to do so. When we got here, we were met by the rest of my family."

Standing next to him, Åse laughed scornfully. "She was certainly shocked to see me, I'll tell you that. 'So we meet again,' I said to her. It wasn't long ago that she'd bragged to me about being pregnant with Henrik's child. She started crying and carrying on. Tried to appeal to some sort of sisterhood she claimed we shared. Not very successfully. It's too bad about the baby, I told her, but being a mother is not a human right."

"Then she started talking about the ritual," said Johannes, taking over again. "She told us what she thought went on here. And she wasn't that far off the truth. 'You are unique,' she told us, 'bearers of tradition. I respect that. I don't have to tell anyone about this.' 'Well,' I told her, 'now you're going to become acquainted with yet another tradition.' And then we stabbed her. All of us did. We'd decided on that beforehand. Everyone would take part. And she ended up in the spring, just like Peter Schram."

Max was feeling light-headed, and he was afraid he might throw up.

"We thought that was the end of it," Johannes went on. "But then the police officer that Jørgen Homme had circulated rumors about suddenly rang the doorbell thirty years after Schram disappeared. And I realized we were in trouble. But it was only when Knut revealed that he knew who Pappa's father was that we decided to grab him. Seemed like he wanted to brag a bit, give us a scare. And he did. That was his big mistake. We knew if he'd figured out that much, he'd be able to figure out the rest. And he wasn't just some student. He was a former policeman. So we drowned him in the sink. Instead of dumping his body in the spring and creating yet another mysterious disappearance in Eidsborg, we drove over to the river late at night and got rid of his body there."

"Wearing cloaks," murmured Max.

"Yes, in case anybody saw us. The idea was that any witnesses would find it difficult to file a credible report, if they said the ghost from the stave church had been involved in the drowning."

"What about the car key? Why did you throw it into the river?"

"We forgot to put it in his pocket before we dumped his body in the river. And we agreed it would seem strange to leave his car unlocked, with his wallet and phone inside. It would make more sense if the key was found in the river. People always close doors and lock them. It's human nature to do that. Even if you're about to jump into a river. So I tossed the key from the bridge."

"Someone saw you."

"Who?"

"Someone who will remain anonymous."

"So be it. Enough talk!" said Johannes, pushing back the handcuffs that were about to fall out of his pocket. Then he waved the gun. "It's time to get rid of you, once and for all."

Max inhaled deeply through his nostrils. The air smelled of the forest floor and the cold marsh. And something else, something spicy that he recognized but couldn't quite place. Bog myrtle, maybe. It wasn't fear alone that was making him shake. The nights were mild and bright, while the days baked under a sun that never went down completely. But the hour around sunrise was always filled with a special, raw chill.

Everything was so familiar. Finally he had returned home, also via his senses. But it was too late.

It was all too late.

Lars Liom checked to see that he'd released the safety and took aim at Tirill. At that moment Åse turned on her heel and ran over to the big backpack that one of them had been carrying. It was still covered with a blanket. The tiny bell on her finger rang, sounding as if it came from a little bird. Max tried to see what she was doing, but she was crouching down with her back turned.

No one spoke for several seconds. The only sound was the crystal-clear ringing, and Max could hear that Åse was speaking.

"Is everything OK?" Johannes shouted at last, without taking his eyes off Max. "Åse?"

Max thought his voice sounded different. Was it fear he heard?

When Åse finally stood up, she was holding something heavy. For a moment she paused, facing away from them. Then she turned around. In her arms she held something wrapped in a gray wool blanket. She took only a few steps before Tirill began to scream. And now Max saw it too. Sticking out of the blanket was the head of a little boy with tousled hair.

Tirill was about to run toward Åse, but Max grabbed her from behind and held her back. The sheer strength he felt in her body scared him. It was as if every fiber of her being had suddenly turned to muscle. He knew that if she managed to pull free, all three of them would be instantly shot.

Max pressed his face against her ear and whispered through her screams.

"Ice cold, Tirill. Ice cold, or Magnus dies."

Probably no one else could hear his words.

Tirill's screams subsided to a barely audible whimpering, and the forward thrust of her body was replaced with a violent shaking. Max continued to hold on to her, stroking her arms to calm her. He had to get hold of one of the guns, but neither Johannes nor his son stood within reach.

Sixty-Nine

ONLY A FEW METERS AWAY, Åse knelt down, caressing the hair of the seemingly lifeless boy she had placed on the sacrificial stone. She hadn't bothered to remove the pig's head, which formed a grotesque contrast to the peaceful face of the little boy wearing Spider-Man pajamas.

"It's only a sedative," said Johannes. "She hasn't done anything to harm him."

Max felt how these words made Tirill shake even more as he kept his hold on her.

"Ice cold," he whispered again, but he didn't know if she heard him.

"Put him back down in the heather," Johannes commanded.

But Åse continued to stroke the boy's hair. Max could hear that she was speaking quietly to him, but he couldn't make out her words. Her face still had that rigid look that had scared him when she pushed back her hood.

Suddenly he realized what it reminded him of. She looked like Tirill's great-great-grandmother. The dead woman in the old photograph. The woman who stood there among the living, with eyes that no longer saw. In the photo there was also a child. A little boy reaching out to his dead mother, in the hope of finding solace and love.

"Mamma?" The voice was no louder than the peep of a bird.

"Mag—!"

Max pressed his hand over Tirill's mouth before she could finish shouting his name. She struggled in his arms after hearing her son's voice.

"Mamma is here," Max now heard Åse say quite clearly. "You've been so nice, not complaining about anything. What a good little boy you are. Mamma's own little boy."

Tirill was madly twisting about like a snake, trying to scream through his hand clamped over her mouth.

"Mamma is going to take care of you until all of this is over," Åse was saying as she knelt by the stone.

"That's enough!" said Johannes Liom harshly. "Come over here. Now."

But Åse gave no sign of obeying his order.

"Now you'll see what it feels like to lose the one thing you need more than yourself," she said, turning to Tirill.

She'd pulled a long knife out of her cloak. Tirill's body was practically convulsing, and she was already halfway out of Max's grasp.

"Åse!" shouted Johannes in warning.

She turned to look at them, her gaze as unfathomable as the spring beside her.

"He should have been mine!" she said. Swiftly she raised the knife in the air, but before she could complete the movement, Johannes shifted the shotgun away from Max and Tirill and shot her in the head. At such close range, the effect was explosive. Her head was brutally flung to the side, and a burst of hair, blood, and brain matter sprayed across the stone and the grass of the marsh.

The tiny bell rang a few more times. Then there was silence. Only a high-pitched whistling in their ears.

Max threw himself at Johannes and knocked the shotgun out of his hands. They both landed on the ground, with Max on top. Out of the corner of his eye, he saw Lars aiming the pistol at him. He seemed to hesitate because of his father. Max grabbed the shotgun and fired the final shot from where he lay on the ground. He saw Lars's arm jolt backward. The pistol sailed in an arc and landed not far away from old Gunstein. In a flash Max was on his feet and reached the old man before he could grab the weapon.

He yanked on the old man's hand until he screamed in pain. Only then did Max pick up the gun. He looked down at Gunstein, whimpering on the ground. His grandson Lars had turned pale, gripping his right arm with his left hand.

There was an acrid smell in the air. Pale blue smoke was still seeping out of the shotgun lying in the heather. Max leaned down and picked it up.

A shrill scream from Tirill made him spin around, gun at the ready, but it was pointless to shoot. Johannes had put one of the handcuffs around his own wrist and the other around the neck of the wooden god. Without a sound, but with a strangely ecstatic look on his face, he jumped into the spring and disappeared.

Max raced over and threw himself down next to the pool of black water. Far below, he could see the white oval of the man's face. He was holding Freyr in his arms as he plummeted down. There was nothing Max could do. Johannes Liom and his god sank through the water. The next instant, both vanished into the eternal darkness below.

Epilogue

MAX SWITCHED OFF THE FLASHLIGHT, and darkness closed in around him. It was pitch black, with not a hint of light, but oddly enough he wasn't afraid. He'd been scared when he first entered the stave church, using the key he'd acquired as part of the bargain he'd struck with the two surviving Liom men. When he opened the creaking church door, he'd felt a gust of something sinister strike him, and it took all his willpower not to turn around and leave. Even worse was when, after fumbling with the tool for a long time, he finally managed to unlock the device that held the big floorboard in place. The moldy, stale air that rose up from the secret space under the church floor had filled him with terror.

But again he refused to flee.

Once he'd made his way down into the dark, his fear had faded as if it had never been. Now he could turn his flashlight on and off at will, without its having much effect on him. He actually preferred the dark. The space was so small that there was only enough room for him to sit down. The floor was of natural stone—not at all comfortable to sit on—and the walls were clad with roughly hewn boards.

This was where the god had lived, as far back as the surviving Liom men could remember. Maybe ever since the church was built. This was where Freyr had sat in the dark with that strange cap and that erection of his, while parishioners had sung and prayed overhead. The Homme family had sat in the front pew, listening to the pastor. But they knew the old god was still there, right under their feet. He was here first, before they built the church where the temple once stood.

It had been a sort of divine alodial right. A right of inheritance.

Max had achieved his goal. He had found out the truth about what happened to Knut Abrahamsen. Yet it gave him little satisfaction. When he closed his eyes, he could still see Åse as her head was shot off. He might never be able to erase that image from his memory.

Tycho Abrahamsen and his mother were grateful. As were Cecilie's parents and Peter Schram's widow. Max had given the gun back to Tycho, since it had belonged to his father, after all.

Lars and Gunstein Liom had confessed to the murders unconditionally: Gunstein to all three; Lars to the last two. That was part of the agreement that had given Max access to the key to their church and to the tool needed to open the floor. He would return both when he was done here. For their part, he and Tirill had promised never to mention the old cult or to publish any of the photographs from the ritual, which were still on the memory card from Max's camera. In fact, as soon as the court case was over and Lars and Gunstein had been sentenced, they were supposed to destroy the card. That was a promise they intended to keep.

The kidnapping of the four-year-old boy from his grandmother's home in Bø, with the subsequent murder and suicide, had been presented in the media as entirely separate from the murders the Lioms had committed previously. Åse Enger Thue had been mentally unbalanced when she abducted Magnus without telling Johannes Liom. They were lovers, but Johannes shot her when he realized she was going to kill the child. After that he took his own life.

When it came to the three murders, Lars and Gunstein explained that they first killed Peter Schram because he had discovered a cache of valuable stolen goods that Jørgen Homme had hidden and was supposed to pass on to his illegitimate son. This seemed plausible, since many people from Eidsborg had heard the rumors about the old sheriff's stealing from criminals. The two other murders were committed to prevent the perpetrators from getting caught.

The case sparked enormous media attention. Yet that was nothing compared to what would have occurred if the thousand-year-old cult had become known to the public.

The police sent a diver down into the spring, but he soon returned, saying that it was too dangerous. They tried all sorts of dragnets and hooks. A camera was also lowered into the water, but to no avail. Apparently there was a subterranean river way down deep that carried off anything that fell in.

Max switched on his flashlight and took something out of his pants pocket. The old clasp that he'd found in the devil's wedding ring. He'd decided to leave it here. It was hard to imagine a more suitable place. Whoever had owned the clasp was most likely a worshipper of Freyr, and this was the space where the god had been kept. So it felt right when he placed the clasp on the stone floor.

Then he turned off his flashlight again, to feel the old darkness one last time.

Author's Note

As far as we know, the Nikuls ritual was performed at the Eidsborg stave church in the manner described in my book. The reenactment of the ritual as a local "play" also took place. As for the saint statue, I've taken certain literary liberties. The statue we can today admire inside the stave church is a replica. The original statue, from the Middle Ages, is in the Collection of Antiquities at Oslo University. For the sake of the story, I decided to change this fact and make the statue in the church the original.

Aside from this, the Eidsborg stave church is described as any visitor will see it today. It's definitely worth a visit, as is the adjacent museum, where you can see, among other things, the house gods as they are described in the novel.

Even though the Nikuls statue now in the stave church is a copy, this situation may well change. The residents of Eidsborg have made several efforts to have the original statue returned from the antiquities collection. And they're not about to give up anytime soon.

Vidar Sundstøl
Bø, in the Telemark region of Norway

Vidar Sundstøl won the Riverton Award for the best Norwegian crime novel for *The Land of Dreams,* the first volume of his acclaimed Minnesota Trilogy, published in the United States by the University of Minnesota Press; the other two volumes are *Only the Dead* and *The Ravens.* He has lived in the United States and Egypt, and now resides with his family in Telemark, Norway.

Tiina Nunnally is a translator of Danish, Norwegian, and Swedish literature. Her translation of *Kristin Lavransdatter III: The Cross* by Sigrid Undset won the PEN / Book-of-the-Month Club Translation Prize, and her translation of Per Olov Enquist's *The Royal Physician's Visit* won the Independent Foreign Fiction Prize. She was appointed Knight of the Royal Norwegian Order of Merit for her contributions to Norwegian literature in the United States.